Hope you enjoy! ^^

~ E. R. Paskey

ONCE UPON A CRAFT SHOP

E.R. PASKEY

CRAFT SHOP MYSTERIES

For my husband, Tim.

CHAPTER

ONE

Golden morning sun poured through a large plate glass window, slanting across the dusty oak wooden floor and illuminating a horde of dust mites floating lazily in the thick air. It was early August, and Kentucky's broiling heat and hazy humidity were in full force. They were especially noticeable in the large, empty front room of this shop.

My shop.

I clutched an ornate silver key and a sheaf of papers to my chest, careful not to wrinkle the papers in my excitement. My chest swelled with emotion, and for a second my eyes burned with hot tears.

It was finally mine. I'd done it.

After years of wishing and hoping, I'd finally made my dream come true. I had leased a little shop and I would be able to open my very own fabric and craft store in Starhaven,

Kentucky—the cutest, sweetest little town I'd ever seen this side of the Appalachian Mountains.

Celia's Craft Shop.

Did I know anybody in town? No. Did it matter? Also, no.

I dragged in a deep breath of hot, humid air, resolve and giddiness twirling together like bright ribbons inside me. I'm fairly approachable. I'd manage to make friends eventually.

A bright smile lit my face, wide enough to make my cheeks hurt. Even better, with any luck, I'd have *customers* soon.

Still clutching the papers, I twirled in a giddy circle, letting the folds of my light summer skirt fan out around my legs. Oh, I was so excited!

My open-toe sandals made little scuffing sounds on the wooden floor that echoed in the large room as I turned. The stuffy heat and humidity in this room grew more oppressive by the moment, causing sweat to bead on my forehead, the backs of my knees, and under my breasts, but I didn't notice. I was too busy painting the room with my mind's eye, imagining what it would look like once I bought rows of shelving and brought in bolts of fabric.

I'd been doing that for the last two months now, though I'd tried to restrain myself in case I hadn't been able to lease the shop. In theory, it was a great thought. Better to guard myself a little and protect myself so I wasn't completely crushed if everything fell through.

Reality worked a little differently.

The truth was, I had fallen in love with this shop and what I'd seen of this town and the sheer *potential* of it all. I had never in my life walked into a place and see *what could be* with such startling clarity before.

I was so wrapped up in my giddy imaginings that it took a few moments to register the weight of the silence filling this room—and the unsettling feeling that I was being watched. Slowly, like a damp fog rising from the Ohio River, it seeped into my delight and tainted it. The hair on the back of my neck prickled.

I blinked once, twice, and the store I'd been arranging in my head fell away to be replaced by the empty reality of the room in which I stood. Despite the heat, a chill crept over my skin. The feeling of bright promise permeating my new shop and making the sunshine glitter even brighter gold seemed to dim.

Even the rays of sunshine slanting through the large plate glass window darkened, as though someone had thrown a lacy veil between the sun and the earth.

Someone was watching me—and I had the distinct impression that they were *not* happy I was here.

Under the guise of smoothing out my sheaf of papers, I swept a quick glance around the room, taking in dingy cream walls and the original molded tin ceiling squares. Nothing.

I was alone in this room—I'd been alone since Mr. Moffat's attorney handed me the sheaf of signed papers with a smile and let himself out.

The hair on the back of my neck continued to prickle.

Doing my best to maintain my giddy smile, I glanced toward the plate glass window. I expected to see a face duck out of sight—though I hadn't thought there had been anyone outside on the sidewalk—but again, nothing.

It was only then that I finally noticed the disapproving heaviness of the silence filling the room. I stood perfectly still, listening. When I'd first set foot in this shop, I'd have sworn that the sounds of traffic from the street outside were audible.

I heard none of them now. The silence seemed to have melded with the heat and humidity to create a heavy layer that pressed down on me almost like a living thing.

Almost like it was trying to force me out. Like it was a disgruntled child trying to tell me I wasn't welcome here.

Words stirred, formed before I could think about what I was doing.

"I signed a lease," I said loudly, though to my own ears my voice sounded muffled. "I have a key."

Instinctively, I tightened my grip on both my lease papers and my oddly antiquated silver key, as though someone—or something—was about to snatch them out of my hands.

But of course, that was ridiculous.

I breathed out a laugh that was only slightly shaky. What was I doing, talking to myself like this? It wasn't like I'd never been alone in an empty room before.

The heat is getting to you, I thought. *Need to get some fresh air.*

Lifting my chin, I marched across the light wooden floor to the front door. In my hyper-alert state of listening for any other sounds, it struck me that this old floor was surprisingly non-creaky. The feeling that I was being watched persisted all the way up until I opened the door and stepped out into golden sunshine and fresh air—if you could call air so thick you could practically cut it with a knife 'fresh'.

It was only when I took a deep breath and looked up and down the street that I realized that nagging feeling of being watched by disapproving eyes had disappeared.

I cast a backward glance over my shoulder. My shop's front room was still empty. Shaking my head, I shut the door and locked it.

I was imagining things. I had to be. But on a practical note… I made a mental note to make sure I bought one of those little bells that jingled when someone opened the door.

A moment later, having safely tucked both the lease papers and the silver key in my purse, I looked around the street again. For a second, I couldn't recall what I'd meant to do next.

A sultry breeze brushed past me, ruffling the leaves of the decorative tree in a large pot that graced the edge of the sidewalk two yards down from my door. My new shop was just off of Starhaven's City Square. From where I stood, I could see similar trees dotting the sidewalks along each of the streets leading into the Square. They gave the downtown area a healthy, outdoor vibe that kept all of the concrete and brick from being overwhelming.

Three doors down from me, a large antique store took up one of the Square's corners. An orthodontist office and a tiny jewelry store stood between us. Directly across the street stood a plant shop. The sign above the door read *Vine Life* in curly green letters.

I liked that. The shop had the same cutesy vibe you see on all those salt life stickers, but I knew the owner had to be dead serious about plants.

At that moment, a woman came through Vine Life's front

door with a large pink watering can and began to water a few hanging planters with vibrant green leaves that were suspended from the awning and hung on both sides of the door. Even from across the street, I could see she had a delicate face with large, dark eyes and a fall of chestnut-brown hair that almost seemed to glisten in the early morning sunlight. Everything about her was slender, from her long limbs and torso to the fingers grasping the watering can.

I almost took a step back when she turned her head and our gazes connected across the street. Those large, dark eyes were full of suspicion and—if I didn't know any better— almost outright hostility.

I suppose I am *staring*, I thought, and forced myself to smile brightly and wave. The plant lady had to know who I was, though. Small towns differed in some things, like location or weather or layout, but there were a few things that remained the same no matter where they were.

One of those things was that everybody knew everybody else's business. Particularly if a new business was coming into town from *out* of town.

For a split second, I debated crossing the street and introducing myself. But then the plant lady's mouth firmed into a thin foreboding line. She broke eye contact and deliberately turned away, tossing her mane of chestnut hair.

My smile froze on my lips and my chest gave a funny ache, like somebody had shoved me really hard. Well, clearly at least one person in Starhaven was not happy I was opening a shop here.

Swallowing a protest that the plant lady didn't even *know*

me yet, I forced myself to turn away. *Don't let one cranky grump ruin your day*, I told myself. *They won't all be like that.*

The law of averages meant that at least a *few* people in this town would be glad to meet me, right?

TWO

I stood in the sunshine on my doorstep for a moment, debating whether I should go ahead and unpack my car or whether I could spare a few moments for a celebratory iced coffee. There was a cute little coffee shop on the corner of the Square opposite the antique shop.

I'd packed my car to the gills, but I'd had to hire movers to bring everything else from my apartment in Louisville. (It was either that or abandon what furniture I had. Unfortunately, none of my friends were available to help me drive a U-Haul.) I would have to drive back to Louisville this afternoon so that I could supervise the movers in the morning.

One of the coolest things about my new shop was the fact that the apartment over it was also included in my lease. My commute to work would literally consist of walking out of my apartment door and down the stairs to street level. It was an older apartment, but it had air conditioning and wi-fi access, and it wasn't moldy.

Also, the combined rent was reasonable. I'd been thrilled.

In case you're wondering, yes, I fell in love with my apartment the moment I saw it, too. Not because of what it was—it was clean, so to speak, but not the kind of clean you want to move all your stuff into—but, again, because of its potential.

Standing in the middle of the surprisingly spacious living room, I'd scanned the interior and seen what could be, with a little love and elbow grease. And new curtains. And a new coat of paint on the walls.

Since I moved out of my dad's when I was twenty, I've rented several different apartments in Louisville, but I've never lived in anything like this. On my off days, sometimes I'd walk the streets in downtown Louisville and imagine what it would be like to live in the apartments that overlooked the stores and businesses along some of those streets.

And now I had the chance to do that too. My shop might not be directly on the Square, but it was close enough that it gave me a fluttery feeling of excitement.

I was so happy to be here it wasn't even funny.

Glancing up at my apartment windows, I decided I'd better unpack first. Then I could grab some coffee and head back to Louisville.

I had just taken the first step toward the alley that lay between my shop and the shop to my left when a disgruntled male voice spoke from behind me.

"What are you doing here?"

Startled, I whirled around, my fingers tightening instinctively on the straps of my purse. The light folds of my skirt tried to stick to my bare, sweaty legs.

"Excuse me?" I asked, before I realized who had addressed me.

It was a little man about four feet tall, dressed in khaki slacks and a dark blue polo, with a faded blue baseball cap pulled over gray curly hair. Arms folded across his chest, he glared at me from beneath his cap as though my very presence—and maybe the fact that he had to literally look up at me—personally offended him.

"You heard me." The little man raised his chin, his scowl deepening. "Why are you here?"

Bewildered, I motioned to the shop window behind me with the hand not clutching my purse. "I just signed a lease." I tried for a friendly smile, despite the fact that the little man's brown-eyed glare could have stopped a flow of lava in its tracks. "I'm planning to open a fabric and craft shop."

"You shouldn't be here. We don't need a craft shop." The little man shook his head, his upper lip curling with disgust. "What was Moffat thinking?"

"Hey." Irritation finally broke through my shock. I posted both hands on my hips. "What are you, one of those small-town people who think nobody should be allowed to move in unless they're already from the area?"

The little man just glared at me mulishly.

I took a deep breath of humid air and mentally counted to ten. I had absolutely no idea who this guy was or how he fit into the dynamics of Starhaven, but I really didn't want to get off on the wrong foot. Of course...I didn't want to be *walked* all over, either...

"I'm Celia O'Malley." I thrust a hand out toward the little man. "I'm from Louisville, originally—"

"At least you're still from Kentucky," the little man grumbled, eying my outstretched hand like it was something contagious.

"—but I fell in love with this town when I visited a while back and I decided to move here." I dropped my hand, not bothering to mask my irritation.

"Why?" the little man's arms were still folded across his chest. "What could *possibly* have made you think it would be a good idea to open a—" his nose wrinkled in distaste, "—*craft* shop here?"

Another light breeze brushed past us, the heavy, humid air tinged with something delightfully floral. I was too focused on the man in front of me to wonder where that lovely flower smell originated.

"I know there are a lot of artists in the Appalachian Mountains." I gestured to the town at large with one hand. "This region of Kentucky is known for the beautifully handmade things that come out of it."

I drilled the short little man with a firm stare. "And I noticed when I was here that this town doesn't have a store that caters to that audience. Somebody who makes things only has three options—buy whatever the big box store happens to have in stock, order it online, or travel to a bigger town that has a craft store."

The little man opened his mouth to make a retort, but seemed to be unable to find the right words. Instead, he snapped his jaw shut and glared at me. "You shouldn't be here."

That again? I took another deep breath. *Consider this practice for dealing with recalcitrant customers*, I told myself, before offering him a tight smile. "You said that already."

"And I mean it." He drew himself up to his full height, bristling with indignation. "Outsiders don't find this place."

A burst of incredulous laughter escaped me before I could stop myself. The little man's expression turned lava-level hostile again, and I bit my lip to hold back another giggle.

"I'm sorry," I said, barely able to contain my laughter, "but have you looked at Google Maps recently? Y'all are on there." I raised my eyebrows at him. "You're on a map on the weather app I've got on my phone, too." I nodded to my purse. "And I have cell service, so..." I shrugged.

A shrewd, calculating look came into the short man's brown eyes. "But cell service was strange when you came into town, wasn't it?"

I blinked at him, caught off-guard. I thought back to my arrival in town that morning—and then tried to recall the details of my visit a few weeks earlier. Come to think of it, my phone *had* acted a little strange, but I'd chalked it up to the peculiarities of the local terrain. Hollers and hollows tucked into the sides of mountains don't tend to get good cell reception.

I decided to switch tactics. Clearly, this man, whoever he was, was one of the locals who resented anybody else coming to live in what he considered his territory.

Setting my irritation aside, I offered him a bright smile. "What's your name?"

If anything, his scowl deepened. He looked downright suspicious now that I was smiling at him. "Why?"

Of *course* he was going to be difficult. Sending up a silent prayer that he would not, in fact, turn out to be one of my neighbors, I motioned to the Square. "Do you own one of these shops?"

"Not exactly."

Oh, dear heavens. I gritted my teeth. This was worse than trying to pry family history out of my great-uncle Terry.

I opened my mouth to ask another question—what, I hadn't entirely worked out yet—but a firm female voice sounded from behind me.

"Dave, are you being obnoxious to this poor girl?"

THREE

I whirled around, but not before I glimpsed the little man's face turn a peculiar shade of purple-red.

A plump woman just a little shorter than I was stood on the sidewalk in front of my new shop. A wild riot of silver-gray curls adorned her head, and green eyes sparkled at me from a round face. She wore a light blue dress with a lacy floral pattern and sleeves cuffed at the elbow with about two inches of lace. A white apron was tied around her waist.

I thought she had to be at least in her fifties, but her faintly-lined light brown skin gave her that indeterminable look that meant she could be anywhere from fifty to seventy.

"Maddie!" The little man, Dave, spluttered. He unbent his arms long enough to throw them into the air in frustration. "You can't just go around town introducing people and handing out names willy nilly!"

"You mean like you just did?" The older woman, Maddie, propped her hands on her hips.

Dave choked back whatever he'd been about to say, falling into grumbly silence.

Fascinated, I watched the two interact. I couldn't explain it, but I had the strangest feeling that I'd inadvertently stepped into an argument years in the making.

"It's fine, Dave." Maddie offered the little man a surprisingly gentle smile, her green eyes full of an understanding I didn't quite comprehend. "Let me handle this."

Dave's face puckered like he'd just bitten into a lemon, but he jerked his head once in a short nod. His surly gaze flicked to me, and then he turned around and marched off without another word.

A faint frown creasing my brow, I watched him stomp away. Another humid breeze ruffled my brown hair. I tucked a stray lock behind my ear out of habit and turned to find Maddie watching me.

"Don't mind him, dear." The older woman offered me a friendly smile. "He's not usually that cranky."

Unwilling to let the little man off the hook so easily for his churlish behavior, I arched an eyebrow. "I suppose he randomly accosts everybody who moves into this town?"

For a second, the expression on Maddie's light brown face could have been carved from stone. Then she sighed. "Believe it or not, dear, people don't generally move to Starhaven."

I wonder why, I thought, but I had the sense to keep the words to myself.

"Dave has had several..." Maddie hesitated, choosing her words carefully. She glanced down the street, apparently checking for Dave's whereabouts, though he'd long since turned the corner and disappeared. "Well, he's had several bad experiences. And he doesn't handle change well."

I remained undaunted. "Most people don't like change." I took one hand off my hip and held it out. "It's part of the human condition." My chest ached with a sudden, old pain, but I resisted the urge to put my hand over my heart. "The only way we can grow is through change." I shook my head slightly. "It's inevitable. That doesn't give him the right to be downright hateful to a complete stranger."

"Agreed." Maddie sighed again, inclining her head in a slow nod. "But before you judge Dave too harshly, I will tell you that he has had a rough time over the years. There is a reason he's so frightened of change."

She held up a hand before I could even open my mouth. "It's not an excuse, mind you. I just think you should know, if you're going to live here, that this town is named Starhaven for a reason."

She gave me a knowing look. "But then, you wouldn't be here if that didn't resonate with you in some level."

Her words caught me completely off guard. I eyed this strange older woman, mentally debating whether this had been a lucky guess or if she knew something about me that she shouldn't.

Lucky guess, I decided. I was a single young woman opening her own business in a new town. If that didn't indi-cate I was making major changes in my life, I didn't know what did.

"Now..." Maddie's face broke into a smile. "I'm sure you have plenty to do, but let me buy you a coffee, Miss O'Malley. I'd love to hear more about this craft store of yours. I can assure you, there are plenty of people looking forward to you opening."

This has been the strangest conversation I've had in a long time, I thought, but I only hesitated a second. "I'd like that."

Maddie smiled at me and swept a hand toward the coffee shop at the other end of the Square. "After you."

I hiked my purse up on my shoulder and started walking, but as I took the first step up the sidewalk, the hair on the back of my neck prickled again.

Someone was watching me.

I suppressed a shudder. *Glaring* at me was probably more like it. The truculent stare didn't feel friendly, whoever was responsible for it.

I darted a glance sideways, but the tall, willowy owner of the plant shop across the street had vanished. Probably not her. My gaze flicked to the apartments and shops that lined the street above the businesses at ground level. Impossible to tell where that stare was coming from—someone could be watching me from any of those windows.

Ignore them, I told myself firmly, lifting my chin and holding my head high. *You have just as much right to live in this town as they do.*

As Maddie and I walked to the coffee shop, however, talking lightly about the weather and the number of shops along the Square, I couldn't help but wonder. If this town was as insular as Dave seemed to think it was, why had it been so very easy for me to move here?

CHAPTER

FOUR

I liked Starbright Café the moment I stepped inside. It had a comfortable, cozy vibe—the kind of vibe that suggested you were among friends and had all the time in the world. Plus, it was laced with fantastic smells that promised all sorts of wonderful delights.

Coffee was the predominant scent, but as I sniffed appreciatively, I caught the underlying scents of chocolate and several teas, along with something floral I couldn't quite place.

Just like in my own shop, the owner had played up the old factor of the building by leaving the original molded tin ceiling squares intact, as well as by restoring the brick walls that lined the interior. The golden wooden planks of the floor were worn, but clean, and they also seemed to be squeak-free. Some pretty sort of Celtic music played quietly over the speakers, though it had a wild feel to it that put me in mind of beautiful women wandering across lonely moors.

The sofas, tables, and chairs scattered around the long, narrow interior were mismatched, but it was the kind of mismatch that ended up blending together and adding to the comfortable vibe. A few other customers were scattered about the coffee shop—a pair of women nestled in a couple of cozy chairs in the corner by the window, and a middle-aged man with a laptop at a table across from them.

I cast an approving glance around as I followed Maddie to the long, smoothly-polished counter made of gray stone, but my gaze was caught and held by the most curious-looking cuckoo clock I'd ever seen. It was mounted high on the wall at the far end of the coffee shop between two doors leading to the men and women's bathrooms. Even from here, I could see the plethora of strange figures carved into the wooden frame that surrounded the clock face. Mermaids, and fairies, bears and dwarves, with a host of smaller figures skillfully carved into the spaces between them.

I started to drift closer, to give the clock a better look, but at that moment I realized it was my turn to place an order.

Turning back to the counter, I smiled at the young man behind the counter. He was short and slight, with wavy golden hair and eyes so dark they were nearly black set in a pale, square face.

"Hi, may I get a feta and egg wrap and one mocha iced coffee with two percent milk, please?"

"It's on me, Rodney," Maddie interjected, before I could pull my wallet from my purse.

The young man nodded and rang me up without saying a word—or returning my smile. In the back of my mind, I thought that was rather odd for a barista in a coffee shop, but after the morning I'd had, I couldn't help but wonder if everybody in town had issues with newcomers.

What did they do when tourists arrived?

Aloud, I said, "Thank you, Maddie."

"My pleasure. Let's go over here." Maddie led the way to a red velvet loveseat nestled in the corner opposite the two women, who were both eying us covertly. Golden morning sunshine still slanted through the plate-glass window, though it was dwindling as the sun rose higher in the sky.

Smoothing my skirt, I took one corner of the loveseat, while Maddie took the other. Neither of us spoke until the short golden-haired barista brought our drinks over. He remained tightlipped and unsmiling, even after both of us thanked him.

I bit the inside of my lip as I stared down into the dark mocha surface of my iced coffee, wondering for a split-second if I needed to worry about what was in it. I immediately chided myself for being ridiculous. Surely the coffee shop wouldn't deliberately open themselves up to a lawsuit like that.

I took a sip and smiled. Delicious—and comfortingly familiar. I glanced at Maddie, who was serenely sipping what looked like green tea from an actual teacup, and raised an eyebrow.

"Is he always like that—" I tipped my head discreetly toward the barista, "—or does he share Dave's opinion of newcomers?"

Maddie's green eyes widened slightly, and then her face smoothed back into its cheerful, friendly expression. "Rodney doesn't talk much, it's true." She took another sip of her tea. "You'll have to excuse him. And Dave."

I lifted an eyebrow at this. It would take a while before my vivid first impression of the little man faded. "Why is he so against new people coming to Starhaven and opening businesses?"

"It's complicated." Maddie lifted one shoulder in another delicate little shrug. "He has his reasons." It was her turn to smile briefly. "I will admit not all of them are valid or rational, for that matter," she added, "but don't worry. I'm sure he'll come around in time."

I bit my lip. I could only hope.

Maddie gracefully changed the subject. "If I may ask, how did you come to discover Starhaven?" She twinkled a smile at me and leaned forward, her posture indicating genuinely curiosity. "We *are* a ways off the beaten path."

It was for that reason—and that reason alone—that I decided to let her change the subject. Well, that and I really didn't want to talk about Dave any more.

I took another sip of my iced coffee. "I was driving through the mountains to Tennessee so I could visit a friend of mine and my car overheated or something." I shrugged—I still wasn't entirely sure what had happened. "Fortunately, I wasn't far from this exit and I was able to stop at the auto shop."

My face creased in a frown at the memory. The mechanic on duty had been surprised to see me. Odder still, he'd taken a look at my car and proclaimed there was nothing wrong with it. I was able to go on my way—but not before I'd had a chance to walk the Square.

That was when I'd gotten the crazy idea for my craft shop. I'd seen a 'For Lease' sign on the shop and I'd taken one look at it and just *known*. This was where I was supposed to be.

It helped that my paternal grandmother had left me a bit of an inheritance when she passed away six months ago. I hadn't known what to do with it until I found myself in Starhaven.

I conveyed as much to Maddie, who nodded with the sage look of someone who'd fully expected that to be the answer.

She took a contemplative sip of her tea. "What did you do before?"

"I was a secretary." I lifted one shoulder in a shrug. "Worked for a law firm in Louisville. I was good at it, but it was kind of sucking my soul dry, you know?"

A faint smile tugged at one corner of Maddie's mouth. "And you thought going into retail would be better?"

"Frankly? Yes." I straightened a little in my seat. "I'm not expecting it to be easy. I know there's a good chance I could crash and burn. But—" I waved the hand that held my coffee, belatedly realizing it was a good thing I had a lid when it sloshed alarmingly inside my cup, "—I love fabric and yarn and thread. I love making things and helping people make things."

"And... "I lifted my chin a little, meeting her in the eye. "This town doesn't have what I'm offering."

Maddie held my gaze for a long moment, and I had the strangest sense that she was taking my measure, probing into things I probably didn't even realize she was probing.

"This town is special," she said at last. "We take care of it, and we take care of our own." That faint smile tugged at her lips again. "We don't much care for strangers, it's true." Her large, green eyes narrowed fractionally. "But you found us, and Old Man Moffat leased you the building." Her tone held the faintest note of amazement.

That statement begged a question—and I asked it. "Is he not normally in the habit of leasing to people? I've never met the man—only his lawyer."

The pause Maddie took before she answered would have told me everything, even if she hadn't replied. "Not to outsiders."

The hair on the back of my neck prickled again. It was funny, Mr. Moffat's lawyer had asked me several times if I was sure—absolutely sure—I wanted to move to Starhaven. At the time, I'd just chalked it up to him being extremely thorough and perhaps a little pedantic. But now...

For the first time, a whisper of a thought crossed my mind. Forget the ups and downs of retail—had I gotten myself into something I'd regret with this town?

"Well, he must have liked me." I offered Maddie my most charming smile. "I *am* pretty likable. No criminal record either," I joked.

She smiled, and the expression was friendlier than it had been earlier. "You're here now, so they'll have to learn to like you—or at least tolerate you."

The look the plant lady had given me returned vividly to the forefront of my mind. I laughed, a little uncertainly. "Yeah...that'd be nice."

I drank some more of my coffee, wondering why the lawyer hadn't seen fit to inform me that my neighboring business owners weren't keen on an outsider joining their ranks. You'd think, if he was trying to discourage me from signing the lease, that he might have mentioned that.

I said as much to Maddie and she just gave me an enigmatic smile over the rim of her teacup. "Old Man Moffat wanted you here," she said, as though that settled it.

Maybe in her mind it did.

Giving my head a mental shake, I decided it was my turn to change the subject. "What do you do here in Starhaven?"

"I work for the Starhaven Community Foundation." Maddie took another delicate sip of her tea. "I am what you might call a facilitator." One corner of her mouth dimpled in a smile. "I help people settle into the town, and I make connections between people."

A town facilitator. I stared at Maddie. I'd never heard of such a thing.

"What kind of connections?" I asked cautiously.

Maddie lifted one shoulder in a shrug. "Oh, you know... Someone is looking for a new employee, I know someone who would be perfectly suited to that job. Helping people find houses in the right part of town." She waved a hand. "Really, the job covers all sorts of things."

"And Starhaven has a *Foundation* for this?" My forehead scrunched into a frown. I'd never heard of a community foundation that did those things directly.

"Oh, yes." A warm smile suffused Maddie's light brown face again. "Over the years, various...citizens...have made generous donations that enable us to help people as needed." Her smile softened. "It's part of what makes Starhaven so very special and unique."

"I see..." I took a thoughtful bite of my feta and egg wrap, chewed, and swallowed. "I'll be honest, Maddie, I've never heard of a community foundation that operates like that."

Part of me was a little worried that she would be offended by my bluntness, but Maddie only twinkled a smile at me. "Like I said, Starhaven is quite unique."

"Oh, I know that." I couldn't help but smile back at her. "That's part of what drew me to this town in the first place." I took another bite of my wrap, enjoying the melted feta cheese. "So do you offer grants?" I'd heard of nonprofits that did that.

Maddie paused, her expression growing thoughtful, as though she had to parse out exactly how to answer this. "Well...I suppose in a matter of speaking, we have grants."

I nodded. "Is there a formal application process?"

Was it my imagination, or did something flicker behind her green eyes?

"No...not quite."

I nodded again. It wasn't like I had any experience with grants, but I wasn't completely ignorant of them.

A thought occurred to me, and I offered Maddie a rueful smile. "Perhaps you can help me with Dave." The little man and his dour expression stood out quite vividly in my memory. "Why is he so against new people coming to Starhaven and opening businesses?"

Maddie's smile dimmed, just a fraction. "That, my dear Miss O'Malley, is a story for another day."

Nodding, I accepted the dismissal for what it was. Ah, well. There would be time to get the whole story later.

"Well," I said at last, crumpling up my empty wrapper. "Thank you very much for lunch and coffee." I made a vague gesture toward the door. "I probably ought to get going. It's a long drive back to Louisville and I have to unpack my car first. But..." I brightened. "I'll be back tomorrow."

Maddie offered me a smile over the rim of her tea cup. "And officially moved in."

"Yes. I can't wait." I smiled at her. "I'm very excited."

"You should be," she said decisively. "I think you'll be good for this town."

"I hope so."

I'd had the feeling that Starhaven would be good for me from the moment I set foot in the place. It would be nice to return the favor.

To my surprise, my overall move to Starhaven wasn't that bad. I'd half-anticipated it being more grueling than my other moves (after all, I was moving several hours away instead of just across the city), but it went pretty well. Amazing the difference paying a moving company makes. I'd never had the money—or the inclination —before, but I will be the first to admit that on this occasion, at least, it made a difference.

After I left Maddie at the coffee shop, it hadn't taken me long to empty out my car, and my drive back to Louisville had been mostly uneventful. I'd hit the tail end of rush hour traffic, but I survived, and finished out the evening with a few last-minute things I couldn't get done any earlier.

The movers showed up bright and early at 8 AM. I packed essential things in my car and dropped off my keys at the apartment office, they played Tetris with my furniture and everything else, and we were on the road less than two hours later. It probably helped that, while it was still unbelievably humid, it was much cooler than it would be by lunchtime.

Our drive to Starhaven was relatively peaceful. The interstate seemed to be ushering us along, and I spent the drive pleasantly engaged in thinking through the lists of things I would need to do once I arrived. We turned off the interstate onto a state highway and navigated it another half hour until we reached Starhaven.

Excitement fluttered in my stomach when I glimpsed the city's welcome sign. Funny how this place already felt like home.

The movers parked the U-Haul in front of my shop, while I parked in the tiny parking lot adjacent to the line of buildings that held my shop and apartment. I then walked to the alley that separating my building from the next one over to unlock the back entrance so they could start carting things up to my apartment.

Slinging my purse over my shoulder, I let myself into the cool darkness of the hall and hurried up the creaky old stairs to the second floor. My apartment was the second to the right. Faded black metal letters said, Apartment 3.

Unable to help a proud grin, I opened the door and stepped into the foyer. A faint smell of cinnamon met my nose, mixed with a faint odor I can only describe as the smell of an old building.

My apartment here in Starhaven was almost double the size of the last place I'd rented in Louisville. The foyer was poky, but it opened up into a decent-sized living room that overlooked the street below, with a partial wall and a relatively new counter separating it from the kitchen. To the left, a short hall led down to a bathroom and two bedrooms.

I'd claimed the larger bedroom with the best view for my office and the repository for the majority of my personal craft supplies. The smaller bedroom would be fine for me to sleep. I'd already anticipated that most of my waking hours would be spent in my office, the living room, or downstairs manning my store.

I drew in a deep breath. I'd done it. I was here. My grin widened, but I barely had time to take everything in before the sound of heavy footsteps told me the movers were on their way up with the first load of my belongings.

It took those three men less than an hour to empty the U-Haul. And that even included them setting the couch and my other furniture in the rooms where I needed them. My mattress, they leaned against the wall in the smaller bedroom. I'd be able to assemble the bedframe and maneuver the mattress into position myself.

And then they were gone, like a burly whirlwind, leaving me standing alone in my living room, surrounded by stacks of boxes all marked in my semi-neat handwriting.

For a second, I savored the silence—and the glimpse of my future opening up ahead of me with glittering possibilities. This was my brand-new apartment, over my brand-new shop.

Talk about a dream come true.

Dropping my purse onto my faded blue couch, I did a little twirl in the middle of the hardwood floor. Hard to believe I was actually standing here, but...I was.

When I came to a stop, I looked around again and realized

that the stacks of boxes cluttering up my living room and foyer lent a strangely claustrophobic air to the place. I propped my hands on my hips, frowning slightly. I'd have to fix that.

If I accomplished nothing else this afternoon and evening, I needed to unpack as many of my belongings as I could. Once the inventory for my store started arriving, I'd be up to my eyeballs in fabric, yarn, and various crafty accoutrements, and it was entirely likely that I wouldn't have much time to deal with my own things for a while. Best to start things off right to give myself the best possible chance to succeed.

After all, I'd used my savings and the small inheritance my grandmother had left me to start this venture.

Moving over to the front door, I locked it and then kicked off my shoes. *It won't take that long to put everything away*, I told myself. It wasn't like I had that much stuff, outside of my personal craft hobbies.

Making a mental note to rent myself a safe-deposit box at the bank as soon as a I could for my lease papers, which were still tucked into my purse, I set about unpacking.

The first things I unpacked were my laptop and my Bluetooth speaker. The laptop went onto my tiny square kitchen table for now, and the Bluetooth speaker went onto a little end table in the living room. I plugged my phone in to charge and then cranked up my favorite Irish rock band. Thus cheerfully motivated, I tackled the first stack of boxes in the living room.

Part of me itched to go downstairs to my shop and start taking measurements so I could start buying shelving, but I forced myself to hold off. Best to take a couple of days and get my own apartment mostly livable, and then I could get down to work.

***

Surprisingly, it took me less time to unpack that I had anticipated. I don't know if it was because I had more space here (probably), but I emptied box after box without much trouble at all. My own personal craft supplies went into my new office—I would sort them out later—but my clothes and books and everything else were relatively easy to put in place.

Truth be told, the kitchen was probably the fiddliest bit. I had a whole box of spices that had to be arranged in a cupboard, along with my dishes. (Mostly matching, though I had a few beloved mismatched pieces, and more coffee mugs than one woman should probably admit to owning. I'd weeded a few of them down when I moved, but I couldn't bring myself to give the rest of them away.)

It was only at a quarter to seven, standing in my now-mostly organized living room with my hands on my hip, surveying my apartment, that I realized I was incredibly hungry. I'd snacked on a couple of granola bars over the past few hours, but the quick lunch the movers and I had grabbed on the way had been hours and hours ago. I'd been so absorbed in unpacking that I hadn't noticed that my stomach was staring to launch a protest.

Right. I rubbed my hands together, proud of what I'd managed to accomplish so far. Supper. That was the next order of business.

After washing my hands and brushing my hair so I wouldn't look too crazy, I touched up my lipstick. Then I grabbed my purse and headed for my front door.

As I stepped out into the hallway, a faint chill swept over me. The corridor darkened as the single lightbulb in the light mounted in the hall ceiling seemed to dim. The back of my neck prickled as though someone unfriendly was glaring at me, willing me to go away.

I froze, and then blinked once, twice. "Is someone there?"

The darkness abruptly receded, the light in the ceiling returning to its usual wattage. Unsettled, I peered around me, searching the nooks and crannies of the tiny hallway for... what, I wasn't exactly sure. *Something.*

In a rush, I recalled I'd experienced that same feeling the day before. "I belong here," I said aloud, with more firmness than I felt. "I have a lease, and a key. This is my home too."

Was it my imagination, or did the lightbulb flicker in what felt decidedly like annoyance?

I blinked again. *Okay, Celia.* I clutched my purse a little tighter. *You really need to get something to eat. You're starting to imagine things.*

I forced myself to walk down the hall at my normal pace, thought part of me itched to turn around and look behind me. If I had, the dark eyes glaring at me from the shadows of a corner at the opposite end of the hall would not have made my assessment of my mental state any better.

Back out on the street, in the hazy early evening heat and humidity, some of my optimism returned. This was my town now. A trill of excitement ran through me. I couldn't wait to explore the place more.

For now, however, I needed a good spot to eat dinner. Eventually I'd be a responsible adult and do some meal planning and grocery shopping, but for now, I really wanted something like...pizza. My stomach rumbled appreciatively at the thought.

Turning onto the sidewalk that led along the east side of the Square, I started perusing shop fronts, searching for restaurants. A decent stream of people flowed along the sidewalks, and cars filled parking spaces along the street. I smiled at a few people who made eye contact with me, but after the first few minutes, it was quite apparent that a good number of these individuals were shying away from me.

When I tried to make eye contact and smile, they would

deliberately ignore me, or turn away and speak to their companions. My smile froze on my lips.

Is it that noticeable I'm not from around here? I wondered. How in the world would they *know*? Just because they didn't immediately recognize me?

Dave's voice floated through my mind again. *We don't get many visitors here.*

My footsteps faltered. Starhaven couldn't possibly get so few visitors that *one* person stuck out like a sore thumb, could they?

A second later, I bolstered myself. Well, they'd just have to get used to me. As of today, I was officially a citizen of Starhaven too. Lifting my chin, I straightened my shoulders and kept walking.

Regardless of its inhabitants' deplorable state of unfriendliness, I couldn't help but be struck again by the beauty in this place. The courthouse stood in its neatly-trimmed green space in the heart of the Square, with decorative paths leading out from it to the four sides of the Square. To one side, a gazebo stood, with a colorful banner proclaiming a floral festival or something. I made a mental note to check that out later.

On the other side of the Square, I finally found what I was looking for: a pizza place. Not a chain pizza place, either. This was a locally owned shop—Tam's Pizza—and if the smells escaping its front door and trailing down the sidewalk were any indication, the food was *fabulous*.

My stomach growled in renewed appreciation. Picking up my pace, I hurried over. I paused outside the door long enough to google the restaurant and pull up a menu...but I couldn't find it. Tam's Pizza did not appear to have an online presence at all, let alone a social media presence.

Huh. I squinted at my phone. That was interesting. But, considering how little information was available about Starhaven period, maybe I shouldn't be surprised. I'd tried to research it when I first decided to move and hadn't found much. Not that it had deterred me, but... it was odd.

With a mental shrug, I let myself inside the restaurant. The second I crossed the threshold, I almost melted in delight. The smell of oregano, tomato, pepperoni, and the underlying amazing smell of fresh-baked pizza crust was even better here.

A corner of my mind noted the smattering of people sitting at crowded tables despite the fact that it was past seven o'clock—couples, a few families with children, and several of men and woman sitting by themselves. Something inside me relaxed. Not that I really cared, but it was nice to know I wouldn't look even more out of place sitting by myself.

I practically floated over to the counter. A short, matronly woman with jet-black hair came over to the cash register. "What can I get you?" she asked, before she got a good look at me.

If I hadn't been looking for it, I would have missed the imperceptible flinch she gave when she saw me. Her dark eyes narrowed fractionally, and the warm expression on her face cooled into something more distantly polite.

I suppressed a sigh. Yep, people in this town definitely knew who wasn't from around here.

Ignoring the doomed little voice inside my head whispering that *maybe* moving here hadn't been such a brilliant idea after all, I held out my hand and offered the older woman my friendliest smile.

"Hi, I'm Celia O'Malley. I just leased the shop across from Vine Life and I'll be opening a craft store."

The woman blinked beady black eyes at me. Then, grudgingly, she reached across the counter and shook my hand. "I heard about that."

I'm sure you did, I thought, maintaining my smile. I gestured to the restaurant's interior, with its original brick walls (my shop probably had those too, underneath the drywall) and rustic wood decor. "It smells absolutely amazing in here. I love pizza. Do you have a recommendation?"

The woman rested an elbow on the worn counter, eying me up and down. I had the sudden, inexplicable feeling that I was being appraised like she was measuring my worth. "Will you eat it if I give it to you?"

I hesitated. *That* was unexpected. Visions of fishy eyeballs or some other strange toppings floated through my head, but I took a firm grip on myself and gave her a decisive nod. "Yes."

Her eyes narrowed further, and then she lightly thumped a hand on the counter. "Okay, then. Have a seat."

And *that* was how I ended up tucked into a corner with a medium spinach artichoke chicken pizza with feta cheese. Apparently, nobody in Starhaven ever asked her for recommendations. The novelty of it seemed to temporarily override her suspicion of outsiders.

After the short woman deposited the steaming hot pizza

on my table, she vanished back behind the counter without another word.

Okay, then, I thought, carefully picking up the first piece. *I can do this.* I'd never had spinach artichoke pizza with feta cheese before, but it was surprisingly really good.

I was hungry enough that the fact that I was the object of covert looks from other patrons in the restaurant didn't bother me at first. I ate my pizza and scrolled through my to-do list on my phone, mentally mapping out my priorities for the next few days.

When I'd polished off three quarters of the pizza, I finally conceded that I was full. Leaning back in my chair, I sighed contentedly and then glanced around the restaurant. A dozen faces immediately turned away as people pretended they hadn't been staring at me.

An uncomfortable prickle crept along the back of my neck. I'd grown up hearing the jokes that people made about rural backwater communities in the mountains, but I'd always dismissed them as just sweeping generalizations.

For the first time, I found myself wondering if, in Starhaven's case, there was a little bit of truth in those jokes. I reached for my Coke, took another sip. It wasn't like I'd expected anybody to roll out the welcome mat, or this big Southern greeting, but...I guess I *had* expected just a bit of warmth.

My thoughts returned to my conversation with Maddie. I'd expected more interactions like her, I guess, and less like my interactions with Dave.

A presence appeared at the table beside me. "How was it?"

I almost jumped. I hadn't even seen the older woman approach. "Good!" I said, with a little more enthusiasm than I'd intended. "Really good." I offered her a friendly smile again. "I'd eat it again. In fact," I waved to my leftover pizza, "I'm taking that home for lunch."

The older woman studied me with those beady black eyes of hers, and then, almost by magic, a few of the wrinkles in her tanned face smoothed out. "I'm glad to hear it." She cast a wry glance in the direction of the rest of her customers, who suddenly were very studiously *not* looking in our direction again. "Nobody around here wants to experiment. It's always the same thing." She wrinkled her nose. "Meat, bread, and cheese."

"Well...that *is* your classic pizza." I shrugged. "I don't think you can go wrong with a classic."

"Eh, I suppose." She eyed me again and then abruptly held out her hand. "I'm Tam. This is my pizza shop."

Quelling a sudden rush of delight, I shook her hand. "Nice to meet you, Tam."

"You're opening a craft store, eh?"

"Yes." I nodded, proud and enthusiastic.

"Well, that ought to be interesting." Tam dropped my check on the table. "I'll bring you a box. Pay when you're ready."

And that was that.

Bemused, I walked back to my apartment a few minutes later, holding the remnants of my pizza. A wash of golden sunlight from the setting sun gilded the tops of the trees along the Square and the domed top of the courthouse. I took the long way around, wanting to reacquaint myself with the remainder of the businesses around the Square.

Starhaven boasted not one, but two pubs, which were already both quite busy. Raucous laughter drifted out onto the sidewalk as a burly man ahead of me opened the door and vanished into the dark, dimly-lit depths. The uncomfortable feeling that I was being watched increased as I strode past the covered windows with their cheerful luminescent lighting.

While I'd unpacked, I'd entertained vague notions of visiting all the businesses in Starhaven, but I wasn't sure about the pubs. I'm not much of a drinker.

Still, it wasn't like I had to visit them in the evening. I could go during the day and introduce myself to the owners. I bit my lip, restraining a slightly hysterical laugh. Frequenters of pubs can have crafty hobbies, right? Or know people who do?

As I let myself into my building and ascended the stairs to my apartment, I suddenly recalled my experience before dinner. I braced myself for more of the same weirdness, but to my relief, the hallway appeared perfectly normal. I shook my head. Clearly, I needed to make sure I ate regularly so my imagination didn't run away with me.

Unlocking my door, I stepped inside—and nearly tripped over a pair of sandals lying in the middle of the doormat I'd laid on the floor earlier.

"Whoa!"

I staggered a few steps, almost dropping my pizza box, but I managed to catch it—and myself—at the last second. Wide-eyed, I stared down at my shoes. I didn't remember leaving those there. I'd taken all my shoes to my bedroom closet, hadn't I? Except for the pair I'd been wearing all day?

I guess not.

Shaking my head at my own silliness, I stowed the pizza box in my empty fridge and then went to take a shower. After that, I had inventory lists to finish putting together.

Giddy excitement coursed through me, overriding the slight disappointment and dismay I felt at my lackluster greeting from Starhaven's residents. Picking out my inventory had proved to be one of the bets parts of my new business venture.

Despite my excitement, I didn't make it much past ten o'clock before fatigue prompted me to put myself to bed. Tomorrow was a bright new day with a million things I needed to do as a newly-minted business owner.

And, hopefully, I thought dreamily, just before sleep claimed me, *I'll make some friends here.*

As far as the making friends part of life here in Starhaven went, it was soon blindingly obvious that I was not off to a great start. I like to think I'm an optimist by nature, but even my optimism wavered in the face of the next morning's interaction.

I returned to the coffee shop to get a mocha iced coffee because I realized when I woke up that I still had absolutely nothing in my apartment. Well, actually, I take that back—I had a Keurig, my favorite coffee, and reusable pods, but I didn't have any milk or flavored coffee creamer.

So, in essence, I had nothing. (I came to terms years ago with the fact that I will never be a black coffee drinker. If that's all that's available, I will never drink coffee again. I've tried. And failed. End of story.)

This morning, a different barista stood behind the counter—a slim young woman with brown skin and black curls named Molly. She was friendlier than the guy from the day before, but not by much. And it definitely *was* me.

I know this because Molly practically lit up like a Christmas tree when the bell over the door jangled to admit the coffee shop's next customer.

"Zel!" Molly squealed, as a short young woman in a flowy floral skirt and pastel pink top entered, pushing a double stroller holding a set of a twins—a boy and a girl, probably about six months old. Unlike most of the babies I'd ever met, these already sported hair. One had golden hair like his mommy, while his sister boasted soft chestnut curls.

I tried not to stare as the young woman pushed the stroller up to the counter and leaned on the handle, tucking a lock of impossibly golden hair behind her ear. She was stunningly beautiful, and quite young, if a little worn around the edges. (Being a mom to twins would probably do it.) She had large blue eyes with long eyelashes and a pale, porcelain complexion that some women would kill for. (I'd worked with a couple women like that at the law firm. Their cosmetics and facial care expenditures were out of this world.)

"Hi, Molly. May I get the usual?" Her voice was sweet and musical, with almost an ethereal quality to it.

Standing off to the side, awkwardly waiting for my iced coffee, I found myself wondering if this girl did any singing— I bet she'd be amazing. Like one of the Celtic Women, or something.

"Sure thing." Molly rang her order up and then leaned over the counter to make silly faces at the twins. "And how are you two lovelies today?"

"Teething," Zel said wryly.

"Aww. Are you two keeping Mommy up all night?" Molly cooed.

My heart almost stopped in my chest. Molly's black curls shifted as she moved, and for a second, I almost *swore* the tip of her ear looked pointed. I blinked and it was gone—or at least, Molly's ear was concealed behind her hair again.

I bit my lip. *Methinks I need coffee more than I realized this morning. Now I'm imagining somebody in this town has pointed ears like an...elf or something?*

"Yes, they are." Zel looked down at her children with a tired kind of fondness.

"Celia." Molly had finished preparing my coffee and set it on the pick-up counter. Her smile vanished as she looked at me. *Intruder,* her flat black gaze seemed to say.

"Thanks," I said, but the barista had already turned around and was whipping up Zel's 'usual'.

Well, so much for that. I took a sip of my iced coffee, careful not to give myself brain freeze. It was amazing. Molly made good coffee, at least. Hopefully I'd win her over eventually.

I paused next to the Zel and the stroller on my way out. Both babies blinked at me. "They're beautiful," I told Zel with a smile.

"Thanks," she said in that soft, musical voice.

In hindsight, I should have kept walking. But I didn't. (There are days I think 'optimist' really means 'glutton for punishment'.)

"I'm Celia." I stuck out my free hand. "I'm opening a craft store across from the plant shop."

Zel didn't shake my hand. She just stood there and stared at me, a look of mild confusion creasing her pretty forehead. "A...craft store?"

"Yeah." I waved my free hand. "You know, sewing, knitting, crocheting, embroidery... That kind of—" I broke off in alarm.

Zel's face had gone very pale, making her green eyes seem even larger.

A thread of panic curled through me. Was that *fear* in her eyes? I didn't know what to do. Usually, the mention of artsy crafty things like crocheting and knitting didn't *scare* people.

"Um...." I held up both hands, nearly spilling my coffee all over myself in the process. The back of my neck felt hot. "I'm sorry, I didn't mean to—"

I didn't even know why I was apologizing. All I'd done was introduce myself.

Zel took a visible deep breath, and then the color returned to her face. "It is all right." Her voice grew stronger, even as a shadow flitted across her face. "I—I really can't stand embroidery."

Okay, then. I didn't know you could have bad memories associated with something like embroidering in this modern age, but what did I know? Apart from the fact that people are just plain strange?

"I'm really sorry." I took a step back, my cheeks flushed in embarrassment. Out of the corner of my eye, I glimpsed Molly giving me a death stare from behind the counter. The back of my neck burned even hotter.

"It's not your fault," Zel said, just as the barista loudly said, "Zel, here's your coffee."

The blonde woman turned toward Molly, and I seized the opportunity to make my escape.

"It was nice to meet you," I said, and then I bolted for the door like my life depended on it.

Half a block later, I finally slowed to something approaching a normal pace and sighed. So much for going back to that coffee shop anytime soon. Now I *had* to go grocery shopping at some point today. No more excuses.

I took a consolatory sip of my coffee, relishing the cold and sighed again. The worst part was that I really liked the coffee shop. And it really wasn't my fault a complete stranger like Zel had been triggered by the mention of embroidery, of all things, was it?

Mentally, I shook my head. Oh, well. At least I had plenty of work to distract myself with today.

EIGHT

I wasn't kidding about having plenty of work to do. It hadn't come up in my conversation with Maddie two days earlier, but my plan was to open my craft shop the first weekend in September. If I was going to accomplish that, I needed to hustle.

I had accomplished most of the business side of things once I'd determined I was, in fact, moving to Starhaven—opening a bank account here, applying for a sales tax permit, and filling out all the other various state and local county paperwork that had to be done in order to open a business. Thankfully, most of it could be done online.

Now that I'd officially moved here, all the physical work began. I had walls to paint, shelving to assemble (once I ordered it and it arrived), and inventory that would soon be arriving and needed to be stocked. The paint necessitated a trip to the hardware store a few blocks away, but I returned with primer, white baseboard paint, pale lavender wall paint, and all the tools I'd need to start the next day.

Setting up my Bluetooth speaker, I put on a playlist from one of my favorite musicals and set to work taping around the baseboards with painter's tape. I've always thought this was the fiddliest part of painting walls—it takes longer to tape everything in order to prepare for painting than it actually does to paint. But...it had to be done. I consider myself fairly good at painting, but I'm not *that* good.

Once I had everything taped, I set to work measuring walls and the floor so I could order shelving and also so I could draw up a rough sketch for the layout of the interior of the shop. In my mind's eye, I pictured where everything would go and tried to commit it to paper. The result rather resembled something that looked like an enterprising five-year-old had drawn it, but...that was fine. I never claimed to be an artist with a pencil.

As I worked, I tried not to think about the fact that when I'd left my apartment this morning, full of bright, cheerful energy for the day, I'd entertained vague thoughts of introducing myself to a few of my immediate neighbors (like the plant lady). Unfortunately, the scene with Zel at the coffee shop had shaken me. I'd anticipated feeling like an outsider in Starhaven for a while because, well, I *was* an outsider, but... I hadn't anticipated feeling completely unwelcome.

Worse, the longer I worked in my new shop, the more the back of my neck began to prickle with that creepy feeling of being watched again. I kept glancing at the big plate window to assure myself that nobody was standing outside peering in, but...

The feeling was inescapable. *Somebody* was staring at me. *Glaring* at me, actually. The vibes I was getting right now were disapproving and absolutely not of the friendly nature.

My thoughts flashed back to the incident two days ago, after Mr. Moffat's attorney had left. I'd felt the same thing then. And—yet another quick glance around the large, empty shop room told me that I was completely alone in here.

Just like I had been two days ago.

Taking a deep breath, I set my tape measure down. I should state here for the record that I do not believe in ghosts or in places being haunted. Never have.

But...I couldn't help but wonder. Just for a second.

I can't say I've ever stayed in a place where I felt so unwelcome before.

My thoughts traveled back to my lease... and the surprisingly affordable rent. Was this why I could afford it? Because there was something *wrong* with this building?

The back of my neck prickled again. And then I laughed. Even though I had music playing, the sound echoed in the large, empty shop room, and bounced back to my ears. It almost held a tinge of hysteria, but I got a grip on myself.

"This is ridiculous," I said out loud. "There's nothing wrong with this building."

Clearly, I was imagining things. I'd probably been on my own too long lately, and most of my encounters so far in Starhaven had not exactly been positive.

Groceries, I thought, taking another deep, bracing breath. *I need to take a break and go grocery shopping.*

As much as I wanted to keep working, this was probably a good moment to stop and take care of mundane things like making sure I had food in the apartment. Particularly if I wanted to avoid going to the coffee shop again tomorrow.

At the thought of the coffee shop, my stomach grumbled, reminding me that it was now late afternoon and I hadn't had lunch yet. Also, another cup of coffee sounded really good.

Stowing my tape measure inside my little toolbox, I left it sitting on the floor by the shop's back wall and grabbed my purse. Time to investigate Starhaven's grocery store. Then I could finish up the last few things I needed to do before I started painting tomorrow.

Starhaven was not big enough to rate its own Walmart, but it did have a local grocery store. Starhaven Food Shoppe was big enough and busy enough that I didn't feel like I drew too much attention, but I was still grateful to get back to my apartment with everything. (And that wasn't even counting being grateful to escape the relentless heat.) I'd grabbed lunch meat and other sandwich fixings, so I ate a quick lunch, and then went back downstairs to my shop.

I picked up my toolbox, intending to retrieve my tape measure, but stopped, frowning. The tape measure was no longer where I had left it. My frown deepened. I'd put it back in here, hadn't I? I *distinctly* remembered doing that.

Still frowning, I cast a sweeping glance around the large, empty room. *There it is.* My tape measure lay on the floor by the baseboard clear on the opposite side of the room, near the front door.

How in the world did that happen? I rubbed my eyes. Maybe I was more tired than I'd realized.

Shaking my head at myself, I crossed the room to retrieve it and set to work.

Over the course of the next hour, I occasionally glanced through the big plate glass window at Vine Life across the street. I really did want to visit the place. I wasn't good with plants—never have been—but I liked them. I just wish I could keep them alive.

I've tried, but it never ends well. There are a few I've managed to keep alive for a few weeks longer than others, but I have what my dad jokingly refers to as an Agent Orange thumb. (I looked that up once and discovered it's a reference to a Vietnam War era chemical used to defoliate the jungle. Lovely.)

It's particular sad because I loved flowers. I loved the atmospheric vibe of a few planters hanging here and there with bright green plants trailing leafy vines. But, as much as I would have loved to buy them and scatter them around my store, I had enough respect for them to save my money and my heart and let someone else buy them.

I'd just be the kiss of death.

At one point, I saw Dave. The short little man crossed the street and traveled down the sidewalk in front Vine Life. He sent a glare across the street in my direction too, almost as though he knew I was looking at him.

That startled me, but I reassured myself that there wasn't any way he could actually see me. Not with the reflection off the plate glass window and the fact that there were no lights on inside my shop. I hadn't seen the need to turn them on yet.

Which reminded me that I needed to decide what I would do for lighting. My shop definitely needed better lighting, but I didn't know if it needed to be box-store bright or if I could get away with something a little gentler.

Maddie's words about Dave floated through my mind. Dave was scowling today, as well. (I had half a notion that a perpetual scowl was his default expression.) He might've scowled in my general direction, but he couldn't be mad down the whole length of the street, could he? Something else had to have upset him.

It occurred to me then, that I didn't even know what Dave did for a living. Did he own a business on the Square? Was he an employee at a business on the Square? Or did he work somewhere else in Starhaven?

As I scribbled down the last of my measurements on my rough floor plan, I resolved to ask Maddie about that the next time I saw her.

At five-thirty, I realized that I desperately needed iced coffee. From the coffee shop. Because, while I had gone grocery shopping, I didn't have anything to make iced coffee myself at the moment.

I talked myself out of it. I'd already been to the coffee shop once today, with semi-disastrous results, and if I wanted coffee that badly, I could just zip upstairs and make myself a cup. (I decided I did not, in fact, want it that badly.)

However, I *did* decide that I needed a break. I wanted to step into Vine Life for a moment, breathe in some plant air and look at all the pretty plants that I would never be able to keep alive.

Hey, a girl could dream.

Brushing off my hands, I put my tools away again and grabbed my purse from its spot against the wall. Whether the rest of the businesses on the Square wanted me here or not, I was here. And I did want to be on good terms with my neighbors, if at all possible.

I mean, good grief, I'm opening a *craft* store. How controversial can it be?

CHAPTER
NINE

As I discovered, it turns out it's really not so much the idea of a craft store that bothers people, but the idea of me running it. Or, rather, I should say it's my presence in this town.

Whatever, I decided stubbornly. *I still intend to win them over.*

I just knew there were lots of people here who needed fat quarters for quilts and chunky yarn for afghans for their grandchildren and all kinds of other cool stuff that I intended to sell them. How could you not fall in love with this brand of creativity?

The second I set foot outside my shop, a wall of hot, humid air slapped me in the face. It might be nearly quitting time for a number of businesses along the Square, but August clearly intended to work overtime. Heat waves shimmered over the sidewalk and the asphalt, and I broke a sweat just crossing the street.

By contrast, even from the outside, Vine Life looked cool and inviting. The leafy green plants in the planters suspended on either side of the front door were vibrant and perky, no doubt partly because they lived in the shade of the awning. To the left of the door, the shop's large plate glass window showcased a small stone waterfall fountain and an assortment of potted plants and plants in hanging baskets. I recognized several of them—purple petunias and a couple of houseplants I'd once tried to grow—but I had no idea what the rest of them were.

Opening the door, I stepped into mercifully cool air. I breathed a sigh of relief...and then I breathed in again, on purpose. The air in here smelled amazing—water and flowers and fresh green growing things. It put me in mind of a rainforest, though I'd never been to a rainforest.

Above my head, the obligatory bell jingled, but it wasn't the usual jingle. This particular bell had a dainty, musical sound that put me in mind of fluttering fairy wings, for some strange reason. It blended well with the gentle rushing sound of the water streaming through the waterfall fountain.

Completely charmed, I wandered away from the front door, looking at everything. Like most of the shops on the Square, Vine Life was longer than it was wide. (Mine was an exception to this, which was one of the reasons I loved it.)

Wire shelves of varying heights lined the brick walls on both sides of the shop, holding a truly amazing array of plant life. A cash register stood on a short desk that had been placed perpendicular to the left wall, while a smattering of end tables holding other plants dotted the rest of the wooden floor. Still more plants dangled from the ceiling in carefully placed locations.

I spotted several small bonsai trees, along with Venus fly traps, and an entire floor-to-ceiling section of succulents. A cascade of rainforest-esque leaves trailing out of one of the baskets next to an absolutely thriving red rose bush in a giant pot left me speechless. The rest were a host of impressive plants of varying sizes in equally impressive pots made of everything from pottery to glass, metal, and stone. There was even a pot that looked like it had been sculpted from delicate pink marble.

At first, I didn't see Plant Lady (as I'd termed her) anywhere. I just meandered around her shop in wonder and not a little awe. A stray corner of my mind wondered how long it took her to tend to everything. When I was growing up, my mom used to have a ton of flowers on the front porch, and I remember it seemed to take her a small eternity to water them all in the summer.

"Can I help you?" inquired a fluty voice from somewhere off to my right.

"Oh." Startled, I turned in that direction to find Plant Lady emerging from behind what looked like a small potted tree. Up close, she was taller—and slimmer—than I'd realized. She wore light brown slacks with a floaty pink silk short-sleeved shirt, and her fall of dark brown hair seemed even darker against the pale skin of her face and arms. Her most startling feature, however, was her eyes, which were the most unusual shade of green I'd ever seen, and—

—those eyes were currently fixed on me with the same kind of suspicion I'd expect from someone who was convinced I was some sort of alien plant. (Pardon the pun.) She did *not* look pleased to find me standing in her shop.

Pasting a smile on my face, I held out a hand. "Hi. I'm Celia O'Malley." I tipped my head toward my shop across the street. "I'm getting ready to open a new craft store across from you."

Plant Lady did not blink, but she tossed her head. "I've heard."

Internally, I winced. If the temperature in here could actually reflect the atmosphere, a layer of frost would be forming on all her pretty plants. Outwardly, however, I maintained a pleasant smile.

"These are amazing." I waved a hand to indicate the shop. "How many different plants do you have here?"

Plant Lady propped a slim hand on her hip. She had long, elegant fingers. "Almost two hundred."

"Wow." My eyebrows shot up. I'd suspected it was a bunch, but... "That's amazing."

Internally, I face-palmed. I'd used that word already, hadn't I? Oh, well.

I tried to rally myself. "What's your name?"

If she wouldn't introduce herself, I'd just have to ask her. Like we were in kindergarten, or something. (It was ridiculous, really, but...what else could I do?)

Those unusually green eyes blinked once and then again second time, as though Plant Lady's mind was racing. After another blink, she said reluctantly, "Marie Claire."

"Nice to meet you." I nodded, still maintaining a smile. *Be friendly*, I told myself.

Plant Lady—Marie—folded her arms across her chest. "Can I help you with something?"

I didn't know how to place her voice. It had an airy, fluty musical quality with a hint of a Kentucky drawl. But just a hint—which meant there was a good chance Marie either wasn't originally from here either, or else she'd learned to suppress her accent for some reason.

"I just thought I'd come by and introduce myself," I said lightly. My smile turned self-deprecating. "I would buy some of these plants, but I'm afraid they wouldn't survive long."

A flash of alarm lit Marie's eyes.

"I can't keep plants alive," I hastened to explain, lest she think I'm some sort of insane destroyer of plants. "I've tried, honest, I have, but I either over-water them or I don't water them enough, or..." I shrugged helplessly. "My dad used to tell me I have an Agent Orange thumb."

The reference apparently went right over Marie's head. She blinked those curious eyes of hers again, and then something in her stance relaxed. She canted her head to one side, surveying me thoughtfully.

"Perhaps you would do better with a succulent."

"You mean like a cactus?" I laughed nervously and held up both hands. "No, no, I'm good. Don't want to be responsible for killing it too. I mean it when I say I'm death to plants."

Marie's gaze flicked down to my hands. "That is curious and unfortunate."

"Tell me about it." I sighed. "My mom loves flowers, but that gene just didn't pass to me."

For a moment, we stood in near silent camaraderie. It *almost* felt like I'd broken the ice.

And then I saw the moment Marie remembered that she was supposed to distrust me because I'm an outsider. Reserve tightened the corners of her eyes, dropping like a wall between us.

Strangely, I wondered if she and Dave were good friends. I wasn't about to ask her that, of course. I have my moments, but I'm not stupid. Usually.

Instead, I offered Marie another bright smile that I knew didn't quite reach my eyes. "Well, I'd better get back to work. Nice meeting you."

A flicker of surprise flashed across the taller women's face, followed by confusion. I had a sneaking suspicion she wanted to ply me with questions, but either couldn't work up the nerve, or didn't know where to start.

Missed your chance, I thought wryly, raising a hand in farewell and heading for the door.

I half expected Marie to stop me, but she didn't. Back out into the oppressive heat I went.

I sent a considering glance up and down the street at the shops and businesses around me. Maybe I'd have better luck trying somebody else. But then I swallowed a sigh.

No, I really did need to get back to work. My gaze strayed wistfully to the corner where the coffee shop stood. Also, if I didn't get back to work, I'd end up over there buying the cup of coffee I really wanted but really couldn't afford, given that my craft shop wasn't even open for business yet.

Honestly, I probably didn't need caffeine as badly as I

thought I did. And I didn't want to trigger anybody *else* with mentions of things like embroidery.

TEN

The next morning, I ate a quick bowl of oatmeal and was out the apartment door and down in my shop before eight AM, hauling a box fan with me. I put on an audiobook I'd been wanting to listen to and spread some old sheets on the floor for drop cloths. After that, I set to work painting a coat of primer on the walls, beginning with trimming out the baseboards and around the window and doorframes.

Several hours later, I set down my roller and surveyed the empty room with satisfaction. Even with just a coat of primer on the walls, my shop already looked brighter and cleaner. I'd turned the box fan on and pointed it toward each wall as I finished. I'd be able to come back after lunch and put on the first coat of real paint.

Unfortunately, that did leave me with a bit of time on my hands. I spent some of it ordering my shelving, and then I fixed myself a sandwich, which I ate standing at the counter in my kitchen while I wrote down a list of the little things I still needed to do in my apartment. After that...I wasn't quite sure what to do with myself.

I drifted over to my living room windows and glanced down at the street below. Cars streamed up and down the street. A group of laughing older women emerged from Vine Life, cradling plants like they were the most precious thing in the universe.

A considering frown creased my forehead. It was Friday— and I really didn't have anything else to do (other than perhaps unpack a little more, but I ignored that particular thought for the moment) until the primer on the walls down- stairs dried.

I glanced down at my hands, which had few speckles of paint on them, but weren't that bad. Maybe this would be a good time to tour another shop or two on the Square. I knew which one I wanted to start with—a lovely-looking antique store on the corner at the west end of the Square, diagonally opposite the street that housed Vine Life and my shop. I'd noticed it several times, during different walks along the Square.

Five minutes later, dressed in regular clothes instead of painting clothes, I exited my apartment building through the back entrance and stepped out into the shadowed alley. When I emerged onto the sidewalk, hot August sun beat down on my shoulders. I slipped my sunglasses on and started walking.

It didn't take long for me to break a sweat. I was keeping the interior of my shop cool enough to work right now, but I didn't have the air conditioning turned up to the level I'd probably use once I'm open for business. Call me cheap if you like, but since I was the only person who had to deal with it, I figured saving a little money on this front was okay for now.

Heat waves shimmered on the sidewalk and the asphalt as I traversed the Square. I sped up as I approached the antique shop, anticipating the wonderful cool air I would encounter inside. (I'll admit it—I'm an outside girl only as long as I'm not freezing my butt off or melting into a puddle of goo.)

Just before I opened the door, I paused long enough to admire the lettering on the big plate glass window. In beautiful calligraphy, it read *Black Forest Antiques*. That was another thing on my massive to-do list—figure out if I was going to buy a sign or just hire somebody to letter it on my window.

Setting that thought aside for now, I pushed the door open and stepped into a welcome wall of cool air that smelled like cinnamon and age. The good kind of age, like visiting my grandparents when I was very young and poking around their upstairs. It made me think of sturdy pieces of furniture full of stories of all the people they'd seen since they were crafted.

A bell above the door intoned a solemn 'ding' to indicate my arrival. I shoved my sunglasses up on top of my head and looked around with eager interest. Black Forest Antiques was as large as I'd expected, given that it took up the corner, and it was crammed full of interesting things.

Along the wall to my left stood a gleaming dark oak counter with glass cases and a sleek, modern cash register sitting one end. The glass cases held all kinds of jewelry—

old-fashioned and otherwise—along with a boatload of other little knickknacks. The high chair behind the counter was empty—the proprietor must be somewhere else in here.

Rows of shelves lined the wall behind the counter, presumably holding more valuable, definitely more breakable pieces. Antique lamps, vases, and some really stunning pieces of crystalware. Also a glass case with what looked like a glittering woman's shoe nestled in a bed of black velvet.

Standing here was almost sensory overload. I'm not an antique expert, but I recognized a few Edwardian pieces, a Princess Anne desk (oh, I wanted that, but definitely could not afford it), as well as a smattering of much more modern pieces of furniture. More Furniture of all sorts lined the walls, while more shelves holding smaller items ran the upper length of the walls. There was even a section of antique rugs and tapestries.

What caught—and held—my interest, however, was a small loom sitting in a corner created by a tall armoire made of black walnut and a gilt-edged mirror facing the other direction. My jaw dropped as I approached it. I don't think I'd ever seen one of these in an antique store before.

Made of what looked like cherry wood, the loom was on the small side—I'm guessing it was mostly used for throw rugs and smaller items. You definitely couldn't weave a large area rug, or a tablecloth or something, but smaller items? Definitely.

I spent a moment walking around the loom. It wasn't set up to weave anything—the warp and weft threads weren't there—but it appeared to work. Gently, I pushed the lever on one side and the loom obediently moved, with barely a whisper of sound. My eyebrows rose in appreciation. Whoever had owned this thing in the past, they had definitely taken care of it.

Brushing a gentle fingertip along the satiny smooth edge of the frame, I imagined what it would be like to work with this loom. I'd had a little plastic loom as a child that I'd used to make thin scarves out of yarn, but I'd never had the opportunity to work with a real loom.

I looked up as footfalls headed in my direction, their owner navigating around pieces of furniture to reach me.

"Can I help you?" began a gruff male voice—and then Dave—the little man who disliked me so intensely—rounded a tall armoire made of black walnut and stopped short in disgust.

"Oh, it's you." His bushy brown eyebrows immediately knit into a scowl. He folded his arms across his chest and glared at me like he'd caught me doing something sneaky. "What are *you* doing here?"

My heart dropped in dismay, but I offered him a smile as a peace offering anyway. "I'm trying to visit all of the businesses on the Square. This shop was next. Only," I felt compelled to add, "I didn't know it was yours."

Dave's scowl deepened. His gaze flicked to my hand, which was still resting on the loom, and he jerked his head to one side. "Unless you plan on buyin' that, don't touch."

I bristled—what did he think I was, some sort of clumsy child?—but I let my hand fall away. He already didn't like me. This was just him being petty.

Taking a deep breath, I shoved my annoyance aside and

nodded to the loom. "Where did this come from? It's beautiful."

Dave's dark eyes glittered. For a second, I didn't think he'd answer me. Then, apparently only because I'd asked an actual question about an item and he seemed to remember I was a potential customer, he said gruffly, "Old family in the mountains east of town. Passed down through several generations, but the current set of youngsters didn't see any value in keeping it."

The tone of his voice told me exactly what he thought of *that* short-sightedness. I nodded slowly, turning away from him to look the loom over again. "I'd love to buy it, but I just can't afford it right now."

Dave snorted, as though to say he wouldn't sell it to me even if I *could* afford it.

I ignored him, mentally scanning through the yarn I'd purchased that would be arriving soon. "I could make some really cool rugs on this. Or some neat place mats."

"But you can't afford it," Dave said smugly, arms still folded across his chest.

It irked me, the way he said it. Like he was oh-so-happy he was losing out on a potential sale. I looked down at him. He was dressed in a green pin-striped suit today, with a matching waistcoat, but he'd taken the suit jacket off. He would have looked quite dapper, if it hadn't been for that ugly look on his face.

"No," I said lightly, "I can't afford it. Yet."

Dave mumbled something under his breath, which I chose to ignore in favor of turning to face him and fixing him with a steely glare of my own.

"What is your problem, Dave?" I deliberately emphasized his name. "I've been here for four days, doing my best to get my shop up and running, and I haven't bothered anybody. I'm friendly. I'm trying to integrate with people here in Starhaven." I threw my hands up in the air. "In fact, you could say I'm trying to help bring more business to this town. So what is the deal? How is my presence here such a bad thing?"

Dave's scowl deepened with every word I spoke, until his eyebrows looked like a short, bushy little line across his forehead. His arms were now folded so tightly across his chest that he reminded me of a pretzel. Fire danced through his dark eyes as he glared up at me.

"You're an *outsider*. You don't belong here."

This again?

I couldn't help it—I rolled my eyes dramatically. "Oh, yes, because nobody in this great country of ours can move to a place they weren't born in and start a new life." It occurred to me that I probably should attempt to deescalate this situation, but...I was tired and I was tired of his attitude.

A faint snort and something that sounded suspiciously like a giggle drifted from somewhere else in the shop.

It shouldn't have been possible at this point, but Dave's dark eyebrows drew into an even more ferocious line. He jerked a thumb over his shoulder in the direction of the door. "Get out."

"Excuse me?" I blinked, taken aback. He was...kicking me out of his store? For being a newcomer to town?

"You heard me. Out." He advanced on me a step. "You said it yourself—you can't afford this loom. So there's no reason for you to be here."

I didn't budge. He was being ridiculous. "What, I can't even look around?"

"Nope. Not today." Dave glared up at me, arms still crossed over his chest. "Now, leave. Before I call the police and tell them you're trespassing."

Stung, I stared back at him, my face flushing. I wasn't totally convinced that he could legally kick me out when I hadn't done anything wrong...but I didn't know for sure.

And I really didn't want to find out. Not when I had so much work to do to get Celia's Craft Shop up and running.

A host of angry words swirled around inside my head, struggling to make it out of my mouth, but I swallowed all of them. "Okay. I'm leaving."

Flipping my ponytail over my shoulder as dramatically as I could (just because I'd always wanted to do that), I spun on my heel and stalked out of the antique store. My face was still burning; the hot August sunshine didn't help.

Breathing hard, I marched right back to my apartment. Any thought I had of meandering through another shop on the Square evaporated faster than a drop of water on the sidewalk beneath my feet. The last thing I wanted to do after this humiliating little interlude was visit another shop run by somebody who didn't like me just because I'd moved here from out of town.

ELEVEN

On the upside, my indignation fueled the rest of my afternoon. I made quick work of the rest of the painting...after I located my paint tray and the bucket of paint again. Somehow, they'd ended up on the floor of the storage closet between the back entrance and a tiny bathroom.

That was even more irritating—how had they ended up in the storage closet, of all places? I *distinctly* recalled leaving them neatly organized on one of the drop cloths before I wrapped the paint rollers in plastic grocery bags and took them up to store them in my refrigerator until it was time to do the next coat.

A prickle of unease had pierced my irritation. Had somebody been in my shop? But in the next breath, I'd convinced myself that was ridiculous. As far as I knew, apart from my landlord I had the only set of keys.

No, I'd probably just forgotten I'd put them there. I had a

to-do list of approximately a million things running in my mind like a background app and apparently it was starting to interfere with my short-term memory.

I made a mental note to maybe start writing more of this stuff down so I didn't have to keep it all in my head. (It's the thought that counts, right?)

That evening, I fixed myself a pack of chicken ramen for supper and gussied it up with some chicken breast, scrambled egg, and mixed veggies and sat down to complete that list. Halfway through, my doorbell rang. Startled, I froze mid-bit. I'd only lived in Starhaven for four days—I didn't expect any visitors yet.

In my haste to leave the table, I hooked my ankle around a chair leg and almost fell face-down on the floor. *Very dignified*, I thought dryly. *You act like you never see people.*

Which...was a *teensy* bit true since I'd moved here. (But was it *really* my fault if half the town was so strangely stand-offish to newcomers? I'd tried to be friendly and introduce myself to people, but most of them hadn't warmed up to me yet.)

Before I unlocked the door and swung it open, I paused to glance through the peephole. To my surprise, a young woman stood in the hall, holding a foil-covered plate in her hands. I gaped at her for only a second before I snapped to and opened the door.

"Hello?" I asked cautiously. A warm, wonderfully fruity smell greeted my nose.

"Hi." The young woman smiled brightly at me. She had curly black hair twisted up into a messy bun, beautiful chocolate brown eyes, and the clearest porcelain skin I believe I've ever seen. "I'm Bianca." She tipped her head in the direction of the street. "I work with Dave at Black Forest Antiques."

"You...work with *Dave*?" My eyebrows attempted to climb up into my hairline, but I stopped them in time. I eyed her, rubbing the back of my neck. "Are you sure you should be here? He doesn't like me very much."

"Well..." Bianca darted a glance left and right along the hall before she leaned in and dropped her voice to a conspiratorial whisper. "Just between you and me, Dave doesn't like most people." She made an apologetic face. "But you're right, he really doesn't like newcomers."

Not much I could say to that except to nod in agreement. I started to hold out a hand, but then my gaze fell on the covered round plate in her hands and I awkwardly retracted my hand. "I'm Celia O'Malley."

"I know." Bianca smiled at me again, her eyes twinkling. "Owner of Celia's Craft Shop." She did a complicated little dance right there in the hall. "I am so excited about your new shop I can hardly stand it!"

I couldn't help it; my eyebrow rose again, this time in wondrous disbelief. Finally, somebody who was actually excited I was here.

Bianca extended the covered plate to me. "A welcome-to-the-Square gift. And—a peace offering." Her expression grew apologetic again. "Don't mind Dave. He's really not as curmudgeonly as he seems."

Nonplussed, I accepted the plate, which turned out to be a really sturdy paper plate.

"Blueberry muffins," Bianca said before I could lift the

cover to peek. She smiled again. "Just took them out of the oven a little while ago. My own recipe."

I lifted the plate to my nose and sniffed delicately. My mouth started watering. The muffins smelled amazing—and they were still warm.

Something equally warm unfurled in my chest. "Thank you." I smiled at Bianca, gesturing with the plate. "This was really, really sweet of you. No pun intended," I added hastily.

She laughed, and the sound was like tiny musical bells. "You're welcome."

Belatedly, I remembered my manners. Stepping to one side of my doorway, I nodded to the interior of my apartment. "Would you like to come in?"

Regret flashed through her dark eyes. "I'm afraid I can't today." A half-wry, half-apologetic smile tilted one corner of her lips. "Dave will be wondering where I am."

That sent tiny little alarm bells off in the back of my mind, though I wasn't entirely sure why. I raised a cautiously questioning eyebrow. "Are you and Dave..."

Bianca blinked at me in sunny non-comprehension. "Related? Yes." Her smile took on a soft cast. "He's my uncle. He's raised me since...well...forever." She shrugged.

That wasn't actually what I meant, but I guess it answered my question. And, really, it wasn't any of my business. I nodded, relieved, and quickly changed the subject.

"Are you a crafter?" I studied Bianca with renewed interest.

Another beautifully sunny smile lit her face. "Yes! I knit." She happily bounced up and down on her toes. "I am so looking forward to perusing your yarn section. And—" She canted her head to one side, birdlike. "Do you crochet?"

"I do. I love to crochet." I made an apologetic face. "I actually enjoy it more than knitting."

I was not prepared for the way Bianca clasped her hands under her chin and looked at me like she was Princess Leia and I was her only hope.

"Can you teach me sometime? I have always wanted to learn how to crochet, but I just can't seem to wrap my brain around how to do it. I am hopeless with instruction books." She scrunched her face into an adorable frown.

"Have you tried watching videos on YouTube?"

Her frown deepened. "Yes. Didn't help."

"Okay." I nodded slowly, my thoughts already spinning with possibilities. "I will...see what I can do."

Bianca gave me a dazzling smile. "Thank you." She glanced over her shoulder, though the hallway was empty. "I must go now." Still smiling, she nodded to the plate of muffins in my hands. "Enjoy them."

"I will."

"Nice to meet you, Celia O'Malley," Bianca called over her shoulder as she headed back down the hall.

"You too," I called after her retreating figure, bemused.

The hair on the back of my neck suddenly prickled, like somebody was staring very hard in my direction. Unsettled, I glanced up and down the hallway, but it was empty. I had neighbors on this hall, but I had yet to meet them. (And I hadn't taken the time to introduce myself yet, either.)

Shaking my head, I pushed the feeling away and shut my front door with my hip before I carried the plate through my apartment to the kitchen. Setting it on the counter, I pulled off the foil to reveal six beautiful blueberry muffins with slightly golden tops. They looked delicious.

I couldn't help but smile, warmth curling through my chest again. I think I might have made my first friend here.

Temporarily ignoring my unfinished ramen, I selected the muffin that looked like it had the most blueberries and bit into it. My eyes fluttered shut in enjoyment. *Oh, that is good.*

The muffin had the perfect blend of sweetness and baked goodness, with plenty of blueberry flavor. The fact that it was still warm made it even better. Opening my eyes, I eyed my butter dish on the counter. A little pat of butter wouldn't hurt either.

Next muffin, I told myself. I had to finished my ramen first.

While I polished off the remainder of my supper, Bianca's earnest expression floated through my mind. Dave. Everything came back to Dave. What was his problem with the world?

I hated to think it, but he really was your stereotypical angry little man.

He's been through more than you might think.

Maddie's words floated back to the forefront of my mind, and a tiny bit of my anger receded, washed away by a little spurt of compassion.

No. I tried to hold onto the anger. I had every right to be angry and exasperated. He was making my life miserable.

Except... Sighing, I set down my fork and rose from the table. I should know better than anyone that things from the past have a stronger hold on an individual's present and future than they'd like.

While I buttered a muffin for dessert, curiosity strong-armed anger out of the way. Why *was* Dave like that? Bianca didn't approve of his attitude, but she also didn't seem to be afraid of him. Which was good, considering he was her uncle.

So there must be more to Dave than his anger and hatred of outsiders.

Munching my muffin, I drifted out of the kitchen and into the living room, coming to a halt in front of my window. I stared down at the street, watching the evening traffic come and go without really seeing anything.

An idea crystallized in my head. I knew what I had to do. Somehow, I had to figure out how to convince Dave that I'm on Starhaven's side. I had to show him I intended to be an active member of the community, not somebody who drained them dry.

A snort escaped me before I could help myself. I had zero idea how I was going to accomplish that feat, however.

And, really, maybe Dave's dislike wasn't that important in the grand scheme of things. Starhaven had thousands of citizens. The odds were in my favor.

That's what I told myself, at any rate.

CHAPTER

TWELVE

Over the next week, Bianca and I chatted a few times, but for me the days passed in a blurry haze of work and more work. Unfortunately, that unsettling feeling of being watched lingered. It was so ever-present that I *almost* grew accustomed to it and it *almost* melded into the background.

Almost.

Some days the feeling increased to the point that I would have sworn an invisible person was wandering around my shop—and, more disturbingly, my apartment—moving things, unplugging them, and generally making a nuisance of themself. Usually, the incidents coincided with some major leap in my preparations to open my shop.

The day I'd finished painting the walls, for starters. The day all of my shelving arrived. (Which was a huge relief, because the cryptic way Dave had talked about cell phone coverage here had made me wonder if I'd have any trouble getting things delivered, but everyone had found my shop just fine.)

On those days, however, the feeling that someone was following me around, practically breathing down my neck, increased to the point that a sense of anxiety pressed down on me so heavily that I ended up concocting ways to escape my own store.

At least until the moment it hit me, sitting in Ed's Sandwich Shop on the other side of the Square, that by allowing myself to be pressured into leaving my store for even an hour, I was allowing whoever was bothering me to win.

I sat frozen with my shrimp po'boy halfway to my mouth, stunned by this internal revelation. It was only when a fat little shrimp fell from my sandwich and plopped onto my plate that I realized how ridiculous I must look. I resumed eating, but I barely registered the spicy deliciousness that was my sandwich.

I'd moved to Starhaven to start over and leave my past behind. I wasn't about to let some strange unknown person (or somebody like Dave) run me off, simply because I hadn't been born here.

I took a fierce bite of my sandwich, before consuming a couple of French fries. Speaking of strange, though... Out of the corner of my eye, I glanced at the plate glass window at the front of the little sandwich shop and the steady stream of lunchtime traffic flowing up and down the sidewalk.

The strangest thing about Starhaven was that its strangeness ebbed and flowed like an odd little current in a tide pool. Some days, things like going into the bank or the grocery store were perfectly normal. Nothing out of the ordinary, nothing I'd think was even remotely different than in Louisville or any other part of the country.

But over the past few weeks, every so often I encountered someone—be it in a store or on the street—who seemed a little...*off*. There really wasn't any other way to describe it. And it was almost always early in the morning or later in the evening.

I didn't think it was the Square itself that was the epicenter of all the strangeness, I think that was just where I happened to notice many of these things because I was currently spending all of my time there.

Taking another bite of my sandwich, I catalogued some of the things I'd noticed. Old women in the grocery store wrapped in old-fashioned cloaks that obscured their faces despite the August heat doing its best to melt the pavement beneath our feet. People who liked to dress up in Renaissance clothing and go strolling about town early in the morning or late at night. (They always seemed to disappear down a side street when I got too close, but I'd made a mental note to do some specific advertising later. Individuals who were *that* passionate about costume design would probably like my shop, right?)

And then there were my fellow business owners on the Square themselves...and their employees.

Marie and her otherworldly eyes crossed my mind, and I thought back to that day at the coffee shop when I'd sworn the barista Molly's ears were pointed. Those weren't the only incidents, however. On another visit to Tam's Pizza, I'd glimpsed one of her employees in the back who could have tried out for a role as a troll or a giant in a movie. (Poor guy—

I felt sorry for him. He'd probably been made fun of his whole life for that lumpy nose, oddly deep-set eyes, and that heavy brow.)

My gaze slid to the order counter as I took a long draught of my water, shivering a little as the icy water slid down my throat. Also, the owner of this restaurant. Ed was a short little man in his sixties, with wizened features, a white beard, and twinkling blue eyes. (Those eyes hadn't twinkled at me, but they certainly twinkled at other customers.)

I couldn't quite put my finger on *why* I thought there was something different about him, but...there was. And his wife too—if that was the identity of the equally short, equally wizened older lady who worked with him. Was it the way those blue eyes seemed to look right through me? The way he'd almost seemed to know what food I was going to order before I ordered?

It wasn't the cool reception I'd received—I'd expected that, given Dave's widespread interference. No, this was something else. I popped another French fry into my mouth, savoring the salty potato goodness. I just wasn't sure what it was yet.

When I'd first started picking up on all these strange little things, I'd scolded myself for being overly imaginative. I'd probably breathed in too many paint fumes, or spent too much time by myself lately. There had to be a logical explanation for what I'd seen.

I told myself that...but it had been weeks now, and I hadn't found that logical explanation yet.

Polishing off the last of my sandwich, I gathered up my trash and moved to throw it away. It occurred to me that I probably ought to talk to Maddie at some point. I'd seen the town facilitator in passing in the last two weeks, but we hadn't spoken.

She might be able to answer some of my questions. Hopefully.

"Thanks," I called out to Ed. "It was delicious."

The short man nodded without looking at me, his attention entirely focused on his next customer, an older man in a suit who probably worked at the courthouse.

Irritation prickled over my skin, compounded as I wove my way around full tables to the door. A couple of people met my eye and offered smiles, but most of them ignored me. That was another thing.

Quite a few of the people in this town tried to avoid me without making it *look* like they were ignoring me. (Except for Dave. He made no bones about the fact that he was actively ignoring me, and it was oddly refreshing.) I didn't know why people thought that would work. Provided the person being ignored has an IQ greater than a flat rock, they can always tell.

But, I digressed. The point was, apart from feeling like I was being watched all the time, it was becoming increasingly obvious that there really was something different about this town...and it *literally* had to do with a chunk of its inhabitants.

Well, I decided, as I marched across the Square to my shop, filled with an excellent lunch and new-found determination, I'd worry about my fellow citizens and their strangeness later.

Right now, I had a shop to finish setting up.

THIRTEEN

The following Monday, my shop sign went up above the awning, right on schedule. Despite the still-broiling heat, I stood outside on the sidewalk and just stared at it in amazement.

In cheerful purple script on a sideways lavender oval, it read simply *Celia's Craft Shop*

My craft shop.

Tears pricked at my eyes. Wouldn't my grandmother be proud?

Clasping my hands together beneath my chin, I took several deep, steadying breaths. *Almost there*, I told myself. Opening day was just around the corner.

Around me, people went about their daily business. I'm sure I drew a few strange looks, but I didn't care. I'd worked really hard for this, and now it was all about to pay off.

"My, that looks nice," said a voice behind me.

Startled, I turned around to find Maddie approaching me

on the sidewalk. The town facilitator wore a different floaty dress today in a pastel lavender that almost matched my sign, as well as a rather becoming straw hat. She looked like she could have stepped foot out of a period piece in England.

"Thank you." I returned her smile with one of my own, giddy excitement rising in my chest again. "I'm almost ready."

"Yes, you are." Maddie turned to survey my sign. "I like it. Simple, not too complicated." She nodded. "Rather elegant, in its own way."

Wow. I blinked at her, and then glanced at my sign again. "Well, I hadn't thought of it that way. I was thinking more that simplicity would be best." Slightly embarrassed, I rubbed the back of my neck with one hand. "I'm not exactly a complicated person. I didn't want to get too fancy."

To be honest, I'd sorted through and discarded dozens of different name ideas and sign shapes over the last few months. Everything from the fanciful to the practical. In the end, it had come down to the simple, basic fact that this was *my* craft shop.

"How are you settling in?" Maddie asked after a moment. "I haven't had a chance to check in with you in a while."

I glanced sideways to find the older woman studying me thoughtfully. Almost as though she knew the kind of troubles I've been having lately. I suppressed a mental laugh. *Just keep telling yourself that, Celia.*

"Fine," I said brightly.

Maddie just continued to look at me, drilling me with exactly the same sort of knowing look my grandmother used to give me.

A slight shiver traveled down my spine. "Well..." I hesitated. It was going to sound crazy. I *knew* that. But...

Maddie raised an encouraging gray eyebrow. She didn't look suspicious or distressful, she just looked kindly curious.

It was the kindness that finally prompted me to spill the tea.

"This is going to sound a little crazy," I began. "And I assure you, I'm not crazy."

Maddie nodded. "You don't strike me as the crazy type, my dear."

"And I don't believe that places are haunted either," I added. "But I have to admit, there is something strange about this building." I waved a hand toward my shop and my apartment above it.

"Strange?" Maddie arched an eyebrow.

"Yeah..." A hot wind blew down the street, carrying with it the smell of exhaust, hot asphalt, and the scent of flowers from the planters along the sidewalk. An odd combination.

Quit procrastinating and just tell her, I scolded myself.

Taking a breath, I plunged into my story. How things moved themselves when I left them, or sometimes seemed to have moved when I turned my back. And the fact that while I might have a lot on my mind right now, I was *not* losing my mind.

"On top of that," I finished, "I constantly feel like something is watching me disapprovingly. It's creepy and as annoying as all get out." Unconsciously, I looked up toward my living room window, which overlooked the street. "Is that why the lease was so reasonable?"

To my surprise, Maddie did not react in any of the ways I

expected. She didn't laugh at my tale, or brush me off as being a single woman with an overactive imagination. Instead, she, too, lifted her gaze to stare thoughtfully up at my window.

"I don't believe this has anything to do with the price of your lease," she said slowly. "Old Mr. Moffat had his reasons for wanting you to be here."

I didn't have time to examine that particular statement before she continued, "No, my dear, I'm afraid you have a different problem." Her forehead creased with a thoughtful frown. "Hmm. What would be the best way to go about this?"

I shifted uncomfortably on the hot sidewalk. She seemed to be consulting herself, not me.

"Are you a messy housekeeper?"

The question startled me, making me bristle. "I beg your pardon?" What did *that* have to do with anything?

Maddie repeated the question, her attention still fixed on my apartment's windows.

"No..." I said slowly. "Not particularly. I mean," I shrugged, "when I have busy days sometimes I don't keep things as clean as I probably should, but I wouldn't say I'm particularly messy."

A thought occurred to me. "Unless I'm creating something." It was my turn to frown. "When I'm quilting or knitting or something, sometimes my workstation gets a little crazy."

"No, no." Maddie shook her head, almost absentmindedly. "That's not what I mean." Tapping one hand on her hip, she turned to eye me speculatively.

I had that strange, itchy feeling she was taking my measure again.

"Set out a plate of cookies tonight, Celia," she said abruptly, with an air of finality. "Homemade cookies, mind you. Not the store-bought kind. Don't ask me why, but it matters. And some sparkly beads, if you have them."

Homemade cookies? Beads? I blinked, wondering if the heat was getting to me—or to her. "That sounds—"

"Crazy?" Maddie trilled a light laugh. "Yes, I imagine it does." She stretched out a hand to pat me on the shoulder. "Just do it. You'll understand later, dear."

I must have looked particularly gobsmacked, blinking at her in the bright afternoon sunlight, because her smile softened. "You may be new to Starhaven, but you're part of it now. You'll have to get used to a few...peculiarities."

Yeah... I swallowed. That didn't sound ominous at all.

Maddie turned away, but I jumped, suddenly recalling the roughly half a million questions I had for her. "Wait!"

"Yes, dear?" She glanced over her shoulder at me.

"I have some questions for you before my grand opening." I gestured to the town at large. "About Starhaven."

"I see." Maddie's tone shifted like an errant breeze, turning from pleasant and amused to brisk and businesslike. "I'll tell you what. Set the beads and the cookies out tonight, and then tomorrow morning meet me at the coffee shop at nine AM and I'll do my best to answer any questions you might have."

The critical part of my brain couldn't help but note that she had neatly sidestepped outright promising to answer my questions. But, what choice did I have, really?

"Okay. It's a deal." The words fell between us and hung there in the sticky air for a second. I had the strangest feeling that I should hold out my hand. I did so, and Maddie shook it briskly.

"Very well." The town facilitator offered me another smile. "I'll leave you to it, Celia O'Malley. Until tomorrow." With a wave, she set off up the sidewalk toward the courthouse, leaving me standing in her wake feeling as though something momentous had occurred and I had missed it.

FOURTEEN

I baked cookies that evening. Colossal Cookies, made from peanut butter, oatmeal, and chocolate chips, so named because they're about half again as large as your average chocolate chip cookie. I didn't particularly want to take the time to bake when I had a store to finish setting up just a couple of days ahead of my grand opening, but...

Curiosity is a powerful thing, let me tell you.

Also, I was tired of feeling like an unwanted intruder in my own home. And I happen to love these cookies. If you can ignore the amount of sugar in them (which I assure you I can), they make a fantastic, easy breakfast. I'd enjoy them in the morning.

On the upside, I got to test out how well the air conditioning in my apartment worked (just fine, despite the building's age), and I got cookies. I suppose I should classify it as a win-win.

After pulling the last batch of cookies from the oven and quickly cleaning up my kitchen, I took a still-warm cookie with me as I strode into my office. It was still an unorganized mess—boxes of papers and craft materials everywhere—but I'd at least cleaned my desk off in between baking trays of cookies.

Munching happily on the cookie, I located a large rectangular plastic box that contained my collection of various beads and set it on the desk. I liked beading—I'd tried my hand at both making jewelry and sewing designs on fabric—but I didn't love it as much as I loved quilting, knitting, and crocheting.

Hence my memory was a little fuzzy on what exactly I had in here. Down in the shop, I had a large box of various beads I'd be selling, but I was loathe to break into my inventory unless I could avoid it.

I took another bite of cookie, enjoying a mostly-melted chocolate chip, and then let out a triumphant laugh as I spotted what I'd been looking for. "Found you!"

Maddie hadn't specified what size these sparkly beads needed to be. Hopefully, this little pack of Swarovski crystal seed beads in all the colors of the rainbow would suffice. I tilted the little plastic bag this way and that beneath the overhead light, enjoying the way the light danced on them.

Oh, yes. If I needed sparkly beads, these would most definitely do the trick.

As Maddie had not specified *where* to put the cookies and the beads (and I'd been too discombobulated to ask her), I ended up setting them on a plate in the center of my kitchen table. I arranged three colossal cookies on one side of a plain white dinner plate and then poured the beads out in a colorful swathe across the other side of the plate.

I even took a picture of the plate, just to prove to myself later that, yes, I had done this. Almost like I was setting out something for a crafty Santa Claus.

In late August.

But if it meant that the weird unpleasant vibes stopped? I'd try it.

Shaking my head at myself, I headed to the bathroom to take my contacts out and then went to bed. Surprisingly, I didn't dream.

When I stumbled out to the kitchen the next morning, dressed in a t-shirt and pajama pants, two of the cookies were gone. So were most of the seed beads. And by 'most of', I mean *all* of the beads except for the weird pale topaz ones. Those were still there, sorted into a neat little pile.

For a second, I just stared at the plate in dumb incomprehension. That the cookies were gone somehow made sense in my brain (probably due to my conversation with Maddie). But the *beads*?

Taking my glasses off, I rubbed my eyes. Then I put them back on and leaned in closer to examine the plate. Nothing changed. Somebody—and it had to be a *somebody*, because I didn't know what else could actually *sort* tiny beads—had taken the time to pick out the colors it—they?—apparently did not like.

My fingers tightened their grip on the back of one of my

kitchen chairs, which I'd grabbed to keep myself from falling over in shock. What the heck was going on here? Had somebody broken into my apartment during the night? Did I need to call the police?

Bad enough that it felt like somebody was rummaging around my apartment and my shop in the daytime. The idea that someone had been rummaging around my kitchen *while I was asleep* made the hair on the back of my neck prickle.

A knot of hysteria rose in my throat. Maybe chucking my life in Louisville and moving lock, stock, and barrel to a tiny town in Eastern Kentucky had not been the great idea I'd thought. Maybe—

"Your gift is accepted," said a reedy little voice somewhere off to my left.

"What?" I jumped, making an undignified little squeak, and looked wildly around my kitchen. Police. Yes, I definitely needed to call the police. What had I done with my cell phone?

"Who's there?" I demanded, even as I scrabbled in the pocket of my pajama pants to find my phone.

"Don't like the soggy-looking brown ones, though," the reedy little voice continued. "No good, those."

Maybe I was asleep and dreaming. Pressing my lips into a thin line, I forced myself to look around my kitchen a little more slowly.

First, the counters. I swallowed. Nothing there except my appliances. My gaze lingered on my Keurig. Maybe I needed to lay off the caffeine.

Next, the worn linoleum floor. Nothing there, either.

That left the kitchen table. Subconsciously, I'd saved it for last. Heart in my throat, I looked over in the direction of the plate again and—

"Eek!" I jumped backward, nearly tripping over my own feet in the process. Hand on my chest, I stared in shock and disbelief at my kitchen table.

A tiny creature stood there, hands on its hips, staring up at me with a frank expression edged in suspicion. If I hadn't heard it speak, I would have thought it was a little clay statue of some sort with a mass of curly hair. It was brown and a little lumpy looking, though—I squinted and adjusted my glasses—on closer inspection, the lumps were actually its nose and ears. It was dressed in a lumpy, raggedy brown dress, and its mass of black curls was tied back with a ragged brown kerchief.

"What—what are you?" I asked faintly. "*Who* are you?"

The lumpy little creature just continued to stare at me.

My heart pounded beneath my fingers. I took a deep breath, willing myself to calm down. Maybe I really wasn't awake yet. Maybe I needed coffee more than I realized. Maybe—

"You've been talkin' to Maddie, ain't ya?" the creature demanded in that reedy little voice. "Only way an outsider like *you* would have known to leave *me* a present."

I was so dumbfounded by this I could only nod. How did it know? How did *Maddie* know? And if she did know about this...this...whatever this creature was...why hadn't she just *told* me about it?

The creature heaved a reedy sigh so deep it must have originated somewhere in the building's basement. Tipping its head back, it stared up at the ceiling, as if asking *why me?*

before it grimly pivoted around and marched over to the plate I'd left on the table. Breaking off a large chunk off of the last remaining Colossal cookie, it sat down on the edge of the table and proceeded to take a bite out of the cookie chunk (which was bigger than its head).

"Can't believe I'm doing this," it muttered to itself. It took another bite, eying me while it chewed. "Not supposed to, you know. Protocol is to only come out at night an' never reveal ourselves." Shaking its head, the little creature swung its feet morosely.

Slowly, my heart rate returned to something approaching normal. I took another, deeper breath and blinked several times, just to make sure I wasn't seeing things. Well, I mean, *clearly,* I was seeing things, but the *thing* I was seeing happened to be sitting on the edge of my kitchen table like it owned the place.

Dimly, I was aware that I was still standing in my pajamas, frozen in place in the middle of my kitchen floor. The creature continued to munch on the cookie, and it was that fact, oddly enough, that finally spurred me to speak.

"Who *are* you?"

The creature pulled a truculent face and kicked its legs through the air beneath the lip of the table for a moment before it finally answered. "Outsider like you can't pronounce my name."

What kind of an answer was *that*? Flummoxed, I stared at the creature, resisting the urge to put my head in my hands. Without a doubt, I could safely say this was the most surreal moment I'd ever experienced. And if I was dreaming...well...I was never buying that turkey from Starhaven Shoppe's deli again.

I tried a different tack. "Okay, so then, *what* are you?"

A shrewd light passed through the creature's dark eyes. It ate another bite of cookie, before shrugging lumpy shoulders. "What do you think?"

Another non-answer. A flicker of impatience curled through me, like a flame devouring a scrap of paper. "I don't know. I'm an outsider, remember?"

"Oh, yes," the creature said glumly. "You are that." It studied the chunk of cookie remaining in its hands. "But you can bake, which is more than the last one could do."

I desperately needed a cup of coffee, but a ray of realization poked through the surreal befuddlement coursing through me. "Do you—do you *live* here?"

The creature gave a reedy snort. "Where else would I live?"

A dozen different memories crowded to the forefront of my mind. The feeling of being glared at. My things temporarily disappearing, or being rearranged.

It was my turn to eye the little creature. "Are you the one who's been causing me all this trouble?"

A shifty look passed over the creature's lumpy brown face and I had my answer.

"What are you?" I asked again. "And why are you bothering me?" I waved a hand to the apartment. "Mr. Moffat rented me this place. I have permission to be here."

An unspoken question hung between us. *Who gave you permission to be here?*

The creature's stubby fingers tightened on the fragment

of cookie it still held. "My home." It jabbed its chin in the direction of the floor. "Been my home since—since That Day."

I nodded as though I knew what That Day meant. Inwardly, I shook my head. *I can't believe I'm standing here having this conversation with...whatever this thing is.*

"Well," I tried to strike a tone midway between gentle and firm. "This is my home now, too."

The creature pulled a terrible face and hunched its shoulders, but then it glanced sideways at the plate, empty save for the neat little pile of topaz beads. In that moment, there was something profoundly lonely about it.

A nascent headache began throbbing in my temples. Pinching the bridge of my nose between two fingers, I closed my eyes and took a deep breath. Before I—we—did anything else, I wanted coffee.

And a cookie.

Opening my eyes, I addressed the creature. "Would you like a cup of coffee?"

"Coffee?" The creature wrinkled its nose. "Why would I want to drink hot bean water?" Snorting, it ate a little more of its chunk of cookie. "No, no, tea's the proper thing, you know."

"Because hot leaf water is so much better?" I asked faintly, before I could stop myself.

"Exactly." The creature nodded firmly, and then tilted its head to one side, looking oddly hopeful. "Do you have any? Tea, that is?"

I must confess I'm not much of a tea drinker except in the winter time or when I don't feel well, but I usually kept some on hand. I motioned to the cabinet on the right side of the sink, near my little pantry. "I have mint tea, cinnamon, and Irish breakfast."

The creature eyed the cookie in its hands and then looked up at me. "Irish Breakfast."

And that was how I ended up having breakfast with the strange little creature that apparently inhabited the part of the building that held my shop and my apartment.

I couldn't *wait* to have a conversation about this with Maddie.

FIFTEEN

An hour and a half later, I met Maddie at the coffee shop at nine AM sharp. Were it not for the strange little creature sitting in my kitchen, I might've needed to gather my courage before I went in, but as it was, that creature's existence blew any residual embarrassment out of the water.

I really couldn't wait to hear what Maddie had to say about *this*.

The town facilitator sat at a little table for two in the sunshine pouring through one of the front plate glass windows. She rose from her seat when I walked in and greeted me with a smile. We exchanged perfunctory greetings and then Maddie bade me to order whatever I wanted.

Once she had her teacup of green tea and I had a mocha iced coffee, she snagged a couple of armchairs in a corner out of the way. That surprised me—for some reason, I'd expected her to return to the table in the sunshine.

Maddie wasted no time in beating around the bush. She fixed me with a half-curious, half-expectant look over the rim of her teacup. "Did you set out the cookies and the beads?"

A burble of hysterical laughter bubbled up in my throat, but I managed to contain it. "Yes, I did."

Interest lit Maddie's green eyes. She arched a graying eyebrow. "And?"

I opened my mouth to tell her about the creature—and abruptly changed my mind. Just how much did Maddie actually know? Shaking my head, I opted for a different approach.

"When I woke up, two of the cookies were gone. And most of the beads."

Something indiscernible—surprised, maybe?—flickered in her eyes. "The beads weren't *all* gone?"

"Oh, no." I shook my head again, before taking my first sip of iced coffee. The combination of chocolate and coffee never got old. "It left all the topaz ones."

"Interesting." Maddie sat back in her seat.

I took another sip and then said casually, "It said it didn't like them because they were soggy brown." I took a third sip. *Wait for it...*

Maddie nodded, as though she'd expected this...and then my words penetrated. Her eyes widened. "What?"

Something that felt suspiciously like triumph curled through the astonished shock still befuddling part of my brain. "Oh, yes." I nodded, before taking another cautious sip. My coffee was deliciously cold, and I really didn't want to give myself brain freeze.

I gave Maddie a chiding look. "You could have told me there was a lumpy little brown creature living in my apartment. Although, to be fair," I held a hand out palm up, "I probably wouldn't have believed you."

"She *showed* herself to you?" Genuine shock flooded Maddie's face. She leaned forward so abruptly she nearly spilled her tea all over herself. "This morning?"

Her reaction confused me even more. I stared askance at her, bemused. "I...take it that's not what you were expecting it—her—to do?"

"No." Maddie stared at me as though she had just realized I was some sort of strange new specimen of human. "I expected you to simply tell me that the cookies and the beads were gone."

"And then you planned to explain?"

"Yes." Maddie continued to stare at me. "That is...very interesting."

We both fell silent, and I became more aware of the sounds of laughter, conversation, and the various coffee machines that had been relegated to background noise.

After a moment, I shook my head. "Maddie, what *is* that thing? It wouldn't tell me its name. Just said I couldn't pronounce it." I waved my free hand. "And then it sat on my kitchen table and ate the other cookie and I made it a cup of tea and—"

"You—made it a cup of tea?" Maddie's jaw actually dropped. She gaped at me, her expression so shocked that it almost made me wonder if I had somehow sprouted a second head.

"Yes. And then it disappeared—" *That* had nearly made me drop my coffee cup in shock, let me tell you. "—and I came to meet you." Frowning at her, I repeated my earlier question. "What *is* that thing?"

For a moment, it seemed all Maddie could do was gape at me. But, gradually, her shock faded and her eyebrows grew into a puzzled frown. At last, she leaned back in her chair and took a long sip of her green tea.

"It's a brownie," she said after she swallowed. "Or, I should say, *she* is a brownie. Quite rare, too, for her to be a female. Most brownies are male."

It was my turn to freeze in astonishment, my coffee cup halfway to my lips. Inanely, my first thought was of the chocolate dessert. But then my mind went back to stories I'd read as a child. Fairytales and folklore, to be more precise.

Belatedly, I realized Maddie was waiting for me to say something. I cleared my throat. "A...brownie? As in those creatures from Irish folklore, and things like that?"

Maddie nodded.

I looked askance at her. "*That* lumpy little hairy thing?"

Something like concern flickered through Maddie's dark eyes. "Don't insult her. They're spiteful when angered."

Oh, boy. I hadn't expected *that*. Weakly, I sank back into my armchair, clutching my iced coffee.

For just a second, the coffee shop spun about me as my brain attempted to make sense of this information and my world readjusted. I really *wasn't* crazy or seeing things. There really *was* a creature from folklore living in my building.

"Is that why the lease was so affordable?" The question popped out before I could stop myself.

Maddie pressed her lips into a thin line before she answered. "I believe that might have been a factor, yes."

I narrowed my eyes at her. What was *that* supposed to mean? But before I could prod further, Maddie continued.

"I can't believe she actually showed herself to you." She shook her head in wonder. "That changes things."

I'd just taken a sip of my coffee, but almost choked on the cold liquid. "What things?"

"How you proceed from here." Expression thoughtful, Maddie swirled her tea around in her teacup. "It changes what I need to tell you about how to handle daily life with a brownie."

Handle daily life...what? I held up a hand. "Wait a minute. Do you mean to tell me that that...brownie is a *permanent* part of my apartment? As in, I can't get rid of it?"

Maddie's eyes flashed at me. "Quiet," she said sternly, though she kept her voice very low. "Don't say that so loudly."

This was nuts. I flipped the end of my ponytail over my shoulder. "My lease didn't say anything about my apartment or shop coming with a roommate, folklore creature or otherwise."

"Are you sure?"

"Yes." I straightened in my armchair, my coffee sloshing in its cup. "I read the whole thing."

A crease appeared between Maddie's eyebrows. "That is... unusual. Most people don't."

"Yeah, well, I worked at a law firm, remember? I learned how important it is to read the fine print before you sign anything." Setting my cup aside on a little square end table beside my chair, I folded my arms across my chest. "And, like I said, I don't recall anything about a brownie."

"You wouldn't, at least not directly." The suddenly severe look on Maddie's face turned to one of weariness. She pinched the bridge of her nose. "I believe she's covered in the lease as one of the 'as-is' features of the building."

My jaw dropped. That was crazy. "But—"

"I know." It was Maddie's turn to hold up a hand. "It doesn't make sense, from your point of view." She offered me a wry, albeit kind, smile. "That's another part of my job as town facilitator, you see. To explain to newcomers that things don't always make sense in this town."

"I'm starting to get that feeling." The brownie's somber little brown, lumpy face appeared in my mind's eye and I made a mental note to read back through my contract.

"She won't be a bother, I assure you. Not now that you know about her and she's accepted your gift." Maddie offered me an encouraging smile. "In fact, if you're kind to her, I think you'll find she'll be most beneficial to you."

It was my turn to sigh and pinch the bridge of my nose. "Will you at least tell me what I'm supposed to call her?"

Maddie regarded me for a few heartbeats—long enough for the chatter of other customers in the coffee shop and the noise of the various coffee machines to seep in the spaces between us again.

"Agnes," she said at last. "We mostly call her Agnes."

Agnes. I turned that name around in my mind. It sounded about right for that lumpy little creature. "Well, that's easy enough to say."

"It'd be best if you got her to tell you her name herself, but..." Maddie trailed off, delicately turning one hand palm up.

"Okay." Nodding, I exhaled slowly. Now that the shock of meeting Agnes had started to fade as my brain processed my new reality, questions began crowding into my mind.

I eyed Maddie. "What else are you supposed to tell me?"

She trilled a little laugh. "That was the extent of it for now, really. Other than the fact that now that you know about Agnes, I am duty-bound to inform you that you cannot break the lease you signed."

I blinked. I wasn't so sure about that—from my experience, leases could always be broken, but most of them resulted in hefty consequences. However, it didn't really matter.

"I'm not planning on breaking my lease." I waved my free hand to encompass the town beyond the walls of the coffee shop. "I'm serious about opening a craft store here." I shrugged, a trifle self-consciously. "I don't really have anything to go back to in Louisville—or anywhere else."

Maddie's expression grew kind. "That would be something you have in common with many of the folk here in Starhaven. We don't really have anything to go back to, either."

I could understand that. But, at the same time...

Taking a deep breath, I made myself look as open and non-confrontational as possible. "Can you answer one more question?"

Maybe I imagined it, but a hint of wariness flickered behind Maddie's otherwise friendly eyes. "If it is within my power."

The phrasing was a little odd, but I brushed it aside. "Why is this town so resistant to outsiders? I mean," I shrugged, "I've visited a few small towns in Kentucky and Tennessee over the years. They definitely have a community vibe going on that's hard for outsiders to break through permanently, but Starhaven takes things to a whole new level."

Silence greeted my words. Maddie pursed her lips and looked down at her teacup. "It is...difficult to explain. Other than to say that we have a disproportionate percentage of a population that is perhaps a little...eccentric. And some of them have trust issues."

I raised an eyebrow. "Why is that?"

Starhaven didn't strike me as the kind of place that had a dark underbelly that left people traumatized, but... My stomach turned over. I hadn't exactly done a ton of research before I'd moved here, either.

Maddie sighed. "I suppose you could say that they feel safe here, which is why they stay. To heal, and to live...normal lives."

Okay. I leaned back in my chair. That didn't exactly answer my question, but...it was probably as close to an actual answer as I was going to get today.

My thoughts returned to my erstwhile apartment guest. "What do I do with Agnes?"

For the first time since we'd started this conversation, Maddie laughed. Her green eyes twinkled at me. "You'll figure it out."

I barely managed to keep from slumping back in my chair. That was *not* what I wanted to hear.

SIXTEEN

When I set foot in my apartment several hours later, after working with the men who arrived to install the extra lighting in my shop, a fresh, lemony scent met my nose. Frowning, I sniffed, trying to place it. Was that...furniture polish?

Huh. That was interesting.

Confused, I locked my apartment door behind me and stepped into the living room. It didn't take more than a quick glance around to see that somebody had been cleaning.

And not just a little tidying up cleaning. *Major* cleaning. The kind of deep, in-depth cleaning I knew I ought to do at least twice a year, but somehow never quite got around to.

I'd done some basic sweeping and wiping things up since I moved in, but I'd been so busy I hadn't had time for things like dusting.

Now...my apartment practically *sparkled*. The glass in the windows shone, the furniture had been dusted, and...I bent down and swiped a finger at the baseboard that ran along the bottom of the wall. Even the *baseboard* was clean.

"Wow." I turned in a little circle in the middle of the living room. There was only one possible explanation for this. "Agnes, did you clean my apartment for me?"

The little brownie didn't answer.

Not that I'd really expected her to. (Honestly, despite our encounter this morning, a small part of me wasn't entirely sure I hadn't just dreamed her up.)

"Thank you," I called out, a little uncertainly.

This was going to take some getting used to. I hadn't had a roommate since the first year I moved out of my dad's house, let alone a creature from folklore. What were you supposed to call a live-in brownie? I sure didn't know.

Part of me felt bad that Agnes had been dusting and cleaning floors when that was my responsibility, but...the larger part of me was relieved—and grateful—that it was done and I didn't have to do it. I know there are people who really enjoy cleaning, but I have sadly never been one of them.

I made a mental note to leave a few more seed beads on the kitchen table for Agnes tonight. She definitely deserved them.

Half-guiltily, half-hopefully, I wondered if this would be an ongoing thing. If so, it would be *amazing*.

I spent the rest of the day putting shelving together. The first massive boxes had arrived after lunch, filling me with excitement. I spread everything out in the middle of my shop's wooden floor and set to work.

About halfway through, I realized that the awful feeling of being watched all the time that I'd been experiencing was gone.

Agnes, it seemed, had been the culprit after all. And, somehow, I had managed to win her over. Or at least prove to her that I wasn't...what? A terrible invader? A threat?

I had no idea. All I knew was that today was the most enjoyable day I'd spent in my shop since I moved to Starhaven—and I took full advantage of it.

That night, I made myself an omelet and tried to look up folklore about brownies. I found a bunch of interesting fairy-tales and stories, but, of course, no 'real' information. Most of the fables talked about how brownies were very particular about how the people in the houses they inhabited treated them or talked to them.

I winced when I read that. *Probably shouldn't have called for her earlier.*

It was funny—some of the things about brownies reminded me of dealing with cats. I would never have expected that.

Just before I went to bed, I set out another little pile of seed beads from my personal collection for Agnes. Pearlescent pink, purple, and cream ones, this time. I hadn't seen hide nor hair of the little brownie, as my grandmother used to say, but I knew she had to be here somewhere. And I wanted to thank her for cleaning my apartment for me.

The beads were gone the next morning. All of them. Agnes didn't mind pastels, apparently.

From that point on, life kicked into high gear. My inventory began arriving and just the sight of those boxes filled me with giddy joy. (Also a tiny bit of anxiety, but that was only because I was putting literally every penny I had into this business.)

Boxes of colorful worsted weight yarn, fingering yarn, and oversized plush yarn. Boxes of embroidery thread, Aida fabric, and notions like needles and embroidery hoops. Sewing thread in all kinds of different colors. Needles, crochet hooks, knitting needles, and more.

And then my favorite part...the fabric. Oh, the gorgeous fabrics I bought. Beautiful cotton solids in a rainbow array of colors. Tiny all-over patterns that would look amazing in quilts. Larger prints and floral patterns. Fun patterns like sandcastles and butterflies. I even threw in a few licensed prints for children.

I'd been tempted to go crazy and buy EVERYTHING, but I'd managed to restrain myself. I was opening a craft shop in a small town, not a full-blown box chain fabric store. Best to start with fabrics suitable for quilting and smaller sewing projects, and then I could branch out into other materials if my customers needed something more.

The day all of my bolts of fabric arrived was probably my favorite. I unpacked them with reverent hands and spent a good chunk of the day arranging them around the shop. I arranged a number of them in the middle of the floor, and lined the rest up along one wall.

The hours flew by—I was totally and completely in my

element. This was so much more fun than the secretarial work I'd done, organizing somebody else's daily work life. I organized an embroidery section, and a knitting and crocheting section, and then organized all the sewing notions.

It was glorious. The harder I worked, the more excited I became. This *had* to succeed. Everything had lined up so perfectly for me to even open this shop, it had to be something that would provide what people in Starhaven needed.

Over the next two weeks, I double-checked that all of my state, county, and city paperwork and permits were in order, double-checked my business insurance, and took care of the rest of the final not-so-fun-but-necessary administrative details.

And then I finalized all of my tech details. I set up an online store so customers (and wasn't *that* a lovely thought!) could purchase online and pick up their orders in person. *That* took me several days and much googling, but I finally managed to do it.

During this time, my apartment remained partially unpacked. I'd unpacked all the essentials and found homes for them, but I hadn't bothered with any of my decorations yet. I had things I wanted to put up, but there just hadn't been time. Not if I was going to get my craft shop up and running—and I needed to get it up and running.

I couldn't make any money to pay bills so I could stay in Starhaven if I wasn't open for business.

During those two crazy weeks, I visited the coffee shop several times, but I mostly subsisted on sandwiches and quick, easy meals I picked up from the grocery store. This was not the time to cook myself four course meals, and while I didn't mind meal-prepping, I didn't have time for that either. Nor did I have the money to eat out much beyond the occasional pizza from Tam's when I was just too tired to even slap a sandwich together.

Every once in a while, I thought I heard a disdainful sniff when I pulled something out of the microwave. Agnes never showed herself, but I had the distinct impression that she did not approve of my meal choices.

Oh, well. I'll bake her something after I open the store, I promised myself.

In the meantime, I left her the occasional present of beads as a thank-you for keeping my apartment—and also my shop, I realized—sparkling clean. That would have to do for now.

Opening Day was just around the corner.

CHAPTER

SEVENTEEN

The last few days leading up to my grand opening, I was so busy I almost didn't have time to be nervous. Almost.

Tendrils of anxiety curled through me in odd moments and the spaces between odd last-minute tasks. *It's not like you have much of anything riding on this*, a wry voice kept whispering in my head. *Just your bright, shiny new future in Starhaven.*

Friday night, I could barely choke down my dinner. Excitement vied with anxiety, rendering my appetite null and void. I'd deliberately picked up a delicious meal from a Chinese restaurant near the grocery store, just to tempt myself to eat, but I was definitely riding the struggle bus.

My mind refused to stop going over the fifteen thousand different things I'd been streamlining all week, prepping for tomorrow—and calculating how they could all go horribly wrong. It was bad enough that I seriously considered a glass of wine. Just to take the edge off.

But, there were two problems with that idea. One, I didn't have any wine in my apartment—it'd necessitate going back to the store and picking some up. And two...I don't drink because of what I watched my parents go through. Sure, I'd probably be fine, but why take the risk?

So instead, I tried to eat while I scanned through all of my lists. My online store catalogue was set up, so I'd be able to actually make sales tomorrow. My inventory itself was ready to go. All in all, Celia's Craft Shop was ready for opening day.

I just hoped the town showed up to take a look.

I was in the middle of negotiating with myself how many bites of broccoli I should eat before I could call it quits and not feel guilty about not finishing my dinner when my phone buzzed with an incoming text, startling me. I hadn't gotten very many texts since I moved to Starhaven.

It was from Bianca. *Rooting for you tomorrow, Celia! You will do wonderfully! :)*

Warmth curled through my chest. I didn't know how badly I'd needed a little encouragement until just now.

Thank you, I sent back. *I'm excited.*

Because I was. I was just also horribly nervous.

Leaning back in my chair, I stared out toward my living room window. I'd done everything I was supposed to do. I could spend the rest of the night checking and rechecking my lists, but it didn't change the fact that my shop was ready and now I faced the ultimate test: would people show up?

We'll find out, I thought.

Biting the inside of my lip, I packed up the remnants of

my dinner and stowed them in the fridge. I couldn't eat anymore. Not tonight.

No, I needed something else.

It was in that moment that I realized that after all the hours and days and weeks I'd spent prepping to open my store, I desperately needed to touch grass. I needed to get outside and be in nature for a little bit. I might be a river city girl, but I'm not a never-gets-outside kind of girl.

The realization brought a wave of relief that left me feeling light. Yes. *This* was what I needed to do. Grabbing my phone and my purse, I headed out the door.

EIGHTEEN

The sun was just starting to set as I made my way down Main Street. A gentle breeze blew, and maybe it was my imagination, but the air felt a little cooler than it had earlier today. When I'd first arrived in town, I'd noticed there was a park down another street a block or so away from the Square. I didn't know much about it, but I remembered it had a lot of trees.

That was one thing I did miss from my neighborhood in Louisville—the maple, oak, and magnolia trees and the little fenced-in back yard I'd shared with the other tenants.

Don't get me wrong—I loved my new apartment, and I also enjoyed being able to look out the window and across the street at Vine Life's storefront. Apartment life just wasn't quite the same.

As I walked, I smiled and nodded to a few of the people I passed. A few of them nodded and smiled back. It filled my chest with a warm sense of belonging. Whatever Dave and his ilk thought, I did belong here. And the fact that other people were starting to recognize that? Well, it just made me feel even better.

A shadow dimmed my happy mood as a tiny voice inside my head whispered, *Will any of them show up at your grand opening, though?*

My footsteps faltered—just for a second. Maybe. Maybe not. It was impossible to say that with any certainty.

I'd done the best I could. I'd paid for advertisements in the local paper, and I'd put up flyers. There wasn't anything else I could do to prepare for tomorrow except perhaps pray. (And I'd been doing that, too.)

As I neared the park, I picked up speed. The heat of the day had definitely started to fade, and combined with the steady breeze, it lent the evening a rather balmy air. *So* much better than the humid oven we'd experienced all week.

The park butted up against the side of a small mountain covered with trees, which had initially surprised me. I would have thought that this close to the center of town, somebody would have decided that a neighborhood full of houses would be better suited here. That they had kept the park so centralized for everyone who lived in town to utilize was heartwarming.

A handful of children played on the playground equipment near the parking lot and little shelter house with its rows of wood picnic tables. The children's shouts and laughter filled the air, making me smile with memories of once being that young and carefree. I moved past them, however, taking a paved path that led past a wide grassy area that was perfect for sunbathing or throwing frisbees, or playing soccer.

Behind that grassy field, a stand of poplars, maples, and oaks provided shade for a few carved wooden park benches set at regular intervals around the gently curved paved path that apparently wound its way through the entire park. Beyond that was a section of woods.

I shifted direction, leaving the path to cross the grassy field and head toward the cool shade of those trees. The sun spilled golden rays across the sky, but its light was somewhat muted once I set foot beneath the leafy canopy stretching overhead. The children's laughter and shouts faded until I didn't even register them. A glance across the field told me they were still there, watched over by parents and grandparents, but the sound had been muted. So had the faint sounds of traffic.

Above me, a few birds flitted about, singing their evening songs. It was incredibly peaceful. I exhaled slowly, feeling as though a weight had suddenly dropped from my shoulders. Tipping my head back, I stared up at the green canopy stretching overhead, leaves dappled brighter shades of green by the setting sun. A gentle breeze susurrated the leaves overhead.

I eyed one of the park benches, wondering if this was a good spot to just sit and *be* for a while, but then, beyond what I had thought was a section of woods, I thought I glimpsed another clearing. A puzzled frown creased my forehead. Just how big was this park, anyway? What was back there?

I started to move toward that clearing, but stopped before I left the edge of the path, suddenly uncertain.

It's just a park, I told myself. *A park in the middle of a rather lovely little town.*

Still...I'd grown up in Louisville. And while there were parts of the city that were perfectly fine and perfectly safe, there were also parts of the city you didn't visit unless you belonged there.

I tightened my grip on my purse, debating with myself. On the one hand, I was a woman out here alone. On the other...there were a bunch of kids just across the field.

Of course, none of them would probably *hear* me if I screamed—I mean, after all, I couldn't hear *them* anymore. Why should I think they'd hear *me*?

But...I glanced down at my purse. I had pepper spray. I'd carried that with me for years. Never actually needed it. (Although there was one occasion I would have dearly loved to use it. That's a story for another time, however.)

Around me, the light started to fade as the sun began to slip behind the horizon. That spurred me to action. The longer I stood here, the more light I'd lose.

And I *really* wanted to see that clearing while it was still daylight.

Leaving the path, I started toward that line of trees. A moment later, I emerged between two massive oaks to find myself in a small clearing. That deep quiet was even more pronounced here.

I paused on the edge of the clearing, struck by its strange solemnity. That was the right word, too. Not peaceful, like the

main part of the park behind me, but solemn. Almost...
expectant.

A soft laugh escaped me. *You're starting to lose it, Celia*, I
told myself. *When in your life have you ever called a park
'solemn'?*

The answer to that was *never*, of course.

Shaking my head at my own silliness, I stepped further
into the clearing. Despite the fact that the sky above my head
was still quite blue, the light seemed dimmer here, like it
couldn't quite penetrate through the canopy of leaves that
ringed the clearing. As my eyes adjusted to the dimmer light,
I expected to find another bench or two here, but to my
surprise, nothing but grass covered the ground. Granted, it
was really nice grass, not prickly crabgrass, but...still...

My gaze caught on a large gray object on the other side of
the clearing and I realized I was wrong—this place wasn't
completely empty. Curious, I started across the grass to
examine the object.

Halfway across, the hair on the back of my neck began to
prickle. Somebody was watching me. I glanced sharply from
side to side, but didn't see anyone. As far as I could tell, the
clearing was empty, save for me.

Well, me and the unidentified object.

When I reached the large gray object, I discovered it was a
massive chunk of granite. Sharp and jagged on one side, but
curiously rounded on the other, as though water or the
constant touch of hundreds of hands over a long period of
time had worn it smooth.

I squinted at the giant rock. That was strange. Did lots of

people visit this clearing? It didn't really seem like it was on Starhaven's *Top Ten Most Visited* locations.

I looked around again, and as I did, I realized that the tree trunks surrounding the clearing formed a perfect circle. My frown deepened. Was it normal for natural clearings to form perfect circles? Or had somebody *made* this one?

Beyond the chunk of granite, the trees at the edge of the clearing merged into deepening shadows. That made sense— from a distance, I had seen that the woods extended much further up the hillside. A shiver trickled down my spine. Not that I had any desire to investigate them further tonight.

Especially when I hadn't told anyone where I was going.

I didn't exactly want to become a statistic here in this town. I could see the headline now: *Single girl goes into woods alone, never to be seen again.* Followed by a short little expose on how small businesses never tend to last.

Oh no. I snorted softly. *We're not doing that.*

No, now that I'd been outside for a while and satisfied my curiosity, what I really needed was to go home and curl up on my couch with Netflix and a knitting project to take my mind off of tomorrow's grand opening. Maybe I'd come back another day, when it wasn't so late in the evening.

With that in mind, I turned around and started back toward the trees and the park benches that separated me from the grassy field in the center of the park. A muffled thud behind me, followed by a low groan, sent me spinning around.

My hand reached automatically into my purse for my pepper spray. (Just because I'd never used it didn't mean I'd never *practiced* using it.) My fingers closed over the pepper spray can and drew it out.

Heart pounding in my chest, I gripped the pepper spray and peered between the tree trunks to see who was there. Where the clearing had been empty just a moment before, a crumpled heap now lay on the grass. Another low, pained groan escaped it—no, *him*.

The crumped heap was a man.

NINETEEN

I staggered back a step in surprise, my heart still thudding in my chest. Where in the heck had he come from? I'd been alone in here—I was *sure* of it.

The man did not move, but another pained groan escaped him.

A little of my alarm faded, though I continued to grip my pepper spray like my life depended on it. Warily, I squinted at the man, trying to size him up. It was impossible to tell from this distance how old he was, but there was no mistaking the fact that he was injured.

You should go, urged the sensible side of my brain. *Run while you have the chance, before he gets up. You have absolutely no idea who he is or what's going on. He could be a crazy homeless guy who's higher than a kite.*

Yeah, well, I'd encountered a few of those before. This guy *was* definitely hurt, though I had no idea to what extent. And, regardless of whether or not he was crazy, homeless, on drugs, or all three combined, I couldn't just leave him here in the clearing. As much for his own sake as to protect those kids back there, or anybody else who might come through here later.

That didn't mean I was putting the pepper spray away, however.

Still holding the canister at the ready, I took a couple of cautious steps toward the crumpled heap of a man. "Hello? Are you okay? Do you need help?"

As soon as the words left my mouth, I winced. That was a dumb question, but it couldn't be helped. I had to ask, didn't I?

In answer, all I received was another pained groan.

Biting my lip, I debated my next move. Whoever this guy was, he needed medical attention. Did I leave him and call the police and give them the vague information I had? Or did I need to find out if I should be calling for an ambulance instead?

"Who's there?" The man dragged himself to his knees and stretched out a trembling hand in the direction of my voice. "Show yourself, you coward! Where is she?" Fury laced with panic temporarily trumped the pain threading his voice, which bore a light accent I couldn't quite place.

I blinked. Okay, so clearly he was embroiled in some drama. Too bad he wasn't in any real shape to spill any more tea.

And then it dawned on me that while this guy was looking in my general direction, he wasn't looking *at* me. Believe me, you can tell the difference.

Frowning, I squinted at him. In the deepening gloom that

was overtaking this clearing, it was hard to make out his features, but... My frown deepened. Was he wearing a *blindfold?*

"Sir," I began cautiously, raising my voice to make sure he heard me properly. "You're wearing a blindfold. That's why you can't see anything. You might want to take it off."

To my surprise, a ragged laugh escaped him. "No," he said, his lightly accented voice full of a sudden bitter hopelessness. "That is not why I cannot see."

He managed to crawl to his feet, though he swayed dangerously like a tree in a fierce gale before he finally found his footing. Through the deepening gloom, I saw that he had wavy brown hair, a little on the long side, just brushing the tops of his shoulders. He was also dressed like somebody I'd expect to find at a Renaissance fair. A loose white shirt with a leather vest over it, with dark trousers tucked into knee-high leather boots, all under a blue cape.

The man turned his head, and then he held both hands out before him and took a tentative step in the direction of the chunk of granite.

I winced, but before I could suggest that he turn a little to his left, he spoke.

"Tell me where I am, milady."

Oh, boy. Mentally, I shook my head. Definitely part of a Renaissance fair. Or maybe an actor or something. The real question was whether or not he was a local or he'd been traveling and something bad had happened to him.

I cleared my throat. "You're in a little town called Starhaven. In Kentucky," I added as an afterthought.

"Starhaven." The man repeated the word with what

sounded like a total lack of recognition. He took another couple of steps in my general direction, no doubt following the sound of my voice.

I gripped my pepper spray, even though I had a strange, sudden instinct that I wouldn't need it. "Where are you from? What happened to you?"

The man hesitated, as though trying to think, and then shook his head. "I don't know. I was somewhere...and then I was here." He swallowed audibly. "Wherever *here* is." He tipped his head back, as though trying to see the darkening sky through his blindfold. "And I've lost her."

The sheer agonized hopelessness in those four words wrenched something deep inside my chest. As oddly dressed as he was, his devastation was clear.

"Who?" I took an unconscious step toward him. "Who did you lose?"

"*Her*. My—my—" the man suddenly gripped his head with both hands, as though dealing with a bout of severe pain. "I—I don't remember." Panic flooded his voice. "Why can't I remember? Where is she?"

His panic was contagious. It infected me as well, making my breath come faster and my heart start pounding in my chest again. *What do I do?* How was I supposed to help this guy?

I finally forced out words. "You're going to be all right. I'm going to get you help, okay?"

Still clutching his head, the man started toward me again. I backed up, retreating out of the clearing into the more spacious section of the park beyond. My footsteps made no noise against the mossy ground.

The man followed me through the line of tree trunks, leaving the gloomy clearing behind—and I gasped.

Beneath the blindfold tied around his head, I glimpsed dried blood on his cheeks. Blood that looked like it had seeped down from his *eyes*.

I gulped a breath, trying to stave off a wave of mild dizziness. *Medical care. Yes.* This guy definitely needed an ambulance.

Shifting the pepper spray to my other hand, I pulled my phone from my back pocket and dialed 911. (Later, I'd reflect on how cool that was. I'd never actually made an emergency call like this before. But for now, my knees were a little wobbly.)

A cool female voice answered. "911, what's your emergency?"

"Uh, hi, I'm at the clearing past the park and there is a man here who needs medical attention." I glanced at the man, biting my lip.

At the sound of my voice, the man's blindfolded head whipped in my direction. "Who are you speaking to?"

I ignored his demand. "I don't know how badly he's injured, but he seems to have been bleeding from his eyes. And he's trying to find somebody he's lost."

Off to the side, the man made a choked little sound, as though this was news to him.

"The clearing in the park?" the 911 operator asked.

I described our location as best I could, and then the operator asked me a couple more questions, including one to ascertain if I was in a threatening situation. I assured her I would be fine until the ambulance arrived.

"You're going to be okay," I told the man after I ended the call. "Help is on the way."

This did not appear to mean anything to him. He sagged against the nearest tree as though whatever energy he'd possessed had been drained away and passed a hand over his face. His fingers encountered the blindfold and jerked away as though he'd been burned.

"Nothing matters. Not anymore." He turned his face away, but I saw a muscle in his jaw work. "I've lost her."

Once more, the grief and anger and sheer *loss* permeating those words made me suck in a breath. I had to swallow hard before I could answer. "I'm so sorry."

I should have left it at that. I *should* have. But my curiosity got the best of me.

"Are you sure you don't remember anything?" I asked gently.

For a long moment, I didn't think he'd answer. I shifted nervously from foot to foot, certain I'd pressed too hard. I shot a pleading glance over my shoulder, searching for flashing blue and red lights. Surely that ambulance would get here quickly.

And then the man pressed his hands to his head again and let out a long, keening cry. He thumped his head against the tree trunk of the oak he'd slumped against as though that physical pain would help. "I don't remember. I don't remember. I've lost her and I don't remember!"

His voice grew louder with every word. I shrank backward, eyes wide, cursing myself for opening my stupid, *stupid* mouth.

And then, in the distance, I heard the whine of a siren. A

sudden wave of relief flooded me, nearly buckling my knees. *Thank God!*

A glance at the man told me he hadn't registered the siren. His mind was elsewhere, battling pain and his memory loss and Lord only knew what else.

The whining sirens grew louder.

A glance over my shoulder told me that an ambulance and no less than two police cars had pulled into the parking lot at the edge of the park, which was now illuminated by the white-blue light of street lamps. I was a little surprised that they didn't drive across the field toward us, but promptly scolded myself for being unrealistic. I've watched too many movies.

What good would it do the ambulance to get stuck in the field on the way to an emergency medical situation?

In the light of the street lamps, I watched as tiny uniformed figures spilled out of the ambulance and the police car and set off toward us. They had a stretcher with them. Another wave of relief coursed through me and I managed to pull myself together.

Turning back to the man, I infused as much gentle hope as I could into my voice. "It's going to be all right. The police are here, and an ambulance, and they're going to help you."

The man muttered something nonsensical about police. A frown creased my forehead. Maybe he was going into shock on top of everything else.

I turned back around to watch the police and the EMT move toward us. At the last second, it dawned on me that I was still holding my pepper spray. Quickly, I shoved it back into my purse, a mortified flush burning my cheeks.

The last thing I needed right now was for the Starhaven police to think I was threatening them with pepper spray. *That* would be a terrible end to this strange evening.

A snort escaped me as a wild thought crossed my mind. *Oh, Dave would* love *that.*

CHAPTER

TWENTY

"Hi," I called out, as soon as the bevy of police officers and EMTs were in earshot. "I'm Celia O'Malley."

I made sure to hold my hands out and away from my body so they could see I was, in fact, not a threat. "The guy I called you about is right over there." I tipped my head in the direction of the man, who had not moved from his spot slumped against the tree trunk.

"Thanks," said one of the EMTs in a deep voice as the group approached, a tall, burly guy with curly black hair pulled back in a short ponytail. He reminded me of a dark-skinned Thor, from the Marvel movies.

He and the taller of the two police officers reached us first. The EMT went to kneel beside the man, while the police officer waved me over to the side.

"Miss, if you would, I need you to come over here so I can take a statement."

My breath caught in my throat. Even in the growing twilight, this officer was probably one of the most handsome men I'd seen in a long time. Definitely the most handsome police officer I'd ever met. (Not that I'd met very many, but still…)

He had tanned skin, chocolate brown eyes, and even in the darkness, it looked like beneath the brim of his hat, his black hair had a faint bit of curl to it. His smile, while perfectly polite, made my insides go all fluttery in a way that my insides hadn't gone all fluttery in a really long time.

I nodded mutely, struggling to regain my composure. My vocal cords weren't exactly cooperating. I had a sudden, intense fear that I'd squeak like I did back in high school when a guy I'd had a crush on forever asked me to switch seats with him one day at lunch. *That* kind of reaction would be even more embarrassing now.

Good grief. What was wrong with me?

Drawing in a deep breath, I sternly reminded myself that this was a serious situation. It didn't take me long to recover. I *was* a grown woman now, after all.

"Sure." I held out my hand. "Celia O'Malley."

It occurred to me a second later that shaking hands with the police officer who came to assist me was probably not a normal thing to do, but polite Southern manners are my default when my brain quits working.

Anyway, this absurdly handsome officer didn't seem to think anything of it. He took my handshake in stride—I almost jumped at the electric spark I felt when his fingers touched mine—and then ushered me to one side.

"If you'll come with me, Miss O'Malley. I'm Officer Nick

Poindexter." He had a pleasantly deep voice, with a slightly more pronounced Kentucky drawl than I'd heard from some of the people in Starhaven. He nodded to the other police officer, a shorter heavy-set man with short brown hair. "This is my partner, Officer Riordan."

Riordan nodded briskly to me, and then his gaze slid past us toward the injured man, who seemed to be arguing with the EMTs.

I glanced that way as well, but Officer Nick drew my attention back to himself.

"We're going to take your statement, Miss O'Malley, and then we'll get you home." He continued to give me that polite smile and my insides fluttered again.

"Okay." I nodded, but I couldn't keep from looking back over at the man I'd found.

"Hey."

My gaze snapped back to Nick's. He tipped his head toward the two EMTs, his smile gentling. "He's in good hands. He'll be okay. You did the right thing, calling us."

I forced a smile. I knew he was trying to make me feel better, but...

"Let's give 'em some room to work." Officer Riordan stepped in. "We'll get that statement, yeah?" He pulled a pad of paper and a pen from one of his pockets. "Come on over this way. Better light."

The two of them walked me through the cluster of trees and benches back out to the grassy field. Above us, the sky had darkened to navy blue around the edges, with just a splash of bright colors remaining on the western horizon. A moment later, we reached the edge of the field and stepped back onto the light brown mulch that covered the ground beneath the playground. A few people hung around several of the picnic benches, watching the proceedings across the field with interest.

They were watching me, too, which made my skin crawl uncomfortably.

Officer Riordan proceeded to take my statement, occasionally asking a brisk question. Strangely, I was grateful it was him and his partner. It was easier to focus on Officer Riordan.

Both officers took the information that Renaissance man was possibly suffering from some kind of amnesia in stride. I figured they would—even in a small town like Starhaven, the law of averages meant they'd have to have a least a *few* crazy things happen every once in a while.

When I finished, the two police officers exchanged some sort of silent communication. Riordan jerked his head toward the two EMTs, though we were too far away to see them, and Officer Nick nodded in response.

He glanced at me, his smile now a trifle apologetic. "Officer Riordan will take it from here, Miss O'Malley."

"I—uh, okay." I didn't know what else to say—and the little I *did* manage made me feel like an idiot. "Thank you."

I just *barely* managed to keep from telling him inanely that it had been nice to meet him. Barely.

With another small smile and a tip of his head, Officer Nick headed back across the grassy field to provide any necessary assistance to the EMTS.

"I'd advise you go home now, Miss O'Malley." Riordan addressed these words to me, but he posted his hands on his hips and gave the onlookers a hard stare. "If we have any further questions, we'll call you."

"Okay. Thank you." I glanced at the onlookers as well, and then quickly glanced away. I didn't really want to talk to them either. This was not the kind of get-to-know-you conversation I wanted with people here...even if tonight's events *did* make me mildly interesting for a day or so.

"What will happen to him?" I blurted out, just as Officer Riordan started to turn away. I jerked my thumb over my shoulder, even though the police officer knew exactly who I was talking about.

"County hospital, and then we'll go from there." Riordan shrugged. "Nothing earth-shattering."

"I hope he remembers whoever it was he lost." The words popped out before I could stop myself.

Officer Riordan slanted a sharp sideways glance at me. "We'll be investigating. Don't worry."

That made me feel better, though the way he said it, so brusquely, as though it was none of my business, put my back up a little. (I mean, don't get me wrong, I *know* it's not really any of my business, but I couldn't help but feel a teensy bit responsible for the guy since I'm the one who found him.)

"Thank you," I said, and then I straightened my shoulders, hiked my purse up on my shoulder, and marched off across the playground to the parking lot and the sidewalk beyond.

From there, I made a beeline for my apartment across the several blocks I'd traversed earlier. They looked different now, in the glow of the streetlights. Despite the fact that the air had cooled marginally now that the sun was down, the earlier breeze had died away and left the still-humid air feeling just a touch stagnant.

It was the strangest sensation, but the farther I got from the park, the more dreamlike the last hour became. I still didn't understand where that guy had come from. Hopefully, he'd be able to get help.

As I caught sight of my shop, my thoughts shifted in a different direction. My grand opening was tomorrow...and I had absolutely no idea what to expect. It felt like I had the sword of Damocles dangling over my head.

Things would either go really well...or this whole adventure was fixing to blow up in my face.

I opted for the positive approach, even though my stomach had started tying itself into knots. *It's going to be fine,* I told myself. Everything had worked out for me to get this far.

It would work out after tomorrow as well...right?

TWENTY-ONE

The next morning, I opened the blinds in my apartment to find the Square swathed in mist and a gray drizzle of early September rain. Not the kind of Labor Day weekend weather I'd been hoping for.

I tasted disappointment, but swallowed it back. It hadn't rained in a couple of weeks, and the weather forecast hadn't said anything about rain sticking around. Surely this would all clear up shortly and golden sunshine would return for the rest of the day.

My phone vibrated with a couple of incoming texts. One was from Maddie, wishing me a wonderful opening day. The other was from my mom, also wishing me a wonderful opening day.

Send pictures! Can't wait to hear about it!

Something warmed in my chest. We might not be all that close, but it made me happy that my mom had remembered about today.

My dad had texted me the night before. *Hope it goes well. Love you, princess.*

He hadn't called me that in a long time. The nickname had brought back a surge of bittersweet memories, but I shoved them aside to focus on the here and now. I wasn't a child any more.

This was my life. This was my store.

I peeked out the window again. Starhaven's usual Saturday morning traffic moved along the Square—businesses revving up for the day, morning people headed to the coffee shop.

And now I was part of that, too.

Unable to suppress an ecstatic grin, I pressed a hand to my chest and practically danced to the kitchen to make myself a cup of coffee. Excitement outweighed nerves. I was opening a local craft store—and who didn't love crafts?

Today, I told myself firmly, *will be a good day, whether you have five people walk in the door or a hundred.*

Reality, however, turned out to be a little different.

At five o'clock, I flipped the sign on my shop's front door to 'closed', a wave of mixed emotions flooding me. Pride. Aching disappointment. Relief.

Tears pricked the backs of my eyes, but I held them at bay. *You're being too emotional*, I told myself, crossing back behind my counter to slump against it. *It wasn't a bad day. Just...not as good as you'd hoped.*

Boy, wasn't *that* the truth. After all the little pep talks I'd given myself about managing my expectations, the truth was that deep down I'd still expected a large number of people to wander into my shop today. I'd advertised in the local paper, handed out flyers around the Square, the library, and everywhere else I could think of.

Having less than twenty visitors over the course of an entire day (with only three actual sales) was *not* what I had anticipated.

Still... A tendril of bright hope poked through the morass of sad disappointment filling me. I'd had my first three sales.

That was definitely better than none—which was what dear old Dave had heavily implied I'd end up with.

Pursing my lips, I glanced around the interior of my shop, trying to see it through potential customers' eyes. I'd done my best to lay it out in an organized way, like you'd find if you went to a big box store. (Albeit a lot smaller.)

Staring at the summer collection of fabrics I'd set up in a beautiful display at the head of the fabric section (all ocean wave blues, beachy yellows, and fun fruit prints like watermelon and lemons), I sighed.

Face it, Celia. You don't have any kind of real gauge for what's normal in a situation like this. This might have been a perfectly good opening day and you just don't know it.

Another heavy sigh escaped me. I'd hoped Bianca would stop in, given her previous excitement, but that was probably foolish. Again, because of Dave.

I frowned, crossing my arms over my chest. At some point, I was going to have to figure out what was up with that guy. Maybe if I knew his story, I could be a little more compassionate—because right now, I really wanted to march over to his store and punch him in his angry little face. He'd sabotaged me, just like he'd threatened.

A watery laugh escaped me. That's not normal behavior for me. I'm not the kind of girl who goes around punching people. I might *think* about it, but I've never actually done it.

And, really, there had to be some major hurt behind all that anger. People don't just live their lives angry like that without a reason. Or at least, if they do, I've never met anybody like that.

All the angry people I've ever known had reasons. Most of them needed to get past those reasons and move on with their lives so they didn't terrorize the people around them, but still...

Sighing, I shut everything down for the night and flicked off the lights. Then I headed upstairs to my apartment.

Maybe tomorrow would be better. Louisville wasn't built in a day, and neither would my business.

Still stung, though.

Just before I fell asleep, tucked into my comfy bed, I remembered the injured Renaissance man. He'd crossed my mind several times over the course of the day, but there wasn't really a good way for me to get information about him.

Maybe, I thought with a yawn, *I can call the police station tomorrow and find out.*

They'd probably tell me it was an invasion of privacy or something, but it wouldn't hurt to try, would it? After all, I was the one who found the guy.

And it gave me something else to think about than my lack of customers.

My second day of business went about as well as the first. Which is to say, as the hours passed, only a handful of people trickled in. It was disappointing, but I'd braced myself for it, and it only stung about half as much as yesterday.

The inactivity, however, was the thing that just about drove me out of my mind. There was only so much admin stuff I could do with only two days and a couple of sales under my belt. I played games on my phone for a couple of hours, but *that* just depressed me because I was *literally* killing time.

The solution hit me while I was fixing myself a chicken Caesar salad two nights later. It was so simple and so obvious that I threw my head back and sighed loudly at the ceiling.

Celia, you own a craft shop, *for Pete's sake. Why don't you just do crafts?*

The sheer *freedom* of that realization filled me with giddy joy. I wasn't just an employee who had to justify their time in the store all day, poking at shelves and helping customers and whatnot. I was the *owner*.

Sure, I still had to poke at shelves and help customers (and please, dear God, let there be more customers!), but I could also sit behind my front counter and knit. Or crochet. Or work on a quilt.

Real-life advertising.

Belatedly, I realized I was standing beside my counter,

gleefully rubbing my hands together and cackling like a loon. Part of me thought I should probably stop so Agnes—wherever she was right now—didn't think I was crazy, but the larger part of me couldn't bring myself to care.

I'd moved to Starhaven for the freedom of it. And it had taken me this long to realize that my newfound freedom extended to my work, too.

Bianca's question about craft classes floated through my brain again, sparking a light bulb moment. I couldn't help myself—I started cackling again.

I hadn't given her question much thought beyond the initial, 'Oh, that would be cool' reaction. It had been on a list of things to implement at a later date, after the shop was up and running.

But, now?

I didn't have anything to lose.

Even if it picked up later, business didn't look good right now. And *that* could probably be laid squarely at Dave's leather-shoe-clad feet.

Grabbing my bowl of salad, I marched into the living room and stopped by the window. Leaning toward the glass (but not so close that I pressed my cheek to it and undid all of Agnes's hard work), I narrowed my eyes in the general direction of Dave's antique store.

If anybody had happened to be glancing up at my apartment windows from the street below, they would probably think I was crazy, but I didn't care.

I'd been going about the last few days all wrong. Instead of being meek and afraid to make waves in this town, I needed to put myself out there. (Sure, I'd thought I'd done that already, with my advertising, but now I realized that it wasn't enough. Oh, no. Not nearly enough.)

A Cheshire Cat grin spread across my face. *Game on, Dave. You won't get rid of me so easily. Starhaven is* my *home now, too.*

And I had absolutely no desire to pack up and move back to Louisville. Or anywhere else, for that matter.

Celia's Craft Shop was here to stay.

TWENTY-TWO

The next morning before I opened for the day, I set my new plan into motion. One of the many purchases I'd made for this shop was a chalkboard triangle sign to stand out front when I wanted to advertise anything. I'd set it up the first two days to advertise my grand opening, for all the good that had done me.

Now, I set the triangle sign up by my front counter and got out my box of chalk. After a moment's thought, I crafted a new sign in careful, bright purple and pink lettering. (I'm no calligrapher, but my handwriting is a lot more legible than some people in my family.)

Feeling Crafty But Don't Know How?
Never Fear—Lessons Are Here!
Ask Me About:
- Knitting
- Crocheting

- Quilting

Stepping back, I surveyed the sign with satisfaction. Was it cheesy? Oh, yeah. No getting around that.

Would it work? I shrugged mentally. Only time would tell.

Flipping the sign on my front door to 'open', I propped door open and carefully maneuvered the triangle out onto the sidewalk. I spent a moment fiddling with its position, before deeming it satisfactory. I cast a quick glance up and down the street, taking in the usual flow of traffic and enjoying the relatively cooler morning air. It would be sweltering hot again by the afternoon.

Movement across the street caught my eye. Marie had just come out of Vine Life's front door to arrange her outside plants for the day. Feeling my gaze on her, she glanced in my direction.

Cheerily, I smiled and waved. Even across the street, I could see the confusion on her pretty face.

Laughter bubbled up inside me. I scampered back into my own shop before it escaped. Probably not a good idea to stand out in front of my shop cackling to myself. Still...the look on her face. Wasn't there a saying about smiling confusing people?

I allowed myself a good laugh before I took a deep breath and smoothed both hands down my light floral skirt. "It's fine," I announced out loud. "Everything will be fine."

Positive. I needed to stay positive and remind myself that everything had worked out so beautifully thus far. This, too, would all work out.

And the especially beautiful thing about this morning? I was going to get a UFO done. The thought sparked another smile.

In the crafting world, UFO stands for 'unfinished object". And this particular project had been lurking in my closet for the better part of four years.

Rounding my front counter, I settled into my chair and turned on the music I'd chosen for the day. As airy Celtic music filled every nook and cranny of my shop, I reached down behind the counter for my favorite knitting bag, which I'd brought it down with me this morning. The bag was a deep purple tote, with wide handles and plenty of pockets for things like needle protectors, scissors, yarn needles, and other accoutrements.

I started to reach into the bag, hesitated, and then shook my head at my own foolishness. It was time. I needed to finish this project, and if doing it in my very own craft shop wasn't the perfect place, I didn't know what was.

Carefully, I withdrew a half-finished shawl on a set of circular needles with metal tips. The yarn was a fine-spun metallic silver, impossibly soft despite the silver threads running through it. I'd found a challenging old-fashioned lace pattern on the internet one night and fallen in love with it. I'd had to adapt the pattern on the edges to work with the triangular shape of the shawl, but it had gone surprisingly well.

At least up until I'd stopped knitting it.

For a moment, I simply sat there and held the half-finished shawl on my lap, staring down unseeing while a host of bittersweet memories flashed through my mind. A year ago, or even six months ago, I'd have still been unprepared to handle that flood of memories.

But now, I was able to let them wash over me without feeling the anger and the pain I'd expected. The remnants of those emotions were still there, but they were blunted and rounded, like sharp edges on a rock that over time a stream had gradually worn to smoothness.

Tracing a finger over an intricate stitch, I exhaled softly. When I'd started this shawl, I had expected to wear it at my wedding.

That hadn't happened.

And, really, it was a good thing. If I'd married Darren, it wouldn't have taken long for me to be miserable. I was much, much better off without him.

But even knowing all that, I hadn't been able to look at this project since.

A half-laugh, half-sigh escaped me. I hadn't been able to throw it away, either. And so, it had lived in a hidden corner of my closet.

Its existence bothered me every so often. I hated leaving projects unfinished, and I had been so very excited about the challenge of knitting this intricate pattern. Occasionally, I'd found myself wondering if I ought to just pull it out and finish it, but I'd never been brave enough to do it.

Until now, I thought with a smile.

Another quick perusal of my knitting bag netted me the instructions. I unfolded them carefully, remembering the way I'd laughed when Darren glanced over at my shoulder at them for the first time.

He'd been completely nonplussed by the complicated

lines of stitch instructions, but then, in hindsight, he'd never really been interested in anything I did. He merely tolerated my hobbies as long as they didn't interfere with his wants or wishes.

It took me a minute to determine which was the right side and which was the wrong side of the shawl. (That was when it hit me again how long it had been since I let myself work on this.) Then, squinting back and forth between my instructions and my shawl, I tried to determine where I'd left off. Halfway through a pattern repeat, it looked like.

Once I figured out where I was, I made a note in my phone. Then I removed the needle stoppers and set to work.

Knit one, yarn over, knit two together. Yarn over, knit one, pull through.

I exhaled slowly. Oh, how I'd missed this. With every stitch, I relaxed a little more. The gentle, rhythmic click-clacking of my knitting needles eased the tension in my shoulders, taking away a weight I hadn't realized I was carrying.

Some people prefer plastic needles, or bamboo needles, but I'd always preferred metal. I thought they were smoother, and yarn didn't stick to them. Plus, I liked the sound they made.

By the end of ten minutes, I'd found my rhythm, like it hadn't been four years since I'd touched this shawl.

Warmth bloomed in my chest, and I found myself smiling. It took me a moment to realize that feeling was... contentment.

My smile dimmed, just for a second. Hard to believe it had been so long since I'd felt contented. And it was a little crazy, given that Dave was attempting to run me out of town. But it had been years since I'd felt like I really belonged somewhere and that what I did mattered.

Even if it was as simple as sitting in a chair knitting.

My fingers worked busily, the metallic blue needles flashing in and out as I knit row after row. My soft, glittery silver shawl took on more shape as the morning progressed. I had no idea where I'd wear it when it was finished, but I'd figure something out.

It was too pretty to leave unfinished just because I'd never wear it to the wedding I'd intended it for.

It dawned on me then that I'd been so busy the past few months that I'd forgotten the sheer joy of creation—even though it was one of those things I *knew* in the back of my mind. *This* was why this shop was my dream. Being able to introduce other people to the beautiful fun of making things, whether it was working with yarn or fabric or beads, or whatever.

I hadn't had much time to do fun, crafty things lately, and I realized now how much I'd missed them.

Every so often, I'd pause to take a drink of water, or glance up and down at the street to see if anybody had noticed the change to my sign. Nobody had. From nine AM to half past noon, when I finally closed the shop long enough to get some lunch, no one even darkened the doorway.

If I hadn't been sitting here knitting my heart out, I might have been tempted to cry—even with my resolve to remain positive and upbeat. But, as it was, I found myself taking an unusually prosaic approach. Things would work out. I had no idea how—or when, for that matter—but...things would work out.

I believed I was in this town for a reason. And so, I had to also believe that I would eventually have customers.

That was why, when the bell over the door jingled at half-past two, I wasn't surprised.

I *was* surprised, however, by the identity of my prospective customer. My eyes widened, my stomach turning over in half-hopeful, half-horrified anticipation.

It was the blonde young woman with the twins I'd encountered at the coffee shop a few weeks ago—the one who'd been triggered by the mention of embroidery.

TWENTY-THREE

I watched in wide-eyed silence as the young woman—I couldn't remember her name—edged into my shop like she was a toddler sneaking into a room that was supposed to be off-limits. She was by herself today—no stroller in sight. She'd could have been any almost-twenty-something out shopping in her green floral print dress, floaty light pink top, and her scrappy sandals.

A thought occurred to me and I almost choked on a sudden snort of laughter. If she was trying to sneak in under Dave's nose, ditching the stroller was a good idea. He probably wouldn't recognize her as easily without her little ones in tow I quickly turned the laughter into a cough when the blonde's gaze swung in my direction.

Her large, green eyes were wide with anxiety and trepidation, but also a little bit of...determination.

"Hi." I nodded in her direction, since I was in the middle of a row and I couldn't drop my needles to wave.

Her gaze fell to my in-progress shawl—and a look of combined longing and hunger flashed across her pretty face. She quickly shuttered her expression, but it was too late. I'd seen it—and now I knew why she was here.

The same reason I was here, actually.

Despite my faux pax at the coffee shop the other day, there was a large part of her that really did love the creative process involved with things like embroidery.

The young woman only hesitated on my brown rubber floor mat for a second before she started toward my station at the front counter. She'd barely taken two steps before she was distracted by, well, *everything*.

She stared at my display of summer fabrics for a moment before drifting close enough to reach out a tentative hand and lightly stroke a bolt of blue ocean waves. Her gaze then caught on the long double-rowed shelf of fabric bolts along the back of the wall and she moved in that direction. She walked along them for a moment, before turning back to explore the rest of the shop.

She wandered down several of my short aisles, and then out of the corner of my eye I saw her stop, as though she'd been frozen in place, in front of the embroidery section, which was on the end of an aisle close to the front counter.

Wincing, I bit my lip, my knitting needles stilling in my hands. Thankfully, the sweet, dreamy strains of one of my favorite Celtic songs hid the lack of click-clacking sounds. Would this be the moment she decided the best thing to do would be to walk out?

After what felt like a small eternity, I watched the blonde's shoulders rise and fall as she drew in a deep, bracing breath. She then pivoted on her heel, very decisively, and turned her back on the embroidery section.

I barely had time to drop my gaze back to my knitting and pretend I hadn't been watching her before she drifted into the next aisle, which held my collection of various yarns and things like knitting needles and crochet hooks.

She didn't stay in that aisle long.

Thirty seconds later, she exited the aisle and marched up to the front counter.

"Hello." She extended a hand toward me. "My name is Zel."

I had to shift my grip on my knitting to return her hand-shake without dropping a knitting needle—and all the stitches on it. "Hello, Zel. I'm Celia."

"Yes, I know." Zel looked around my shop again, smoothing her hands down her skirt in a vaguely anxious motion.

"Can I help you?" I asked tentatively. "Is there something in particular you're looking for?"

Zel pressed her lips together in a thin line before she slowly nodded. "I would like to learn how to do that." She motioned to the shawl in my lap with a pale, slim hand.

"Knitting?" I glanced down at my lap without thinking about it.

"Yes. Knitting." Zel clasped her hands behind her back, before nodding over her shoulder. "Your sign says that you will teach classes."

Well. I hadn't expected the sign to pay off so quickly.

"Yes, I will." I straightened my shoulders and nodded,

before gently patting the half-constructed shawl in my lap. "I want to pass on what I know if anybody is interested."

"Good." An expression of relief flashed through Zel's green eyes, as though she had taken an unexpected leap of faith and was quite relieved to find solid ground beneath her feet when she landed. The relief turned to hesitation.

"How...how much will you charge?" She tucked a lock of blonde hair behind her ear, her fingers slipping through it with a jerky motion like she'd recently cut it and forgotten her hair was shorter.

Huh. I blinked, taken aback, and then I laughed. "You know what? I hadn't even thought about that yet." I grinned ruefully. "Terribly impractical of me, as a new business owner, isn't it?" I lowered my voice dramatically. "Don't tell Dave."

This startled a giggle of out of Zel. "Dave?"

"Oh, yes." I nodded, schooling my features into an expression of mock-solemnity. "He's so glad I've come to Starhaven, he just can't stand it, don't you know?"

Zel giggled again, and then her giggle turned into full-blown laughter so contagious that we both doubled over, wheezing.

I hadn't laughed this hard in a long time. It felt good, like something inside me had released. Finally, I straightened, wiping tears of laughter from my eyes.

From the look of Zel, who was doing the same thing on the other side of the counter, it had been a while since she laughed this hard either. The diminutive blonde braced herself against the counter, still chuckling. Her green eyes danced, and her fair cheeks were flushed.

She reminded me in that moment of a princess out of one of the fairy tales I'd read as a child. I blinked, and the next instant that thought was gone.

"Well…" I cleared my throat, an idea coming to me. "I'll have to figure out pricing eventually, but for you, to start…" I offered her a bright smile. "How about just the cost of your supplies?" I gestured to my shop. "It's not like I'm drowning in business at the moment. Frankly, I could use the company."

A small smile tilted the corners of Zel's mouth as she looked around. "You're not drowning in business *yet*. It'll come."

"Dave or no Dave?" I asked wryly.

Zel just let out a breathy little laugh and shook her head. Her gaze sought the yarn aisle, and then she turned her attention back to me. "What do I need?"

Setting my knitting aside, I jumped up and made my way around the front counter, rubbing my hands together in undisguised glee. "You're going to like this."

TWENTY-FOUR

I might not have thought about how much to charge for classes, but I *had* thought about good projects for beginners. And, frankly, projects that would be useful after the fact. For knitting and crocheting, I'd settled on dishcloths.

Zel trailed me as I snagged a little blue shopping basket from a stack by the front door with one hand and strode over to my yarn aisle. Stopping about halfway, I pointed to a section that held a selection of small balls in a variety of colors ranging from pastels to bright and vivid colors.

"This is cotton yarn. It's good for making things like dishcloths, which is what I recommend you start with."

"I can use more dishcloths." Zel drifted closer to the yarn, as though drawn by an invisible magnetic force. After a sideways glance at me, she ran her fingers over a pretty aquamarine ball of yarn. "It looks different from the other yarn."

"That's because it's cotton. Those yarns—" I pointed to a

selection of Red Heart yarn, "are worsted weight, which is wool and polyester." I indicated another section farther down the aisle, on the bottom row. "Those are wool fingering weight yarns, which are good for things like gloves or socks."

"I saw an old woman in the park knitting socks once," Zel murmured. "It seemed like her hands were full of needles."

That was a creative way to put it. I nodded in agreement. "Yeah, if she was making socks, she'd have used at least four double-pointed knitting needles." I frowned suddenly, contemplating a new thought. "You know, I can't remember if they make circular knitting needles small enough to do something like socks."

I made a mental note to check later.

"*Four* knitting needles?" Zel's golden eyebrows practically disappeared into her hairline. "With points at both ends? How in the Forest do you handle that many?"

Now *that* was an expression I hadn't heard before. Where in the world had Zel picked that up? My gaze flicked back to her, but the small blonde was still staring at me in wonder.

"It's really not as complicated as it sounds. You only ever work with two knitting needles at a time."

Zel looked doubtful, but then she shrugged. "Perhaps I can work my way up to it." She wrinkled her nose. "I don't think I want to make socks, though."

"I'm sure you can. And you don't have to make socks." I motioned to the cotton yarn. "Pick a couple of colors that you like, and we'll get you a pair of knitting needles and a few other notions if you don't have them."

As soon as those words left my mouth, I suppressed a wince. That was a dumb statement. Other than maybe a pair of scissors, it was a pretty safe bet that Zel didn't have any knitting notions at home.

If she noticed my inanity, Zel was kind enough not to mention it. She contemplated the rows of yarn for a long moment, her eyes tracking back and forth from color to color.

I wouldn't exactly call it a hidden talent, but I have a pretty good feel for people and colors. (Another reason I thought I might be good at running a craft shop.) I figured Zel would take the aquamarine yarn, and she did. She also picked out a lovely deep rose pink and pale cream variegated yarn.

"Those will make pretty dishcloths." I smiled encouragingly at her as she turned toward me with her choices. She put them into the basket I carried, and I then led her down to far end of the aisle and the shelves that held all of my knitting and crocheting-related notions, along with crochet hooks, knitting needles, and pattern books.

I pulled a set of pink metal knitting needles off the shelf and handed them to her. "Size 7. Good for cotton yarn and for beginners." They went into the basket. "Scissors." A dainty pair of purple-handled scissors followed the knitting needles. "Needle stoppers. I love these things—they've saved my bacon on more than one occasion."

The last thing I added was a pack of plastic yarn needles. "I think they work just as well as the metal ones," I said with a shrug, dropping them into the basket with everything else.

I extended the blue plastic handles to Zel. "Here."

She hesitated before slowly taking the shopping basket, her gaze traveling past me again, this time to land on my small selection of knitting bags. She bit her lip, clearly debating something with herself, and then slowly moved over to them.

Not wanting to crowd her or make her feel like I was pressuring her into purchasing anything, I hung back. It felt awkward to stand there and watch her decide if she wanted to spend money, which surprised me. That part of owning a shop had never occurred to me before. My first few customers had more or less known what they were looking for.

After a moment, Zel selected a knitting bag covered in delicate pink roses. She gently set it into her basket and then turned back to me. Her expression seemed lighter than it had just a moment before.

"I don't have anything to keep all of these things in."

"I should have asked you about that." I smiled wryly, unable to keep from flushing a little. "I told you I'm new to being in business for myself, right?"

Zel favored me with a genuine smile that lit her entire face. "That's all right." Still smiling, she glanced down at her full shopping basket. "Is that everything?"

"Everything except a pattern, but you don't need to buy anything for this project. I'll write down what I'm going to teach you—it's easy enough."

Zel nodded enthusiastically, a blend of excitement and eagerness lighting her eyes. She tucked a lock of hair behind her ear again. "When can we begin classes?"

Her question caught me a little off-guard. "Shouldn't I be asking *you* that?" I laughed, excitement bubbling up in my chest and making me want to bounce on my toes like I was six again. "I'm not the one with babies."

At the reminder of her children, Zel's smile softened. "That is kind of you, to work around me."

"I told you, it's not like I've got a lot going on right now." I motioned to the shop with an over-exaggerated sweep of one hand as we headed back to the front counter.

Zel set her basket on the counter and I started scanning her items with the little scanner that connected to my tablet. "Speaking of which," I glanced up at her through my eyelashes, "may I ask where your babies are right now? If it's okay," I hastened to add. "I'm not prying or anything, I just know how busy you must be with two little ones and I know it's hard for moms to get away sometimes."

"It's all right." Zel's smile shifted again, this time to one of bittersweet weariness. "They're with their godmother, Maddie."

I glanced up sharply at Zel, pausing in the middle of scanning her balls of yarn. "Maddie? As in Town Facilitator Maddie?"

"Yes." Zel gave me a curious look, her eyebrows scrunching in puzzlement. "You know she's our Facilitator?"

Something about the way she said that seemed odd, but I wasn't sure why. "Yeah." I pasted a bright smile on my face, shrugging one shoulder as though it was no big deal. "She introduced herself to me when I moved here." My smile turned a shade mischievous. "She even saved me from Dave, that first day."

"Oh. I see." It was Zel's turn to smile, her puzzlement smoothing itself from her forehead as though it had never been there at all. "Well, from time to time she watches the twins for me so that I can have a little break." She glanced down at a delicate silver watch on her left wrist. "I have to leave soon—they'll be up from their nap shortly."

"That's all right." I finished scanning the last item—her yarn needles—and gave her the total. Zel pulled a debit card from her purse and handed it to me. A moment later, I returned the card along with her receipt and handed her two plastic bags filled with her purchases.

"I put a business card in there." I nodded to one of the bags. "It has my work number on it. If you want, you can text me the times that would work best for an hour-long class and we'll go from there." I paused. "Right now, I can do Monday through Saturday."

"Thank you." Zel cradled her bags as though they held some precious treasure.

It made my chest warm again. Seriously, I think there are so many people in the world who have no idea how therapeutic and fulfilling things like knitting, crocheting, or sewing things are. I think we were designed to create things and enjoy the amazing feeling of satisfaction that they bring.

"One more thing." I motioned to Zel's bag, smiling conspiratorially. "If you want to get started right now instead of having to wait for a class, you can look up tutorial videos on YouTube. That's how I learned how to knit with double-pointed needles, actually. Watched some videos on YouTube."

I was not prepared for Zel's astonished little gasp.

"I did not know that was possible." She stared at me with wide eyes, like I'd just imparted some secret of the universe. "That is amazing." Her green gaze slid past me, suddenly going distant as though she was considering something far beyond my ken. Then, slowly, she shook her head. "It seems everything is on YouTube."

It was my turn to frown in confusion. What was *that* supposed to mean? Before I could ask, a musical trilling sound interrupted us.

"Oh. I am so sorry." Zel juggled her bags in order to pull her phone from her purse. She glanced at the display and then shot me an apologetic look. "My children are up. I need to go now."

"Oh, no, that is quite all right." I flapped my hands at her. "You do whatever you need to do. We'll talk more later."

Zel nodded, already heading for the door. Just before she pushed it open, she paused and glanced back over her shoulder at me. "Thank you, Celia."

Then the bell above the door jingled and she was gone.

TWENTY-FIVE

After Zel left, part of me wanted to close up shop early. The boost of encouragement I'd received from her threatened to dry up without leaving any trace of its existence, like water poured on the summer-baked ground outside. Again, I found myself confronting the fact that having hardly any customers walk through my door in my first week did not a recipe for long-term success make.

Settled back down in my chair, I picked up my knitting again, but did not resume. Instead, I stared down at the lacy silver stitches.

It was tempting—very tempting—to lay every bit of the blame for my lack of success at Dave's feet. He was most definitely responsible for the larger part of it, but...common sense dictated that at least a small part of the blame was on me. I *was* a new business owner, after all. And didn't the statistics state that most small businesses failed in the first year?

Well, I told myself firmly, before glancing at my pattern to see where I'd left off. *I'll just have to hang on.*

Resolve curled through me, lending me strength. I was *not* going to be a statistic.

Nobody else ventured into my shop the remainder of the afternoon. I was prepared for it, but I won't deny that it still stung a little. At five o'clock, I brought my triangle sign back inside before I flipped my 'OPEN' sign to 'CLOSED'. I then locked the door and headed back to the front counter to shut my tablet and the lights off for the night.

Knock. Knock.

The sound of someone knocking rapidly on the glass window in my front door startled me. Caught off-guard, I glanced over at the door—and almost dropped my tablet in shock. Bianca stood on the welcome mat outside, smiling at me, but even through the glass I could see the sense of urgency in her eyes.

A million different thoughts raced through my brain as I rushed over to unlock the door, nearly tripping over my own feet in the process. As soon as I swung the door open, Bianca slipped inside and motioned for me to shut it again.

"Hi," she said breathlessly. A hint of mirth danced in her eyes, temporarily replacing the urgency. "I'm sneaking away for a minute."

"Oh. Okay. Hi." I blinked at her, uncertain how to follow that up.

Bianca nodded to my triangle sign, which I'd set off to one side beside the door. "That's a good idea."

"Uh, thanks." I glanced at the sign as well, before returning my attention to her. "Can I...help you with something?"

A look of regret chased itself across Bianca's beautiful porcelain face. "Yes, but not yet." Tucking a black curl behind one ear, she looked around with interest, bouncing on her toes a little as she took in the array of colorful fabrics and aisles of yarn and beads and notions. "It's terrible timing— you've just shut everything down for the night."

That was true, but... I shrugged. "It's not like I have anything else to do at the moment."

Movement beyond the large plate glass windows to our right caught both of our eyes—but it was only Marie, across the street, starting her nightly process of relocating the plants that couldn't spend the night outside. I noticed that Bianca's gaze narrowed as she watched the taller woman, as though holding an internal debate with herself about something.

At last, Bianca returned her attention to me. She bit her lip, and then, with a gravity that almost made me laugh, announced, "I want to make socks."

"Okay." I nodded encouragingly.

Bianca canted her head slightly to one side, her expression still grave. "You...do not think that is strange?"

Strange? Making socks? I wrinkled my forehead in a frown. "Why would making socks be strange?"

Bianca blinked at me, as though she had never seriously considered this before. "It...seems like it should be strange, when you can walk into a store and buy them." She waved a hand.

It was my turn to look askance at her. "Lots of people make socks, Bianca. There are tons and tons of patterns out there." I shrugged. "Sure, you can buy socks, but if you want to make them..." I spread my hands. "Why not?"

Something about the set of Bianca's shoulders relaxed. "I see." Her tone held a note of faint relief.

I had a flash of inspiration. "I'll tell you what. Yes, I closed things down for the day, but—" I jerked a thumb over my shoulder, "—if you want to place a mobile order for in-store pickup, I'll just go ahead and bag everything for you."

"You...can do that?" Bianca stared at me, the expression on her face turning wondrous.

"Oh, sure. Lots of stores have in-store pickup."

I could probably get my point-of-sale software back up and running for her, but it occurred to me that her ordering online had its benefits.

Still looking as though she'd received an amazing gift, Bianca took one step toward the yarn aisle—and then stopped. Looked back at me. "You're sure? It's not an imposition?"

"No." I shook my head. "Like I said, I don't have much else to do at the moment."

"I'd have sneaked away earlier if I could have managed it." Bianca smiled wryly. "I've been thinking about socks all week. I'd love to try them. I love knitting, but I haven't knitted anything in a long time." She cast a longing look toward the yarn aisle. "I'll be quick."

"It's all right." I watched her hurry away, feeling

bemused. "If you need any help," I called after her, "just let me know."

"Thank you!" she called back.

Bianca spent a few minutes lingering over different types of yarn before she returned with a pack of fine double-pointed knitting needles, a pack of needle stoppers, and an armful of wool fingering yarn in an array of softer, feminine colors, and bolder, more masculine colors.

"Just put everything on the counter," I told her, "and we'll get you set up with an account on my store."

"Okay." Bianca did that, and then pulled her phone out of her back pocket. A moment later, we'd pulled up my online store and she'd put everything into the cart. Within another minute, she'd paid for everything and I put it all in a bag for her.

"The good thing about this," I nodded to her phone, "is that you can place an order whenever you need to and then just come in and pick it up when you have time."

Bianca's face lit with joy. "That sounds delightful."

"Does Dave not...allow you to knit?" I asked carefully, as I handed her the bag with her purchases. Sure, the question sounded absolutely ridiculous leaving my mouth, but...

To my relief, Bianca laughed. "Absolutely not. He just—" she flashed me a guilty look, "—doesn't want anybody frequenting Celia's Craft Shop."

I waved an airy hand, though I wasn't quite sure the sting of that would ever go away. "We already know *that*."

This prompted a relieved smile from Bianca. "Well, he'll have to get over it eventually." She looked around my shop again, before giving me a sweetly mischievous grin. "Once people actually set foot in here, they'll be back."

"I hope so." Sighing, I posted my hands on my hips, but I didn't let myself dwell on it. Instead, I turned back to Bianca. "You're all set." I nodded to her bag. "I hope you enjoy."

A beautiful smile lit Bianca's face, making her even more stunning than she already was. "I intend to. Thank you, Celia."

I jerked a thumb over my shoulder. "Do you want to go out the back?"

Bianca hesitated, something warring behind her eyes. "Maybe today?" Her smile slipped, losing a fraction of its brilliance. "I'm sorry."

"Don't worry about it." I brushed her apology aside. "It'll be fine."

I directed Bianca to the back entrance, and, with another small, grateful smile, she slipped out into the alleyway behind the building. Shaking my head again, I locked up behind her and trekked up to my apartment.

Was this a strange way to do business? Yes. Was it still business? Also, yes. In the grand scheme of things, I couldn't really complain.

Much.

CHAPTER
TWENTY-SIX

When I walked through my front door, a single glance at my apartment told me that Agnes had been busy in my absence. I still hadn't seen much of her, but she certainly kept my apartment clean for me. And she seemed to like the occasional colorful beads and snacks I set out for her.

A single glance at the contents of my refrigerator told me I should probably fix myself a big chicken Caesar salad for dinner. But...I bit my lip, studying the lettuce in the vegetable drawer. I didn't really *want* a salad tonight.

What I really wanted was a big burger and an equally large serving of crispy, golden French fries. (Yes, I know, very healthy.) Normally, I'd talk myself out of it, but tonight...I gave in.

It had been a rough week, even though it wasn't quite over, and I was still recovering from a double whammy of moving and starting my own store. Even the thought of chopping a few vegetables for a salad felt like too much work tonight.

And I knew I could probably get a really good burger at one of the restaurants on the Square.

As I let myself out of my apartment and tromped back down the stairs to street level, I reflected that maybe I should have thought this whole living-next-to-the-Square-thing through a little more. In my little neighborhood in Louisville, I'd never been far from a number of restaurants, but this was ridiculous easy. I didn't even have to drive. I could just walk.

Making a mental note to create a menu and do more meal prep next week to keep myself within my food budget, I stepped out onto the street. A warm early evening breeze ruffled my hair and I smiled. Today had been a little cooler than earlier in the week, and right now it felt amazing. I decided I wanted to eat outside, too.

As I crossed the Square, my phone vibrated in my back pocket. It startled me at first—I hadn't received many texts since I moved to Starhaven. Pulling my phone out, I saw that it was Zel, texting me to thank me again for being willing to teach her how to knit and giving me her schedule. After a little back and forth, we settled on Wednesday afternoons around two.

I shoved the phone back into my pocket, a thrill of excitement humming in my veins. The more I thought about teaching others how to do some of the things I loved, the more excited I became. The idea resonated inside me, like the beautiful clear tone of a bell being struck deep inside me.

I was still smiling as I approached the Starhaven Grill. The scent of grilled meat wafted through the air, making my stomach grumble that it had been a *long* time since lunch. Like most of the restaurants around the Square, a handful of little patio chairs and tables dotted the sidewalk in front of the Starhaven Grill. Most of them were full, with people eating and laughing and discussing their days.

My steps quickened. Oh, it smelled so good. A burger and fries were definitely the right choice for dinner tonight.

I crossed the crosswalk with a handful of other people out walking the Square and made a beeline for the Starhaven Grill's front door. As I did, however, the back of my neck prickled.

Somebody was staring at me.

Without letting my cheerful smile slip, I scanned the area. Nobody sitting in front of the restaurant was paying me a bit of attention, but...

There. My eyes widened a little, and then narrowed. Dave. Of course it was Dave.

The little man stood next to a police car parked in one of the slots across from the restaurant. He'd been talking with the officer driving the car, but apparently, he had eyes in the back of his head and those eyes had spotted me. Also apparently, he'd been unable to keep himself from glaring at me.

I almost waved at him and kept walking. Almost. But then I glimpsed who he was talking to and my steps faltered. It was the handsome young police officer from the other night. Officer Nick...Nick something, right?

A blush threatened to burn my cheeks even as I *thought* the word handsome, but I did my best to tame it. What in the world was that about? When was the last time I blushed when I saw some guy I'd only just met?

Good grief. Mentally, I shook my head at myself and reminded myself *why* this mattered. Renaissance Man had crossed my mind several times throughout the course of the day. This police officer—Nick—*might* be able to tell me what had happened to him.

Instead of heading to get some dinner, I instead shifted my angle and marched straight over to Dave and the police officer.

It was almost worth it just to watch Dave's eyes just about pop out of his head with shock. His grumpy, sour expression flashed to one of panic before he managed to cover the emotion with an irritable scowl again.

"Well, good evening, gentlemen." I offered both men my sweetest butter-wouldn't-melt-in-my-mouth smile. My cheeks tinted just a little under Officer Nick's scrutiny, but I hoped he and Dave would both chalk it up to the heat.

Bristling silently, Dave drew himself up to his full height and fixed me with a glare that could have frozen molten lava. "What do *you* want?"

Part of me (the part that thought it would serve him right for being so mean) wanted to snort in laughter—he was still so much shorter than I was and I just knew it would bother him. But my momma, whatever her faults, raised me better than that.

"I'd like to speak with Officer...Nick, was it?" I lifted a questioning eyebrow at the dark-haired police officer in the driver's seat.

"Nick Poindexter." His smile could have lit the entire Square.

The force of it hit me square in the chest. I almost took a

step back out of shock, but managed to control myself. No need to give Dave the dwarf yet another reason to belittle me.

"Right," I said, just a tad breathlessly.

Dave muttered something unintelligible under his breath. Nick and I both ignored him.

It was Nick's turn to lift a questioning eyebrow. "What can I do for you, Miss O'Malley?"

He remembered my *name*. If I'd been ten years younger, I probably would have swooned. As it was, now that I'd come to it, my courage almost failed me.

Almost.

I could still see Dave in my peripheral vision, and *that* alone would have been enough to spur anybody in my position onward.

I took a deep breath. "I know you might not be able to tell me, but I've been wondering what happened to the man I found in the park. Is he okay? He was hurt, but I wasn't sure how bad."

A slight crease formed in Officer Nick's forehead as he surveyed me. Our gazes locked, making me feel like he was taking my measure—and I wasn't sure what he'd found. The sounds of laughter filling the balmy evening air faded away, until it was just me and Nick...and Dave.

All at once, Nick deliberately blinked and shifted in his seat. Oddly, his gaze flicked to Dave before returning to me. "You said in your statement you'd never met him before."

"That's true." It was my turn to shift from foot to foot. I should have left it at that, but a burning compulsion to explain myself overtook me. I'm not even sure why. "I have no idea who he is."

"Then why are you so interested?" This from Dave, who was still scowling at me. He'd shifted positions too, crossing his arms across his chest.

"He was hurt." I narrowed my eyes at Dave, unable to completely quell a flash of irritation. I directed my attention to Nick again. "And he was really upset about somebody he'd lost, but he didn't seem to be able to remember who she was. And I guess I can't help but feel slightly responsible for him, seeing as how I'm the one who found him."

Nick started to respond, but Dave cut in before he could utter so much as a syllable. "That's part of an ongoing investigation, isn't it, Officer Poindexter?" He offered me a scathing smile. "Which means it's none of *your* business."

"Dave..." Nick said with a sigh.

"I'm not wrong," the short man said confidently, without looking at Nick.

A glance at Nick told me that Dave, unfortunately, was right. The police officer's handsome face wore an expression of regret. He offered me a slight smile.

"I'm afraid he's correct, Miss O'Malley. We're in the midst of an ongoing investigation and I am not at liberty to disclose those details. All I can tell you is that he's received medical attention."

"No, no, it's fine. I understand." I held up a hand, mirroring his smile. "Like I said, I was just curious because I found him and he needed help."

"Don't believe everything you hear around here," Dave muttered.

I ignored him. So did Nick, though his gaze darted to Dave

again before returning to me. He opened his mouth, but another voice cut him off before he could speak.

"Hey, what's happening?"

I turned to find another somewhat familiar figure crossing the street toward us from the restaurant. The heavyset policeman, Nick's partner. He held two brown bags of food.

"Hi." I greeted him with a polite smile too, trying to remember his name. Officer...Riordan, was it? "I was just asking about Renaissance Man."

"Renaissance Man?" The heavyset man actually stopped mid-stride, confusion wrinkling his round face.

A hot flush worked its way up from my neck to my hair-line. "Oh, sorry, I meant the man I found in the woods by the park." Embarrassed, I twitched one shoulder in a shrug. "That's what I've been calling him in my head."

"Oh." Still looking confused, the heavyset man approached the squad car to hand one bag of food to Nick through his open window. "Well, I'm afraid we can't discuss that, ma'am. It's an—"

"—ongoing investigation," I finished ruefully. "Yes, I understand." Glancing at Nick, I inclined my head in a nod. "Thanks anyway. Good night."

With that, I stepped off the curb and headed across the street toward the restaurant. My cheeks still felt hot, but I resisted the urge to press my hands to them. Honestly, I prob-ably should have realized they wouldn't be able to tell me anything.

It had been worth a shot to allay my curiosity, though.

Now, on to dinner. The farther I got from Nick and the

closer I came to the delicious smells pouring out of the Starhaven Grill's open door, the more the butterflies subsided and hunger pains took over. Even across the street, however, I still felt Dave's glare boring into my back.

Just before I crossed the threshold, a dark thought struck me. Should I *really* be spending money on dinner out again when I'd barely made any money so far in Celia's Craft Shop's first week open?

Probably not from a monetary aspect, I admitted to myself.

But from a celebratory aspect? Heck, yeah. Best thing I could do was celebrate having had the handful of customers I'd had so far, including Zel and Bianca.

That was most definitely a win.

CHAPTER

TWENTY-SEVEN

Monday morning found me back in my shop, sitting behind the front counter with a cup of coffee. (My own, not a latte from the coffee shop, as tempting as it was.) My glittering silver shawl knitting project sat in its tote on the glossy hardwood floor next to my chair, but I let it be for now.

Too early to pull that out. Best to save it for the inevitable mid-afternoon slump.

Taking slow sips, I glanced around my shop, looking for anything out of place, or anything that I needed to straighten or organize. There was nothing, of course. Thanks to my rather desultory lack of customers, everything was exactly as it should be.

I blew out a sigh. I'd wait Dave out. I *would*. It was just... hard.

Week two of my own business, beginning with a whimper.

Ah, well. I shook my head and picked up my phone to scroll through my music choices for today. If nothing else, I had Wednesday's knitting class with Zel to look forward to.

I'd just settled on an upbeat collection of Owl City songs when the bell above the door jingled merrily. My heart skipped a beat in anticipation.

"Morning," I called out, looking up with a smile. My smile froze as I took in my potential customer.

A short, hunched figure wrapped in what I could only describe as a gray cloak and clutching an old carved cane of dark wood stood on my welcome mat. An old woman's pale face, as wrinkled as a crumpled piece of paper, peeked out from beneath the hood, along with a few wispy gray strands of hair. Her dark eyes swept a searching glance around my shop before settling on me.

Faced with her sharp, oddly bright expression, the hair on the back of my neck prickled a little. I had the sudden—and keen—awareness that this woman, no matter how old she might appear—was a force to be reckoned with.

"Good morning." Her voice held a thin, reedy quality, but with a depth that almost seemed to resonate in my small shop.

I half-rose from my chair. "Can I help you with anything?"

The old woman studied me, unblinking, and then glanced around again. "I am looking for knitting needles. And tapestry needles."

Those were two very different things for two very different crafts—and I loved it. I offered her a friendly smile. "Knitting needles are on aisle three." I pointed to the clearly marked short aisle. "You'll find tapestry needles on aisle four." I hesitated. "Would you like me to show you?"

"No need." The old woman raised her free hand and then moved slowly toward the knitting section. A scent of lavender and something sharper—hawthorn?—lingered in her wake.

I watched her go, trying not to stare. Outside of television, Halloween, and a Renaissance Fair, Starhaven was the only place I'd ever seen a grown adult swan around in a *cloak* before. Let alone a woman as old as she appeared to be.

Either I was attracting this kind of person all of a sudden or... My thoughts stilled.

Or there really is something different about this town, whispered an oddly knowing voice in my head. *Just like you've suspected. Let's not forget you have a* brownie *living in your house.*

I hadn't forgotten. But I had kind of...acclimated to it? Enough to the point that I was edging into used-to-it territory and Agnes's presence no longer brought me up short.

Funny how fast we humans adapt to things.

The old woman took her time exploring my selection of knitting needles. She lifted several packages off of the shelf and examined them closely before replacing them. At last, she found the one she wanted and moved on to the tapestry needles.

I found myself extremely curious to see what she had decided on, but in order to keep from staring at her, I picked up the tote with my silver shawl. I could not, however, bring myself to resume knitting. I'd have to put it down whenever the old woman finished and was ready to check out, and I didn't want to stop in the middle of a row.

My gaze returned to the old woman. I desperately wanted to ask her about the cloak—usually I wouldn't have had any trouble making small talk and asking a question about why she chose to wear a kind of fashion statement—but I couldn't get the words out. My tongue seemed to stick to the roof of my mouth.

It was a most curious feeling, sitting there not knowing quite what to do with myself. I bit my lip and reached for my coffee and my phone instead.

No new texts and a bunch of spam emails, but I *could* work on some advertising graphics in Canva for a minute.

Over the weekend, I'd discovered Starhaven had its own social media community. I'd already created a page for my shop and now I was just waiting for one of the admins to let me join. Curiously, no one that I actually knew in Starhaven had a social media account. I'd thought for sure that Maddie, as the self-proclaimed town facilitator, would be active on social media, but she wasn't. Nor was her foundation.

And I couldn't find Zel, either. *That* wasn't as surprising— she might not be on social media for safety reasons. You never knew.

"Excuse me."

The old woman's reedy voice startled me. I jumped a little in my seat, looking up wide-eyed from my phone to find my sole customer standing at the counter opposite me.

My heart turned over again in my chest. Wow, she was quiet. When had she left the aisle and come to the front counter?

And how had I not *seen* her?

"I'm sorry." I pasted a smile on my face to cover how badly she'd startled me. "Did you find everything all right?"

"Yes." The old woman inclined her still-hooded head in a nod. Her bright, dark eyes could have belonged to a woman fifty years her junior. "These will do nicely." She set a pair of size 5 knitting needles and a pack of regular tapestry needles on the counter.

"I'm glad." My smile grew more genuine. I rang her items up and put them in a bag for her. "What are you making?"

"Scarves."

I waited a second, but the old woman provided no further information. Okay, then. A woman of few words. That was all right. At least she was here.

I gave her the total and she handed me a twenty. Close up, her hands were even more wrinkled than they'd seemed before, but they had a look of surprising strength about them.

"Here's your change." I handed over her money and her bag. "I put the receipt in the bag."

"Thank you." The old woman gave me one more piercing look, before glancing around my shop again and nodding. Bag in hand, she then made her way out of the shop and back out onto the street.

Once the door had shut behind her, I sank back into my chair. "Well," I said aloud, "that was interesting."

I waited a moment, out of an odd feeling of anticipation, but no one else walked through the door. Feeling a little let down, I went back to my social media graphics. Despite that, I couldn't quite shake that odd sense of anticipation, like today was the start of something big.

It was, but I wouldn't know that for another couple of weeks.

TWENTY-EIGHT

Over the course of the day, a few more people—normal people, in normal getup—trickled in and out of my shop. I sold a few beading kits, enough fabric for a whole Lone Star quilt in summery blue, yellow, and white fabrics, and more yarn.

Was it enough to pay my rent yet? Nope. But was it progress? Absolutely.

That slow trickle of customers continued through Wednesday morning. I greeted everyone with a smile, a buoy of hope in my chest. I sold more fabric, chunky yarn for several afghans, and more sock yarn and knitting needles.

My posts on social media hadn't gotten a lot of engagement, but they'd gotten a little. And I'd noticed that the Black Forest Antique's page had carefully avoided commenting—probably because Dave knew as well as I did that his vendetta against me would come off as exactly what it was: a vendetta.

By the time the door jingled just before 3 PM, I was

writing myself some notes to restock certain yarns in the next week or so. That would be particularly important as we neared fall and people started doing more knitting and crocheting. There are people who knit and crochet all year round, and then there are the fall and winter hobbyists who prefer not to work with warm yarn things when it's ninety degrees outside. (I know, I know, it does sound like a contradiction in terms, but I've met them. These people do exist.)

I looked up with a smile to find Zel standing on the welcome mat. Once again, she was sans children. "Hi, Zel."

"Hi." The short blonde flashed me a small, but excited smile and motioned to the knitting bag she'd brought with her in addition to her purse. "I came prepared."

"Excellent." I clapped my hands together. "Oh, I'm so excited."

"Me, too." Zel tucked a short golden lock of hair behind one ear. "I've been looking forward to this all week."

"I am so glad to hear that." Beaming at her, I rounded the counter and grabbed a couple of black folding chairs I'd leaned up against the wall. I'd had to buy them over the weekend; I didn't have anything like this yet for the shop.

"I'm sorry I don't have really comfortable chairs," I said as I rounded the front counter with the chairs and set them up in the space between the counter and the aisles and in front of the door that led into my back room. (I'd made a sign that said 'Staff Only' in what I'd hoped was friendly lettering and hung it on that door.) "I wasn't really sure how many people would take me up on classes, and I realized I couldn't leave the shop unattended."

"Oh, it's all right." Zel drifted after me, clutching her knitting bag. "Those will work fine." She settled down on one of the chairs and looked at me expectantly.

A hint of anxiety filtered through my excitement as I took the chair next to her. I'd never actually tried to teach anybody how to knit before, but I could knit in my sleep and I'd spent time over the weekend brushing up on my terminology. Surely it wouldn't be that hard.

"Did you watch any YouTube videos?" I motioned to her knitting bag, just to see where we'd need to start.

Zel shook her head. "I don't spend a great deal of time on my phone." She lifted one shoulder in a shrug. "Rowan and Rosalie usually keep me pretty busy."

"I can imagine." I nodded slowly. "Okay, so we'll start with the basics. May I have your knitting needles and some yarn?"

Obligingly, Zel handed over a skein of aquamarine yarn and her knitting needles.

For the first time, I noticed the slender band on the ring finger of her left hand. It looked like it had been woven from blades of grass, or a couple of very thin vines.

A wave of sympathy crashed through me. She was married—or had been. Where was her husband? So far, she hadn't mentioned anything about having one. That wave of sympathy deepened. Had something happened to him?

I almost asked her, but bit my tongue before the words could escape. That probably wasn't appropriate yet. We didn't know each other that well, and that was a pretty personal question.

Instead, I focused on the task at hand.

"Okay, so before we can knit anything, we have to cast on

however many stitches we need. That's what we call putting the initial stitches onto your knitting needle." I made a slip-knot with one end of the yarn and slipped it over both of the knitting needles.

Zel leaned forward, her eyes intent on my hands.

"There are two main methods of casting on. One is basically like regular knitting, and the other involves looping the yarn. Personally, I find the second method easier, and I think it makes your initial line more stable, but once you know how to knit, I'll show you that one, too."

I demonstrated how to use my fingers to loop the yarn around both knitting needles to make stitches.

"Why do you use both needles?" Zel's forehead puckered in a frown.

I grinned at her. "That is an excellent question. The answer is that it keeps the tension from being too tight."

"Oh." A light came on in Zel's blue eyes. "I understand that. One has to be careful of tension in—in embroidery, as well."

"Exactly. You don't want things to be too loose, but they can't be too tight, either." I demonstrated a few more stitches, and then walked Zel through how to do it herself.

Her fingers worked awkwardly at first, but within ten minutes she'd got the hang of it. She looked up at me with a smile. "This is easy."

"I agree." I smiled back at her, and then proceeded to show her how to hold both needles in her hands, as well as how to hold the yarn in the fingers of her left hand. "There are several ways to do this, too. And, eventually, you'll learn how to knit with two different colors."

Zel's eyes widened. "You can do that?"

"Oh, yeah." I nodded solemnly. "It's not that complicated."

We then moved on to actual knitting, and I explained that there are two basic knitting stitches: knit and purl. I then explained that a yarn-over was a common method of creating an additional stitch and that knitting or purling two stitches together decreased the total number of stitches.

"Basically," I finished, "every knitting pattern is some combination of these four things." Well, that and a few other things like picking up stitches, but she wasn't ready for that yet. We'd get there.

It didn't take Zel long to get the hang of knitting. Her only initial problem was adjusting to holding the needles. Once she grasped that, well, all bets were off.

She knit slowly, but steadily. When she reached the end of the row, I showed her how to switch the needle with all the stitches back to her left hand, and she started again, carefully knitting each stitch along the entire row.

I'd been playing classical music most of the afternoon, and right now the quiet strains of Debussy's *Clair de Lune* filtered through the shop as Zel worked. Afternoon September sunlight spilled through the front window, turning a swathe of the hardwood floor to burnished brown.

No one else had come in the shop since she'd gotten here, which was fine. It meant I didn't have to split my attention.

"Did your mother teach you how to knit?"

Zel's soft, almost tentative question drew my attention back to her. "What?"

Her fair cheeks pinked, but she repeated the question.

"Oh. No." I shook my head, chuckling. "My mom is more of a gamer, but if she was going to do anything, it'd involve a puzzle." I motioned to the dishcloth slowly taking shape beneath Zel's fingers. "She thinks this stuff is too fiddly."

"I see." Zel spared me a glance and then refocused on her knitting. "Then who taught you? Your grandmother?"

"No." I shook my head again. "My grandmother—my dad's mom, I mean; my mom never had much of a relationship with her parents—encouraged me, but she didn't knit herself. I pretty much taught myself. Found a book at the library, and then I found videos on the internet."

Zel spared me another glance, this one impressed. "That is quite an achievement."

A little embarrassed, I lifted one shoulder in a shrug. "It's not that hard."

"Celia, as a friend of mine is fond of saying, what one person finds easy, another person may find rather difficult." Zel paused her knitting long enough to give me a knowing look.

"That's true." I've heard versions of that before myself. "But, Zel, I'm serious—this really isn't that hard."

She laughed softly. "If you say so."

At the end of our hour, Zel's phone vibrated softly in her purse. She spared it a semi-regretful glance and then looked down at her lap. "I am in the middle of a row. What do I do?"

"Well, unless it's an emergency, I recommend you finish

the row." I made a face. "Sometimes, stopping in the middle of a row creates these weird gaps."

"I do not want a weird gap." Zel kept knitting, until she'd finished the row. She held up the knitting needle, where a good inch and a half of a pretty aquamarine dishcloth in garter stitch was taking shape.

"Now we put a needle stopper on it so all your stitches can't fall off." I reached into her knitting bag and pulled out the package she'd bought.

Zel carefully fit the little rubber ends onto one needle, and, after a moment's consideration, the other as well.

I didn't comment. If she wanted to use both, she could certainly do that.

"Thank you," Zel said as she tucked everything back into her knitting bag. "That was...fun." She rose to her feet and hiked both her purse and her knitting tote over her shoulder, offering me shy smile. "I enjoyed it."

"Well," I motioned to her knitting tote. "I know you're probably super busy with your twins, but keep practicing. Next week, I'll teach you how to purl."

"That sounds good." Zel glanced at our chairs. "Do you need help?"

"Oh, no. I've got this." I grinned at her and flapped my hand in a shooing motion. "Have fun with your babies."

"Thank you, Celia."

Zel disappeared out the door, while I folded up the black chairs and, after a moment of thought, carried them back into my back room. Probably the best place to keep them for now, considering I currently only needed them once a week right.

As I turned back toward the front counter and my own

knitting, a flash of movement across the street caught my eye. I glanced out my big plate glass window in time to see Marie duck back into Vine Life.

A puzzled frown knit my forehead. Had she been watching Zel leave? If so, why?

Dave's face floated through my mind, but I pushed it aside. What did a single mom with twins have to do with a grumpy antique owner?

Maybe it doesn't have anything to do with Zel, a voice in the back of my mind whispered. *Maybe she'd like to come in here, too, but doesn't feel like she can.*

Again, because of Dave. I rolled my eyes and settled in my chair behind the front counter, before leaning over to pick up my silver shawl. If this kept up, that man was going to have a lot to answer for.

TWENTY-NINE

I texted Maddie that night, after I finished eating a grilled cheese sandwich for dinner. I told her I had more questions and asked if it would be possible to meet for coffee soon. I wanted to poke around for more information on Dave, predominately, but I also wondered if she'd know anything about Renaissance Man.

Maddie didn't respond immediately. Not that I expected her to. Her job at the Starhaven Foundation as Town Facilitator, or whatever her actual job title was, seemed to keep her quite busy.

I was halfway through washing up the dishes when my phone finally buzzed with an incoming text.

MADDIE

Friday morning. 8AM at Starbright Café.

Excitement flared to life inside me. Friday morning would

be perfect—plenty of time for a chat and I'd still be able to open Celia's Craft Shop on time. Wiping off my hands, I picked up my phone and tapped out a response.

Sounds great. Thank you.

Humming a little tune under my breath, I turned back to the griddle pan I was washing and smiled. It was only a matter of time before I wore Maddie down enough for her to spill the tea about Dave and others like him in Starhaven.

I was nearly done with the dishes when a reedy voice said behind me, "You have no idea who came into your shop."

Startled, I jumped—and almost dropped the glass I was holding. Whirling around, I found Agnes standing on the edge of my kitchen table, staring at me with an expression on her wrinkly brown face that I couldn't decipher.

"Agnes!" I gasped, my free hand reflexively going to my heart—and leaving a wet handprint on the center of my t-shirt. "What are you talking about?"

I hadn't seen a trace of her since the morning I met her, and now she was commenting on my craft shop's clientele?

The brownie just continued to stare at me, as though she had rediscovered I was some especially strange sort of alien.

My heart rate slowly returned to normal. Taking a deep breath, I set the glass in the drainer and dried my hands with a dishtowel. Once I'd hung it up on the oven door, I waved a hand in the general direction of my shop below our feet.

"Do you mean Zel? She's a mom with twin babies. I hardly—"

"No." Agnes shook her head once, never removing her eyes from mine.

I listed off several of my other customers, only for the brownie to shake her head after each one.

A peculiar feeling trickled down my spine, like somebody had dripped ice water down my back. Belatedly, I recalled my first customer of the week: the old woman in the hooded cloak. That was Monday, though, I argued with myself. Surely Agnes hadn't waited until *now* to talk to me about her.

Posting both hands on my hips, I narrowed my eyes at the brownie. "Agnes, are you talking about anybody I had here today?"

She blinked once, canted her head to one side, and then slowly shook her head.

The hair on the back of my neck prickled; I resisted the urge to shiver. "Do you mean the old lady from Monday?"

Agnes inclined her head in the barest of nods, one of her little brown hands playing with the strands of seed beads around her neck.

"What about her?" I shook my head. "Sure, it's a little weird that she showed up in an actual cloak, but..." I trailed off, noting that Agnes's expression had grown a little pinched around the edges. It was my turn to cant my head to one side. "Who is she?"

"Can't say." Agnes shook her head and actually took a step back on the tabletop.

I couldn't help myself. "Can't, or won't?"

"Can't. Won't. Doesn't matter."

Part of me wanted to argue that technically it mattered a lot, but the saner part of me (and, boy, wasn't *that* a dizzying revelation) reminded me that I was literally arguing with a creature I'd thought belonged to myths and fairytales. What did I really know at this point?

"Be careful," the brownie hissed quietly, her large, dark eyes suddenly darting around the kitchen as though she expected intruders to magically melt from the baseboards. "Not what she seems." She sucked in a breath through her teeth. "None of them."

My frown deepened. "Agnes, what are you—"

The sudden loud blare of a horn on the street below drew my attention toward the window, just for an instant.

When I looked back at my kitchen table, the little brownie had disappeared.

I blinked. "Agnes?"

But of course, she didn't answer. I stood, frowning at the spot on the table she'd occupied, for longer than I should have. Finally, I shrugged to myself.

A brownie's presence in my life was probably the tip of the iceberg in terms of strangeness these days. And I'd already gotten the sense that there was a lot more to Starhaven than anybody was letting on.

My thoughts returned to that old woman. I didn't know who she was, but she was definitely memorable. My eyes narrowed. *Memorable enough that Maddie probably knows who she is.*

I made a mental note to ask the town facilitator about her on Friday.

That night, I left out more beads for Agnes. Maybe she didn't need them, but what could it hurt?

CHAPTER

THIRTY

Thankfully, it wasn't as awkward to walk back into Starbright Café as I'd been afraid it would be. Friday morning found me nestled in an old brocade armchair in the corner of a few minutes before 8AM, ice cold mocha frappe in hand. I'd decided to splurge this morning. (Once upon a time, I'd considered attempting to make these at home, but I'd come to the conclusion that it was entirely too much work for this season of my life.)

The big cuckoo clock with its mythical carvings had just chimed eight when Maddie sailed in the coffee shop's front door. She looked as elegant as usual, in her floral dress (pink, today) and every gray curl in place. She ordered her usual cup of tea and joined me in the corner.

"Let me guess," she said without preamble, one corner of her mouth tilting up in a smile. "More questions about Dave?"

"You got me." I offered her a rueful grin. "Although, in my defense, you did tell me when I first came here that he was a story for another time."

Maddie considered me for a second, before she allowed her half-smile to bloom into a full smile. "That is true."

She waited until Rodney brought her the tea she'd ordered before she settled back in her armchair and stared thoughtfully down into her tea's milky brown surface. "I cannot give you the full details of Dave's story. It is not my place. But I *can* tell you that he loves Starhaven and does not want to see its old-fashioned charm destroyed."

My jaw dropped. "He actually thinks somebody like me coming in and opening a craft shop is going to *destroy* the town?"

"Dave is—" Maddie stopped, frowning, as though choosing her words carefully. She took a ladylike sip of her tea, and then set her teacup back down on its saucer. "Well, to be perfectly honest, Dave is angrier with the Mr. Moffat and the Council than he is with you."

"Mr. Moffat and the Council?" I felt ridiculous repeating her, like I was lagging behind a half-step the entire conversation, but I couldn't help myself.

"Yes." Maddie sighed, her smile taking on a wry tilt. "The Town Council."

I looked askance at her. "This is another Starhaven peculiarity, isn't it?" It wasn't a question.

A startled look flitted through Maddie's green eyes. She paused, her teacup halfway to her lips. "What makes you say that?"

"Because I've never heard of a Council in a town that determines whether or not people are allowed to move into said town." I paused, shaking my head. "At least not in the last century."

"Your shop is just off the Square," Maddie pointed out. "That is slightly different from someone buying a house here in Starhaven."

"Oh, I get that there are more regulations for business on the Square." I held up a hand. "But it sounds like this Council apparently has a lot more control than normal." I didn't have a lot to base this observation off of, other than what Maddie was telling me, but the moment the words left my mouth, I felt the *rightness* of them settle around me like a warm blanket.

I lifted an eyebrow at Maddie. "Otherwise, why would Dave be so angry with them?"

Maddie pressed her lips into a thin line, acknowledging the truth in my words. For just a second, her blithe, cheerful persona slipped and I caught a glimpse of a woman who seemed much older and much wearier.

At last, she exhaled slowly. "It is a long, rather boring story, Celia, but the truth is, Mr. Moffat found a...loophole in Starhaven's ordinances. He had a good feeling about you—" here she flashed me an approving smile, "—and he wanted to rent to you regardless of what the Council might have decided."

I leaned back in my seat, digesting this. "Okay, that kind of makes sense. But..." I shrugged, shaking my head. "Why in the world would the Council *not* want a craft shop on the

Square?" I waved my free hand. "Crafting is good for people's mental health. It encourages creativity. Why would anybody think that was a bad idea?"

Maddie sighed again. "It's nothing personal, dear." A slight frown puckered her forehead. "I do believe I told you that once. Unfortunately, there are...town politics at play here."

When she did not elaborate on what those town politics were, exactly, it was my turn to press my lips into a thin line.

"I see. Well, if they're hoping I'll give up because of a lack of business, they've got another think coming." I offered Maddie a thin, wry smile. "This is it for me. I don't have a backup plan."

To my surprise, Maddie threw back her head and laughed. "And that is what I love about you, Celia O'Malley. Your indomitable spirit." Green eyes twinkling, she smiled fondly at me, like I was a grandchild she was particularly proud of. "You're here now, so a good deal of that is water under the bridge, but there are those who are still a little miffed that Mr. Moffat went around the Council."

"Like Dave," I said flatly.

"Like Dave," Maddie agreed, before eying me speculatively. "I think, however, that you'll eventually wear him down." Her eyes sparkled with mischief. "Especially since Bianca likes you."

Surprised flooded me, followed quickly by concern. "I hope Dave hasn't found out about that yet." I bit my lip. "He won't be happy."

Instead of sharing my concern, Maddie only waved a

dismissive hand. "He'll get over it. Too protective of her for his own good, sometimes. Although," she added contemplatively, "one can't blame him."

"Why is that?" I asked quickly. "What's their story?"

But Maddie was already draining the last of her tea—when had she managed to drink it all?—and gathering her purse to rise to her feet. "That, my dear Celia, is a tale for another day." She reached out to pat me firmly on the shoulder. "Don't give up. I believe you're already having more of an impact than you realize."

In a rustle of soft floral skirts, she was gone, leaving the faintest scent of lavender in her wake.

I stared after her, frustrated again. I was beginning to sense a theme here. She was like the Starhaven equivalent of Scheherazade, finishing a story but then starting another and leaving that one hanging. Getting answers out of her was about like pulling teeth.

I rubbed a hand over my face and then rose to my feet as well. Maybe by the time I'd lived here a decade, I'd have some idea of these people's stories. The thought brought a burble of hysterical laughter—which I promptly swallowed, of course.

The coffee shop was still pretty busy. No need to give anybody in this town fodder to think I was crazy or anything. Oh, no.

Pasting a confident smile on my face, I made my way through the coffee shop and back out onto the sidewalk. I was halfway across the Square when I realized I'd forgotten to ask Maddie about both Renaissance Man and that old woman.

Wrinkling my nose at my own forgetfulness, I tipped my head up to the beautiful blue sky. Ah, well. It'd just give me an excuse to meet her for coffee (and tea) again later.

Because I *did* want to know about both of them. And, I realized suddenly, I wanted to ask her about that clearing in the woods as well.

THIRTY-ONE

That afternoon, I closed up shop at four-thirty. I reasoned it was highly unlikely I was going to have any new business waltz through the door before five o'clock. And besides, remembered that clearing in the woods had piqued my curiosity.

I wanted to go back there again. Especially while there was a lot more daylight than there had been last time.

I'm not sure why, but my thoughts had been drifting back to that dark circle of trees all day. Maybe it was the fact that it still stood out so vividly in my mind. Maybe it was the fact that I still couldn't quite understand where that man had come from.

Regardless, it didn't settle. And the mystery of it all was driving me a little crazy.

Flipping the little 'open' sign on my door to 'closed', I locked up, stowed the keys in my purse, and set off down the sidewalk toward the park. The late afternoon air was quite warm and still humid, but considerably better than the sweltering heat we'd had the first week of September. And after the coolness of the air conditioning in my shop, the golden sunshine felt delightfully warm. I tried not to keep it too cold —I did have bills to pay after all—but I wanted the shop to be comfortable for my customers.

But, I will say, the sunshine felt incredible. I soaked it in like a cat all the way to the park and across the grassy field to the little stand of poplars, maples, and oaks that obscured the opening to the clearing. A group of children played on the playground and several groups of teenagers were shooting hoops on the basketball court while a handful of parents and grandparents kept an eye on everything. None of them paid me much attention.

A few moments later, I reached the carved wooden benches beneath that scattering of trees. Golden late afternoon sunlight filtered through the green leaves, sending fingers of sunshine to the mossy ground below. Bypassing the benches, I approached the two massive oaks that stood at the edge of the woods and offered the best entry into the clearing. I pulled my pepper spray out of my purse, just in case, but I had a strange feeling that I wouldn't need it today.

The moment I stepped between the oaks, I noticed two things. One was that strange, solemn hush I'd registered the last time I was here. The second thing was the light immediately grew dimmer.

Confused, I glanced up at the canopy of leaves high overhead, stretching branchy fingers toward the center of the clearing. Last time I'd noticed the light dimming, but I'd chalked it up to the time of day. Now I could see that though the center of the clearing was open to the blue sky above, the light just didn't seem to penetrate to the ground.

That was odd.

Puzzled, I tilted my head to one side as I studied the oaks, maples, and silver birches ringing the clearing in that strange, perfect circle. Was it possible for some trees to have extra thick canopies of leaves? I didn't remember ever learning about something like that, but...I'll admit I know as much about trees as the average person. But even that wouldn't explain how it was possible for light not to filter down through that opening in the center.

Shaking my head at myself, I moved forward into the clearing. That massive chunk of granite remained the only object here apart from the soft green grass underfoot. I walked over to it and examined it again, but it hadn't changed. The granite was still jagged on one side and curiously smooth on the other.

I blew out a breath. *Nothing to see here*, I told myself. Just a weird rock, a lot of grass, and a whole lot of peaceful—albeit somewhat strange—quiet.

Meow.

As if to mock that last thought, a plaintive little sound came from somewhere behind me. Startled, I turned around, trying to place the source of the sound.

At first, I didn't see anything. Then in the strange twilight that permeated the clearing, I saw the faint outline of a cat appear around the base of the chunk of granite. A beautiful fluffy calico—orange and black and white. A female, then.

"Hi," I said. "Where did you come from?"

The cat stared at me, unblinking, as if deciding whether

or not I was trustworthy. After a second, she gave a soft meow and approached me. She started rubbing around between my ankles, purring loudly.

Slowly, I bent down and extended a hand toward her. She gave me an obligatory sniff before resuming rubbing against my legs and purring. As I stroked her soft, fluffy fur, I felt the ridges of her spine. For all her fluffy appearance, she was quite thin and scrawny.

"Who do you belong to?" I asked gently.

The cat meowed plaintively again.

I loved on her for a few moments, before I gave her one last gentle stroke and reluctantly stood up. "I'm sorry, kitty, but I've got to go. If you have a home, you probably should go to it."

I felt silly saying the words. This calico was probably a stray, especially given how scrawny she was underneath all that fur.

For one wild second I thought about taking her home with me. *Don't be ridiculous*, I told myself. *For all you know she could belong to somebody and even if she is a stray, you don't know what your lease policy says about animals.*

I didn't remember. I haven't had animals since I moved out of my dad's, so whether or not my current lease allowed them had never been a concern.

Besides, I realized suddenly, *what about Agnes?*

Thoughts of the little Brownie flooded my mind. Would she want a cat in the apartment? Even if it was allowed?

Or would I have to worry about the cat *eating* Agnes? The thought made me shudder.

I shook my head at myself. *Now there's a conversation I never thought I'd have.*

At my feet, the cat meowed again.

"I'm sorry, kitty." I looked down at her, biting my lip. "I can't take you home."

The calico just tilted her head to one side as though questioning why, her eyes huge and plaintive in the dim light.

I forced myself to move toward the edge of the clearing before I could change my mind. As soon as I passed between the two oaks, it was like the world snapped back into focus again. I heard birdsong and laughter from children playing on the playground, mixed with the distant sounds of traffic going up and down the streets along the square.

The suddenness of it almost made me stumble. Startled, I glanced behind me at the clearing. Was it *normal* for tree trunks to absorb that much sound? (City girl, remember?)

I didn't recall that happening the night I'd found Renaissance Man, but I'd also been pretty distracted at the time.

Making a mental note to Google it later, I headed home to fix dinner.

THIRTY-TWO

I made myself Hawaiian pizza for dinner. Store-bought dough and pasta sauce, covered in shredded mozzarella cheese and smothered it in chunks of pineapple and ham. I hadn't made one of these in a while, and just the thought of it made my mouth water in anticipation.

I took a shower while it baked, and then I curled up on my couch in comfy pajamas with a couple of slices and watched a new chick flick I hadn't seen yet. It was a great diversion for a little while. The story was about as predictable as you'd expect—but if I'm honest, I don't watch chick flicks for new and exciting plotlines. I like them because at the end of the story, true love has won and the characters live happily ever after.

Unlike real life, where sometimes the guy you thought was your one true love turns out to be something else.

I sighed, and then stood up from the couch, firmly

pushing thoughts of Darren out of my mind. That relationship was over and done and I was the better for it. And it wasn't like I needed romance right now anyway. I had my craft shop.

That was enough of a dream come true for me.

Crumpling up my paper plate and napkin, I walked into the kitchen to throw them away in the trash.

"You are crazy," intoned a flat, reedy voice.

I jumped, one hand flying to my chest. Gasping, I looked around for the little brownie. "Agnes! Don't *do* that!"

I spotted her sitting on my kitchen counter, eating a slice of Hawaiian pizza. It was quite the show—the pizza slice was about as tall as she was. Agnes had torn off small chunks and was chewing experimentally.

As my heart rate slowed to something approaching normal, I noticed that she'd turned the last batch of beads I'd given her into another series of necklaces. A stray corner of my mind noted that at this rate, I'd need to switch to something else to give her or she'd wind up being smothered by her mass of necklaces.

Agnes swallowed a bite and met my gaze. "You are crazy, Celia."

Annoyance flooded me, subsuming the lingering remnants of my surprise. Still clutching my paper plate, I posted my free hand on my hip and shot her a wry, betrayed look. "Not you too. I've already got enough people in town—"

"In a good way," Agnes continued placidly, which brought me up short. I stared at her in confusion while she licked her lips and dove into another chunk of pizza. When she surfaced, she said, "Town needs somebody like you, to help them make beautiful things." One long-fingered hand rose to touch her layers of beaded necklaces, a little reverently.

Oh. That's what she meant. My annoyance faded, to be replaced by a small swell of gratitude.

"Thanks." I gave her a smile and then crossed to the trashcan. That done, I moved over to the refrigerator and opened the freezer door, hoping a container of chocolate ice cream would magically appear inside.

It did not.

Sighing, I shut the freezer. When I was at the grocery store the other day, I'd deliberately chosen *not* to buy myself chocolate ice cream precisely because I was afraid I'd wallow in it if Celia's Craft Shop's first several weeks of business weren't great.

A small snort escaped me. If my past self had known it was going to be this rough, I'd have relented and let my future self have the ice cream.

Oh, well. Lesson learned, I supposed.

Turning around, I rested a hip against my kitchen counter and watched Agnes continue to systematically demolish her pizza. A sudden thought occurred to me, sparked by my research the other day and those odd comments Maddie had made earlier, and I frowned.

"Hey, Agnes. I thought brownies didn't like to be seen."

Maddie's words of warning flitted through my mind just in time—I barely managed to keep myself from blurting out the obvious question.

Agnes stiffened alarmingly, her expression growing fierce...and then her little brown body deflated like a balloon that some kid had given a slow leak. Her little shoulders hunched as she dropped her eyes to her spindly fingers.

I froze, pressing my lips shut in mild consternation. I shouldn't have said anything. Didn't that mean that—

"Lonely," Agnes muttered, her reedy voice barely audible.

I froze again, this time for a completely different reason? Lonely? Agnes?

Eyes still downcast, Agnes waved a hand. "Apartment's been empty for a long time. Got used to it, but..." She twitched her shoulders in a semblance of a shrug.

The corners of my world seemed to tilt and then realign themselves in a different configuration. It had never occurred to me that the little brownie might actually be lonely.

"But you didn't want me here." I straightened up, completely gobsmacked. "You glared at me when I couldn't see you, and you moved my things, and I was really starting to think I was losing my mind." I waved my hands for emphasis.

Agnes nodded slowly. "Didn't want you. Yes. But you stayed." She finally looked up at me, her dark, somber gaze meeting mine. "And you like strange music and you cook strange foods, but you like to *make* things. Useful things. Beautiful things."

This time, she lifted both hands to finger her necklaces. "Reminded me that—that *I* used to like to make things too. Before."

Silence fell over my—no, *our*—kitchen, broken only by the hum of the refrigerator. I pressed a hand to my heart again, this time for a completely different reason. It was the strangest thing, but this little brownie—this creature of myth and lore and the stuff of fairytales I'd only ever read about—had succeeded cheering me up where Maddie (and even Bianca) had failed.

Tears welled in my eyes, a tangled mix of gratitude and warmth swelling in my chest. I wiped my eyes with the back of my hand. "Thank you, Agnes. I think—I think that's the sweetest thing anybody's said to me in a long time."

The little brownie regarded me with her somber dark eyes. She nodded once and then, in the space between one eyeblink and the next, she vanished. All that remained was the remnants of her pizza crust.

Maddie's words from this morning floated back through my mind. *I believe you're already having more of an impact than you realize.*

Sniffling a little, I wiped the last of my tears away and took a deep breath. Maddie hadn't exactly specified how large this impact might be, but...I think she was right about part of it.

I went to bed that night feeling a little more encouraged.

CHAPTER

THIRTY-THREE

The calico cat showed up at my apartment the next morning. This probably shouldn't have surprised me, but it did. I mean, who seriously expects a cat to follow them home from the woods outside the park all the way to a second-story apartment?

Not me, that's for sure.

I don't even know how she got in the apartment building. What I *do* know is that I was halfway through breakfast when I heard a faint *scritching* at my front door, followed by several plaintive meows. Startled, I went to the door and opened it to find the little calico cat sitting on my doormat in the hall.

She looked up at me and gave another plaintive meow before she brushed past me and let herself into my apartment. Bemused, I shut the door behind her and watched her take stock of my living room.

"Now, wait a minute," I told her. "I don't know that you can be in here. I don't know what my lease says. And—" I hesitated. "I don't know what *Agnes* is going to think about this."

The cat gave another meow, sat down in the middle of the living room floor, and looked up at me. Her entire posture exuded a vibe of *Let me stay. I like it here.*

As though my saying her name had summoned Agnes (even though I was pretty sure it didn't work that way), her thin, reedy voice spoke from behind me.

"What is that cat doing in here?"

I turned to find Agnes standing on one of my bookshelves, her hands propped up on her hips and her little brown face wrinkled in glare directed at the cat.

"She...uh...apparently followed me home from the woods," I explained, a little helplessly. "I'm not really sure how she managed it."

The cat purred, looking pleased with herself.

If anything, Agnes's glare deepened. "Well, it can't stay here."

"I didn't think so," I assured her.

We both watched as the cat strolled over to sniff my couch before sauntering over to inspect my armchair. She apparently decided that was a good spot because she hopped up onto the chair and stretched out on the back, looking quite at her ease.

"Fluffy fur everywhere," Agnes muttered.

I looked askance at the brownie. For all of her glaring and her grouchy words, there was something in her tone that was decidedly *not* grouchy. My forehead creased in a frown. *What is going on here?*

Glancing from Agnes to the cat and back, I opened my

mouth to tell the brownie I would figure out where to take the cat, but Agnes spoke first.

"She looks hungry."

At those words, the cat started purring. My frown deepened as I considered her. "I don't think she's going to eat you, Agnes."

The brownie directed her glare towards me instead. "That's what you think." She tipped her head towards the kitchen. "You have cream in that thing you call a refrigerator, don't you?"

Bemused, I nodded.

"Well?" Agnes turned on her heel. "What are you waiting for?"

I blinked, but the brownie had already disappeared. I shook my head. "How does she do that?"

Returning to the kitchen, I crossed to the refrigerator and pulled the door open. Yes, I did have cream. Not very much, but enough to give the cat a little dish.

When I closed the refrigerator door, I nearly dropped the pint of cream in shock. Agnes had appeared on my kitchen counter. She did not seem to notice that she had startled me, but eyed the cream with some satisfaction.

"Agnes." I set the cream on the counter and pulled out a little saucer dish. "Can I even have a cat in this apartment?"

The little brownie shrugged her shoulders. "Don't know." She frowned again. "More work. All that fur."

"I'll feed her and take her back outside."

"She'll just come back."

Agnes's tone was so matter-of-fact that I found myself

even more confused. I set the saucer of cream down on the floor. "Come here, kitty."

The cat didn't have to be called twice. She rushed in on silent paws and settled down in front of the cream as though it had been ages since her last meal.

I looked up at Agnes. "Well, then I'll find an animal shelter for her."

Propping her hands on her hips again, Agnes scowled down at the cat. "Stuck with her now, aren't we?"

This was enough to give me a headache. I pinched the bridge of my nose and tried to keep my tone reasonable. "Agnes, it sounds an awful lot like you want to keep the cat."

"Why would I want that?" The little brownie sounded scandalized. "Although," she added thoughtfully, "cats are good to keep mice and pixies down."

A surreal feeling washed over me again. Pressing my lips together, I counted to five before I trusted myself to speak. "I wasn't aware this building had a mouse problem. Or a—a pixie problem."

"Not usually." Agnes continued to stare at the cat. "But sometimes they get a mite uppity, don't they?"

She wanted to keep the cat. But, for whatever reason, she couldn't just come out and *say* that. I pinched the bridge of my nose again. "You're not afraid the cat is going to try to eat you?"

Agnes blinked and then gave me a withering look. "Why would I be afraid of a fool thing like that?"

I started to point out that the cat was quite larger than she was and fully capable of eating her like a mouse. But I held my tongue. *You're arguing with a brownie*, I reminded myself. *Nothing about this conversation makes sense.*

"Okay, then." I held up both hands. "She can stay. As long as I'm not going to get in trouble with Mr. Moffat."

Agnes just muttered something about the carpet needing extra cleaning from now. And then, in the space between one eyeblink and the next, she disappeared again.

The cat raised her head and meowed. It sounded like a question.

"Yeah." I sighed. "She does that."

CHAPTER

THIRTY-FOUR

September slipped past in a slow, day-by-day inexorable succession. Business picked up gradually, but with a steadiness that strengthened my hopes of longevity. I'd had a couple of other women take me up on the offer of classes—a grandmother who wanted to learn how to crochet afghans for her grandchildren, a girl my age who wanted to make pretty scarves to relax from the stress of her job in middle management, and a middle-aged woman who needed a hobby and wanted to knit baby blankets for friends.

I enjoyed teaching those classes, but the highlight of my week was definitely my Wednesday afternoon class with Zel. She had taken to knitting like a duck to the water in the lake on the other side of Starhaven. I'd taught her how to purl and how to increase and decrease, and now we were working on more complex stitches.

Her dishcloths would be the prettiest in Starhaven, that was a fact.

One of the things I loved the most about our weekly class was that it gave me a chance to talk to somebody around my age. (And, okay, I'll admit it. I loved seeing her twins as well —Maddie couldn't always watch them for her.) The other young woman had gradually relaxed around me, to the point that I think she considered me a friend.

I set the black folding chairs up in our usual spot, the space between the counter and the aisles and the door that led into the back. Today, Maddie'd had a meeting or something, and Zel had texted to ask if it was all right if she brought her twins.

I told her it was fine. Best case scenario, both children slept and we got to knit as usual. Worst case scenario, we didn't actually knit and I got to hold a baby. There really wasn't a downside to that.

When Zel arrived at my shop with the twins in tow, however, they were both asleep in the double stroller. I studied them for a moment, inwardly squeeing over how adorable they were. Especially while they were asleep.

I turned to Zel with a smile. "I still can't get over how beautiful your children are."

A soft smile spread over her face. She tucked a lock of hair behind her ear again, her fingers still slipping through it like it was shorter than she'd expected. "Thank you."

"Here." Zel reached down into the net bag beneath the stroller and emerged with two frappes in a cardboard holder, one caramel and one mocha. She handed me the mocha drink. "For you."

"Thank you." I beamed at her, already anticipating how wonderful my frozen coffee would taste.

It probably wasn't the best business decision in the world, but I'd decided not to charge Zel for knitting classes. I was having too much fun with them, I wasn't terribly busy, and I'd decided I loved her company.

Zel couldn't bring herself to accept classes for free, however, so she'd compromised by bringing me coffee once a week.

I think it was a pretty sweet setup for both of us. She learned how to knit, and I had some company and didn't have to feel guilty about buying fancy coffee.

After taking a sip of her own coffee, Zel pushed the double stroller over to our usual spot. She pulled her rose-patterned knitting bag out of the bottom of the stroller (I was always amazed by how much she could pack in that thing) and settled into her chair.

"How are things this week?" She glanced around the shop before extracting her current half-finished dishcloth from the bag. This one was the pretty shade of rose pink she'd bought.

"Better, so far." I shrugged as I took a sip from my coffee. "I've had a few more customers." *Normal customers*, I wanted to add, but didn't. I'd have to explain, and trying to explain suddenly seemed very awkward inside my head.

"That's good." Zel began knitting, and for a moment, the only sounds to be heard inside my shop were the faint click-clack of her needles and the subdued strains of Celtic music I was playing over the Bluetooth speaker I'd set up in corner.

This week, I'd decided to start my own set of dishcloths. I needed a few more, and why buy them when I could de-stress and make some at the same time? I'd chosen a pastel purple and blue variegated yarn that would probably work up into a beautiful design, especially when paired with a small, slightly lacy stitch pattern.

Occasionally glancing at Zel's sleeping babies, I cast on the requisite number of stitches for the size dishcloth I wanted. Comfortable silence enveloped us, but as the moments ticked past, words crowded their way onto my tongue.

Words that wanted to form nosy questions, actually. I'd known Zel for a few weeks now, but I'd never asked her about her family...and she had never volunteered any information. I knew it was a touchy subject.

But...I really wanted to get to know her better. And at the same time, I didn't want to hurt her or offend her.

It was quite the dilemma, let me tell you.

Sighing, I took another pull from my frappe and then set it down on the floor beside me before resuming knitting.

"What is on your mind?"

Zel's quiet words startled me. Guiltily, I glanced up at her. "What?"

Tucking a lock of short golden hair behind her ear, she regarded me with a smile. "You keep sighing. What is troubling you?"

"Oh." I flushed in embarrassment. If my hands hadn't been full of knitting needles, I would have rubbed the back of my neck. "It's nothing."

Zel just lifted a dubious eyebrow at me, even as she kept knitting.

A swell of pride rose in me at that—she had come so far in just a few weeks. It was pretty amazing.

She was still looking at me, however, so I dragged my

attention back to the matter at hand. "I—uh—actually, I don't know how to say this." I sighed again.

"Why don't you just say it?" Zel looked amused now.

"Yeah, but I don't want to offend you or anything."

Zel canted her head to one side, eying me curiously. "It can't be that bad."

It could be if the subject of her family was painful. I shifted uncomfortably on my chair, my gaze darting to the shop's front door. For the first time, I wished a customer would come in and interrupt this conversation.

Finally, I shrugged both shoulders awkwardly. "Well, I guess I'd like to think that we're becoming friends, Zel, and I'd like to know more about you. Like where you're from, how you ended up here." I smiled wryly. "I've told you my story."

"Where I'm from." A flash of something I didn't understand lit her green eyes. Breathing out something halfway between a laugh and a sigh, Zel finished her row and dropped her needles in her lap to rub her eyes. "I'm afraid it's not much of a story."

"Well..." I looked back down at my dishcloth. "I'd love to hear it, if you don't mind sharing it with me."

Zel dragged in a deep breath before she shrugged and offered me a wry smile. "I'm from Tennessee. Little town you've probably never heard of." She waved a hand. "Anyway, my husband and I were high school sweethearts. We got married after we graduated and came to Kentucky for school. I got pregnant and then—" Her voice wavered unsteadily.

Apprehension rose inside me. Zel might not have said the words yet, but I had a strong feeling that her husband was not in Starhaven with her and their twins. My stomach twisted itself into a knot. What had happened to him?

"And then he was gone," Zel finished softly.

My breath caught in my throat. I bit my lip and then asked gently, "Gone, as in—"

"I don't know." She shrugged, ducking her head to hide the sheen of tears in her eyes. "I've never known. All I know is that he's gone."

As though sensing his mother's grief, Zel's little boy stirred. We both looked down at the stroller and watched him wave a tiny fist, his eyelids fluttering, before he subsided back into sleep.

Empathetic grief clogged my throat as I nodded in silent understanding. That was awful. To have no idea where your husband was?

"Anyway," Zel wiped her eyes and tried to smile, though it was a tiny thing that lived more in her eyes than in the corners of her mouth. "We ended up here and Maddie helped me find a place to live and get back on my feet."

My fingers stilled on my knitting needles. That was interesting. "Maddie and the Starhaven Foundation?"

Zel nodded, reaching down to smooth a light hand over her daughter's downy head. "I don't know what I would have done without her."

"I'm glad she was able to help you." Mentally, I shook my head. The longer I lived here, the more I began to realize how many different things Maddie was involved in.

"Well, thanks to her, I've been able to make a life for us here." Zel waved a hand to indicate the town at large.

I swallowed the lump in my throat. "I'm really glad, Zel."

We sat in silence for a moment, letting the strains of sweet Celtic music wash over us, and then Zel roused herself.

She smiled at me, though her eyes still held lingering sadness. "I told you it wasn't much of a story."

That startled a laugh from me. "That's what you think." I leaned forward to touch her arm. "Thank you for sharing it with me. I really didn't mean to pry or make you cry."

Zel studied me for a moment, and then her smile widened. "I have not had many friends, Celia, but I believe I can count you among their number."

"You can." I nodded solemnly, though a broad smile stretched across my face. "You absolutely can."

I was about to ask her how long she'd been here in Starhaven when the door jingled, and a familiar figure slipped into the shop.

My eyes widened. "Bianca! What are you doing here? It's the middle of the afternoon!"

THIRTY-FIVE

Bianca's rosy lips curled in a mischievous grin. "I'm sneaking out." She tipped her head toward the antique shop up the street. "Dave is busy with a call, and he can't stop to yell at me." Her grin widened, completely unrepentant.

Once again, I marveled at the relationship those two had. Dave seemed to have so much control over her, and at the same time, none at all.

"Besides," Bianca pulled a plastic container of food from the large tote slung over her shoulder. It was glossy black, with pink sparkles, "I'm taking a late lunch. He can't complain about that."

I raised my eyebrows at her. "He can't complain about where you go to take your lunch? Are you sure? Given his boycott of my shop?"

Bianca just laughed as she strode toward us. "He can complain all he likes, but he can't dictate where I go to lunch." Her smile softened. "Besides, he's only trying to help to protect me."

"Protect you from what?" I gestured to the inside of my shop. "Marauding bolts of fabric, manic knitting needles?"

Bianca laughed, but there was a shadow behind her blue eyes. "Something like that." She glanced from me to Zel and back. "So...I know I'm inviting myself in, but can anybody join this mini club of yours?"

Zel and I both shared an excited smile and then I beamed at Bianca. "Sure! We'd love to have you. That would be awesome." A dour thought threatened to burst my bubble and I eyed her dubiously. "Are you sure it's going to work with your schedule?"

Bianca just brandished her container of food. "Late lunch, remember?"

"Well, if you're sure." I canted my head to one side. "Can you manage eating lunch that late? I get hungry. I don't know that I could skip lunch and eat at three PM. Not unless I was slammed."

I glanced around the shop with a self-deprecating smile. Obviously, I have not been that busy.

Bianca just grinned and waved a careless hand. "Oh, I always bring snacks to work with me. I'm not worried about that."

"Okay, then." I nodded to Zel. "Have you met Zel?"

"Oh, yes." Bianca gifted Zel with a warm smile. "I'm glad you're here."

Zel returned her smile. "Me too."

I went to the back room to fetch another chair, and Bianca

joined us in a little circle. She cooed over the babies, before settling down on her chair.

Zel leaned over to peer into her tote bag. "What are you making?"

"Oh, socks." Bianca pulled out a half-finished striped teal and blue sock. "I like making socks. There's something very comforting about going round and round in circles." She said this with a tongue-in-cheek smile, and Zel and I both laughed.

"Seriously, though," Bianca said. "I really do love socks. My next project, once I master these, is fingerless gloves. I want a pair. I think Dave could use a pair too."

I brightened. "Oh, those are fun. I have a pattern that I like if you're interested, although there are lots to choose from. But this one uses a fingering weight yarn, and they aren't as bulky."

"Wool yarn?" Bianca eyed me with interest.

"Yes." I nodded. "They're quite warm, just not bulky."

"Ooh." Bianca brightened. ""That would be good. I think we could use that."

The three of us knit in companionable silence for a little while, the only sounds the clicking of our knitting needles and the soft music playing over my Bluetooth speaker.

After a moment, I glanced over at Bianca. "I was about to ask Zel this, but how long have you lived in Starhaven, anyway?"

Bianca actually stopped knitting halfway through a stitch. Her forehead crinkled in a frown, as though she was trying to remember. "Not long in the grand scheme of things. Just a couple of years. I think," she added vaguely.

"Where did you live before here?" I finished a row and switched needles to begin the next row. "I came from Louisville, but where did you come from?"

"Oh, I don't think you would have heard of it." Smiling, Bianca shrugged easily. "It's a really small town in Nebraska."

Any other day, I'd have smiled and nodded. But...coming right on the heels of my conversation with Zel, my internal alarm bells went off. Unbidden, my gaze flicked to Zel, who was studiously bent over her own knitting.

The hair on the back of my neck prickled uncomfortably. What were the odds of Zel and Bianca both being from a small town neither of them wanted to talk about? What was up with this?

I bent my head over my own knitting as a crazy thought occurred to me. Maybe they were both part of the witness protection program.

Almost immediately though, I had to rethink that. Biting my lip, I considered the fact that the witness protection program probably didn't put witnesses in the same general vicinity. It would be an odd way to operate if people knew that someone else around them was also in the witness protection program.

Maybe I'm just crazy, I told myself. But at the same time... I couldn't shake the feeling that something was not right here.

I looked up as Bianca set her knitting aside and fished out a fork from a side pocket of her tote. She opened her plastic container of food. "Anybody want some?"

She'd brought some sort of chicken pasta with vegetables that looked absolutely delicious and smelled even better. Zel and I both shook our heads. It might smell amazing, but we didn't want to literally eat her lunch.

Bianca glanced at me as she took her first bite. "Do you have family in Louisville?"

I sighed. Turnabout was fair play. I braved a smile.

"In a matter of speaking. Technically, my dad still lives there, but he's never home." I went on to explain that my parents were divorced and I was an only child. And that of my parents, one had been an only child and the other had been the older of two. So my extended family was quite small.

Bianca nodded slowly, an expression of sympathy crossing her face. "So you are here without much family either."

I shrugged, glancing back down at my own knitting. For some reason, the topic made me uncomfortable. Either they were rubbing off on me or maybe the lack of having a large family bothered me more than I was willing to admit.

"Sometimes." I shrugged. "But I think if I had had a large family, it would have been harder to leave Louisville and come here and start my craft shop." I smiled at both women, waving a hand to my store. "And this really has been a dream of mine."

"Do you want to go back to Louisville in the future?" Bianca asked me in between bites of her pasta.

I started to say no, but stopped, considering. "No," I said at last. "There are things I love about that city, but I think I will do just as well here." I grinned at them. "After all, I've met both of you. I can't say I have a lot of good friends at home. They've all moved away, or gotten married and had families and they're too busy to spend much time with anyone else. Not for lack of wanting to, but just because life's busy and a lot goes on in a day, especially if you have kids."

They both nodded emphatically.

"This is true." Zel smiled, one hand reaching up to tuck a lock of golden hair behind her ear. Her fingers still slipped through it like she hadn't gotten used to it being shorter. "There are times I wonder what I did with myself before I had children."

Bianca gave her a sympathetic look, which I caught out of the corner of my eye. It was the sort of look that said Bianca related to her, or that she understood what she had been through. Which in turn told me that Bianca and Zel were more than just casual acquaintances.

Keeping my voice light, I asked, "How do you two know each other?"

Bianca and Zel exchanged smiles. "Maddie," they said together with a laugh.

Maddie. Of course.

I matched their smiles. "All roads in Starhaven lead to Maddie, apparently."

"She takes her job as town facilitator very seriously." Bianca's grin turned impish, highlighting a dimple in one cheek.

Well, that just brought up more questions in my mind, but the odds of Maddie actually answering some of them was probably slim to none. My fingers stilled on my knitting needles as another thought lanced through my brain. Did either Bianca or Zel know about Agnes?

Was it possible there were more brownies in Starhaven?

My heart started thudding in my chest and my mouth

went a little dry. I took a breath, intending to casually ask if either of them had ever seen a brownie in Starhaven...but at the last second I chickened out. I knew I wasn't crazy, but asking a question like that would definitely make it sound like I was.

I didn't know what to do. So, instead, I drank my frappe and worked on my dishcloth, knitting stitch after stitch and trying to quiet the questions running rampant in my mind.

CHAPTER

THIRTY-SIX

The rest of the week passed uneventfully. On Sunday, I visited a church on the other side of town (I'd been making the rounds since I arrived in Starhaven) and took the time to fix myself a good lunch. I baked a couple of hamburgers in the oven and made a batch of my favorite pasta salad with garden rotini, balsamic vinaigrette dressing, and a bunch of delicious veggies.

I even spent an hour working on a pair of fingerless gloves I'd decided to knit on the weekends. Dark heather gray, with little squares of bright purple. They'd come in handy when fall arrived and the weather grew colder.

The cat curled up on the back of the couch beside me while I knitted the ribbing on the second glove. I'd named her Sassy, on account of the way she'd showed up at my apartment and taken over. Her quiet purrs accompanied the steady click-clack of my knitting needles as I repeated the knit one, purl one pattern around and around in endless circles.

Part of me felt at loose ends. I enjoyed spending my days in my craft shop so much that I almost didn't know what to do with myself on my day off. And I'd decided from the start that I wasn't going to be open on Sundays. Whether I felt like it initially or not, I figured it was a good idea to build in a little breathing room for myself.

Business *would* grow, and eventually I really would need a day to myself.

At the moment, though, the only downside to this plan was that I didn't have enough friends in Starhaven yet to have concrete weekend plans.

After a few moments of indecision, I decided to treat myself to some iced coffee from the coffee shop and take a walk around the Square to peruse more of the shops I hadn't had time to visit yet. Starting with the bookshop on the other side of the Square, opposite the library.

Frankly, I was impressed that Starhaven was big enough to boast both a public library and a bookshop, and I hadn't had time to visit either of them yet.

The idea filled me with excitement. As far as I'm concerned, bookshops rate just under craft stores and libraries. I love libraries—they're fantastic and I couldn't tell you how many books I've checked out from the Louisville Public Library over the years—but there are some books you just have to own yourself.

And while I don't mind shopping online, there's something to be said for being able to pick books up and hold them.

It didn't take long to stow my half-finished glove back in my knitting bag and grab my purse. Sassy opened one eye long enough to watch me go, and then promptly went back to sleep. Clearly, I was not that interesting.

The coffee shop was reasonably busy, but not too crazy. I bought a small iced coffee and then emerged back into the bright golden September sunshine. It was cooler now than it had been a few weeks ago, but still warm enough that you didn't need a jacket.

I was grateful for that. I love the long, slow slide from summer into fall that we usually have here in Kentucky. It's harder the years when the weather does strange things and we have an abrupt transition from warm to cold.

Sipping my coffee, I strolled along the Square, passing Black Forest Antiques on the corner and taking the crosswalk to the other side of the Square. I eagerly scanned the signs above the line of shops, searching for the bookshop.

There it was, nestled between a shoe store and a cake shop. Thornfire Books. I'd never heard of them before—probably a local owner instead of a larger chain.

Excitement lent wings to my feet as I hurried toward it. This was an interesting location, but as I'd already learned, when one runs a business sometimes one can't be particularly choosy about locations.

Besides, the cake shop was probably a better neighbor for the bookstore than the smoke shop.

An obligatory little bell above the door tinkled as I stepped inside and inhaled that beautiful, wonderful smell of ink and paper that permeated every bookstore I'd ever visited. The floor beneath my feet was the same polished hardwood as the floor in my craft shop and many of the other old buildings around the Square. Sunlight poured in through a wide plate glass window, but the shelves of books and racks of books had been carefully arranged to prevent sunlight from reaching the books directly.

Clutching my half-empty coffee cup, I began wandering through the shop, glancing at books and shelves and searching for, well, I wasn't even sure what I was looking for. Maybe a new release from one of my favorite authors. Or maybe just a new book whose cover caught my eye.

I read a wide variety of genres, so I was always on the lookout for new books.

Maybe they have a craft section. My eyes brightened at the thought. If they did, I could see what they had in terms of knitting, crocheting, or quilting.

I had a nascent idea of teaching a quilting class, but I didn't have many books on it. It was too early to launch that, of course, but I could plan it for this winter or perhaps next spring.

Thornfire Books did have a craft section, though it was fairly small. I trailed my finger along the spines of a row of books on knitting, trying to determine which ones might help me teach better.

"Excuse me," said a deep, gruff voice from behind me.

I was so absorbed in my thoughts that the sound of that voice just about scared the tar out of me. I jumped, one hand flying to my chest, and nearly dropped my coffee cup.

Whirling around, I found a tall man with unruly dark hair and the brightest blue eyes I'd ever seen in a human being. He wore gray slacks and a dark blue button-down with the sleeves rolled up to his elbows. He'd have been handsome, if it weren't for the black scowl on his face.

"You can't have that in here." He nodded toward my cup, glaring at me. "Didn't you see the sign?" He jerked a thumb over his shoulder in the direction of the door.

It was only then that I saw a sign mounted by the front door. In large letters, it read: NO OUTSIDE FOOD OR DRINK ALLOWED.

"Oh," I said quickly, though my heart was still hammering in my chest. "I'm sorry. I did not see that when I came in."

The man just continued to glare at me, as though he found that excuse unacceptable.

My mouth went a little dry, but I swallowed and forced myself to smile at him. He was either the owner or an employee, even though he wasn't wearing a name tag. "Hi. I'm Celia O'Malley." I held out a hand. "I own the craft shop that just opened up on the other side of the Square."

The man glanced from me to my hand and made a noncommittal sound in the back of his throat. "Got a trash can over by the checkout counter. Use it."

And then he walked off. leaving me standing there by myself.

My jaw dropped. *Wow. Who* is *that guy?*

If he was an employee...did his boss know how terrible he was on the customer service front? I shook my head as I turned, not toward the trash can, but toward the exit. No doubt his boss got plenty of complaints about him.

But if he was the owner...how in the world was he still in business?

A niggle of compassion worked its way through the indignant outrage coursing through me. *Maybe he's just having a bad day.*

I could relate to that. Some days are just tough, regardless.

But then I shook my head. *He works in customer service. Even if he has a bad day, he still has to try to be polite.*

That's probably one of the most challenging things about the service industry—being polite and professional about everything while dealing with the general public. (The law firm I'd worked for was not exempt from this—there were clients whose phone calls I dreaded having to take.)

Making a mental note to come back to the bookshop on another day, I walked out. I didn't blame Thornfire Books for their policy—I can't say I particularly want people wandering around my shop with food and drinks either.

But I really hadn't seen the sign.

Oh, well, I thought, taking another sip of my coffee as I ventured into the cake shop instead. *Just chalk it up to another experience in my slightly bumpy history here at Starhaven so far.*

THIRTY-SEVEN

Business continued to pick up over the next few days, which was encouraging. On Wednesday, it was such a gorgeous day—bright and a little cooler than it had been—that when I closed the shop for lunch, I decided to eat at the park.

Settling onto a park bench not far from the playground, I tipped my face up to the sky, closing my eyes and basking in the warm sunshine on my face. I breathed in the scent of fresh-mown grass and couldn't help but smile. It was moments like this that made me so grateful I'd been able to leave my old job and come to Starhaven.

Opening up my lunch bag, I pulled out a turkey sandwich, a small bag of tortilla chips, and a little glass container of salsa. My stomach gave an appreciative rumble. I don't know if it was the cooler air or what, but I was hungry today.

Just as I unwrapped my sandwich, I caught sight of a

familiar figure strolling along the sidewalk leading past the park. It was Maddie, and with her was...

I squinted, my forehead crinkling in a frown. *Hey, that looks an awful lot like Renaissance Man.*

Granted, he was dressed in modern clothes and had a pair of sunglasses perched on his nose instead of his old-fashioned getup and blindfold, but...I was pretty sure it was him. It looked like he was carrying the same walking stick.

A jolt of mingled excitement and relief shot through me. I hadn't been able to find out any more information on him, but apparently he was doing well enough to be released from the hospital. I was really glad to see he seemed to be better.

Physically, at least. I bit my lip, eying Maddie and the man sideways to avoid outright staring. The man's entire posture radiated misery, and it wrenched something in my chest.

I looked down at my lunch, my appetite suddenly gone. *I wonder if he's regained his memories yet.*

Hopefully, he'd been able to find whoever it was he'd lost. A darker thought strayed into my mind and I firmly pushed it away. I was going to be optimistic about this and not assume the worst.

Another glance told me Maddie and the man were still walking my direction. They soon stopped at one of the benches on the edge of the park in the sun and sat down. Renaissance Man immediately tipped his face up to the sun the same way I had earlier.

It only took me a second to make up my mind. If I wanted answers, I couldn't have asked for a more perfect opportunity.

Cramming my lunch back into my lunch bag, I walked

over to join them. Renaissance Man tilted his head at the sound of my approaching footsteps, but he did not otherwise move.

Maddie, however, met my gaze. Her expression was somber, but it quickly morphed into its familiar, good-natured pleasance.

"Hi," I said brightly, though my heart had started pounding in my chest like I was running a marathon.

"Hello." Maddie was dressed in pink today—a lovely floaty floral dress. (She must have a whole collection of them.) She nodded to my lunch bag. "A picnic lunch today?"

"Yes." I nodded, perhaps a little too enthusiastically. I waved to the park in general, though I doubted Renaissance Man could see me. "It's such a beautiful day I couldn't bear to stay inside any longer."

I glanced at the man, hoping Maddie would introduce him, but the town facilitator did not immediately venture any information.

Instead, she raised an eyebrow at me. "Can I help you with something, Celia?"

Inexplicably, for a second, I felt like I was ten again, in trouble at school for daring to have a question about something that wasn't quite on topic. But then I raised my chin. I was the one who'd found Renaissance Man and surely it wasn't against the rules to want to see how he—

"I know that voice," Renaissance Man said, before I could get a word of this out. His head swiveled in my direction, his fingers tightening on the head of his walking stick.

Maddie and I both stared at him. Now that he'd had a shower, and a shave, and the blood had been washed away, I could see that he was quite attractive. He had light brown skin, thick black hair pulled back in a little ponytail, and a narrow mustache. I had no ideas what his eyes looked like, hidden behind his sunglasses, but, then…it was pretty obvious he was blind.

I blinked away the memory of his blood-streaked face.

"I know that voice," he said again. "Who are you?" His tone was imperious, like he was a man used to commanding answers from people.

I blinked again. Maybe he was CEO in real life and the Renaissance Fair thing was just a hobby.

"Ahem." Maddie cleared her throat and gave me a measured glance before she placed a hand on the man's shoulder. He stiffened imperceptibly beneath her touch, like he wasn't used to being touched. "Cedric, this is Celia. She owns a craft shop on the Square. She is also the woman who found you the night you—the night you arrived in Starhaven."

The man's expression did not change, but I felt the tension that suddenly engulfed him.

"You found me?" he asked, in that same imperious tone.

"Yes." I glanced from him to Maddie and back. "I was visiting the park that night and you…needed help."

That was one way to put it.

Maddie and I both started in surprise as, in one fluid motion, the man—Cedric—rose to his feet and swept me the most perfect bow I'd ever seen.

"Thank you, Lady Celia," he said gravely, "I appreciate your help."

I gawked at him, my cheeks burning with a sudden blush. *Lady Celia?* Was he for real?

I was so gobsmacked that it took me a second to remember my manners. "Uh, you're welcome. I'm glad you're feeling better."

Cedric's mouth twisted into a bittersweet smile. "Comparatively speaking, yes."

I glanced from him to Maddie, tilting my eyebrows in a silent, unspoken question.

Maddie considered me for longer than I thought she should have before she shrugged. "We are out for the same reason you are—to get some fresh air."

I smiled and nodded, but I couldn't shake the sudden—and strong—feeling that something really strange was going on here. Something I did not understand at all.

Why was Maddie walking around with this guy? Was the Starhaven Foundation helping him too?

I opened my mouth to ask him if he was from around here or if he was a newcomer like me—but a sudden warning glance from Maddie stayed my tongue.

The older woman shook her head at me, her gray curls bouncing with the motion. Her green eyes were sharp and her pleasant expression had sharpened around the edges.

My confusion only deepened. She didn't want me asking him questions. Why?

Cedric continued to stand between us. He might be unable to see our interchange, but he was apparently not blind to the tension suddenly curling through the air. His fingers tightened ever so slightly on the head of his walking stick again.

All at once, Maddie's expression softened. My compliance with her silent warning seemed to have reassured her about something.

"Celia," she said lightly, "I believe we are due for a chat over tea and coffee."

I blinked at the abrupt segue, but rolled with it. "That sounds lovely." I tried to infuse my voice with a smile to reassure Cedric that everything was fine.

I'm not sure why I did—he didn't know me and it probably didn't matter. And I wasn't entirely sure things *were* fine. But...it seemed like the right thing to do.

If anything, Maddie's expression softened further. "How would eight AM Saturday morning suit you?"

It meant waiting a couple of days and having an earlier morning than I'd intended for Saturday, but if it meant I finally got some answers?

"Sounds good to me." I smiled at Maddie, before glancing at Cedric. "Nice to meet you, Cedric."

"And you, Lady Celia."

I suppressed the urge to shake my head as I turned and headed off to find another park bench so I could eat my lunch. That honorific *still* sounded odd.

Maybe it was his way of coping with whatever injury had caused his amnesia. I supposed that was better than brain damage, but still...

It was strange.

THIRTY-EIGHT

After that awkward encounter with Maddie and Cedric in the park, I felt like I'd gotten sucked into a time warp. The rest of the afternoon seemed like it took *years* to pass, which wouldn't have been so bad if I hadn't been so excited about Zel and Bianca coming for class.

When the clock finally struck three PM and the bell above the door jingled to admit Zel, I looked up with a smile of relief. The short blond was juggling her knitting bag and two frappes, no stroller in sight.

"Hey," I said brightly. "Where are your babies today? Maddie?"

Part of me had wondered if Maddie would be able to watch them today, since she was out with Cedric. Although it was entirely possible she'd finished whatever she was helping him with and taken him back to...wherever he was staying.

"No." Zel shook her head, smiling. "Not today. Maddie

introduced me to a lady down the street from us who can babysit for me occasionally. She's quite trustworthy, Maddie assures me, and my little ones will be fine with her."

A shadow flitted across her face as Zel handed me my usual mocha frappe.

I accepted it, but didn't take a sip. "What's wrong?"

"Nothing." Zel sighed, reaching up to tuck a lock of golden hair behind her ear. This time, the movement was so natural I didn't think anything of it. She flashed me a small, rueful smile. "Just...dealing with life."

We both looked over at the door as the bell jingled to announce Bianca had arrived.

The dark-haired young woman greeted us both with cheerful smiles. "Hello, ladies. I brought snacks." She produced a plastic container from her black tote bag with a flourish and handed them around. "Oatmeal raisin cookies. Baked them last night."

I grinned at her, even as I accepted a cookie. "Is this your lunch today?"

"No, although that's a great idea." Bianca grinned back at me, before setting the container on the floor between her chair and Zel's.

We spent a few minutes catching up on our various weeks, and then I reached for another cookie. The sight of it brought Thornfire Books to mind—and its 'no food or drink' policy. I turned the cookie over in my fingers. I hadn't made such a sign for Celia's Craft Shop, but at some point I might need to.

That man, though...

"Who is the guy who works at Thornfire Books?" I

directed this toward Bianca, figuring she was more likely to know the answer to this than Zel. "Really tall? Bright blue eyes? Extremely grumpy?"

Recognition lit Bianca's dark eyes, and then her mouth crimped in a mischievous smile. "Oh, that's Killian Thornton. Did you meet him recently?"

"I did." I shook my head, smiling wryly. "Made the mistake of taking a coffee cup from Starbright Café in with me."

Bianca made a clucking sound. "Ooh, yes, that would do it."

"He came up behind me and scared the tar out of me." A shudder wracked my shoulders at the memory.

"He owns the bookstore, and he's quite protective of the books." Bianca's expression grew sympathetic. "He's not very good with people, though."

That was an understatement. I managed a weak grin. "Kind of like Dave?"

Bianca laughed, her dark eyes twinkling. "Maybe."

I took a sip of my frappe and then picked up my silvery shawl. It took me a moment to retrace my steps in the pattern. Apparently, I had forgotten to mark where I left off the last time I worked on this. Not sure why, but I had.

Bianca ate a peanut butter and honey sandwich and then pulled out the sock she was currently knitting. She chatted away, telling us about a few interesting customers they'd had earlier, but Zel was strangely quiet.

Out of the corner of my eye, I studied the small blonde. I couldn't help but notice that her gaze kept straying to the cell phone peeking out of her knitting bag.

After a few moments of this, I finally asked gently, "Zel, is everything okay?"

Zel started as though she had been lost in thought, and my words had yanked her back to reality. "Oh, yes, everything's fine." Her cheeks pinked a little. "I'm just—well, I'm just waiting to hear back on a job application."

She twitched her shoulders in a shrug. "Part time, you know. I can't afford a babysitter to watch my children the entire day, but I also need to work." Her expressions softened. "And really, I don't want to be away from them. I love them, and I want to give them the best chance in life they can have."

"That is an admirable aspiration for a mom." I smiled at her over the top of my knitting needles.

"Where did you apply?" Bianca paused mid-stitch to fix Zel with a curious look.

A darker blush tinted Zel's cheeks. "Thornfire Books, actually. Mr. Thornton is looking for part-time help, and I like books."

I managed to control my astonished expression with an effort, while Bianca made a humming sound.

Zel shrugged again, a trifle self-consciously. "He strikes me as grumpy, but not mean. I—I think it'll be all right."

"I think you're right." Bianca offered her an encouraging smile.

When Zel's green eyes flicked to me, I offered her a smile as well. "Just don't take coffee in with you unless you get permission."

We all shared a laugh, and the conversation moved on.

Over the course of the hour, I had to get up a couple of times to help customers, but I didn't mind. For one, it meant I had business, which was fantastic, and for another... Every time I looked over and saw Zel and Bianca laughing together while they both worked on their individual projects, it made something warm bloom in my chest.

This was what is so amazing about the world of crafts. Apart from being a wonderful outlet for stress, things like knitting and crocheting bring people together. They give shy people who might have trouble with conversations (more Zel than Bianca, for sure) something to do with their hands so that they don't feel so awkward.

And they definitely make life a little brighter.

Beaming, I settled back into my chair and picked up my never-ending silver shawl. Starhaven might be a little odd around the edges (and I was *really* looking forward to my upcoming chat with Maddie), but I could say without a shadow of a doubt that Celia's Craft Shop and I were both meant to be here.

THIRTY-NINE

Saturday morning dawned cool enough that I regretted not grabbing a lightweight hoodie on my way out the door. The morning air had a crispness to it that promised fall was on its way, even if it had been a little delayed so far. The poplar, oak, and maple trees along the Square still held their lush green color, but I knew it wouldn't be long before they became a blaze of red, orange, and yellow.

I made it to the Starbright Café ten minutes before eight —only to discover that Maddie had beaten me there. When I walked in the door, relishing the warmer air laced with the delightful aroma of brewing coffee, I glanced around and immediately spotted her ensconced in our usual corner.

Either she really wants to talk to me, I thought wryly, *or she's got a busy day planned.*

I waved to Maddie and the older woman waved back, before holding up an iced coffee clearly meant for me. The fact that she'd bought me coffee warmed something in my chest...but it also made me think she felt a little guilty about Wednesday.

"Good morning," Maddie said briskly as I approached her. She handed me the iced coffee and barely waited until I'd settled into my armchair before she fixed me with a piercing look over her teacup. "Thank you for not asking Cedric questions the other day. He's settling in well, all things considered, but he still has a little difficulty handling reminders of the night he arrived here in Starhaven."

I matched her piercing look. "Is he from here? Starhaven, I mean."

For a second, I didn't think Maddie would answer. Then she shook her head, smoothing the front of the lacy white cardigan she'd paired with her leaf green dress. "No. And he doesn't remember where he is from."

Sympathy welled in my chest. I clutched my iced coffee, the cold seeping into my fingers, and contemplated again how terrible it would be to not know who I was or where I was from.

It was my turn to shake my head. "Did he not have any ID on him?"

"No." Maddie sipped her tea. "The police department has made inquiries, of course, but they don't currently have anything to go on. As far as we can tell, he is alone here in Starhaven."

"Which is where you and the Starhaven Community Foundation come in." I nodded slowly, already putting the various pieces together.

Maddie's only response was a slight smile. She took another sip of her tea, a faraway look in her green eyes. I could only imagine what was running through her mind right now.

I stifled a grin. Probably sifting options in her mind for half a dozen people, strategizing the best ways to help them all. Helping Zel take care of herself and her babies, helping Cedric cope with amnesia... Helping *me* settle into town and deal with the strange intricacies of local politics...

"You know, Maddie, I'm not sure calling you a 'town facilitator'—" I made air quotes with the fingers of my free hand, "—does you justice." I shook my head, laughing as a whimsical thought occurred to me. "You're more like a real-world fairy godmother."

The moment the words left my mouth, I felt the truth of them settle around us. My eyes widened. That was the *perfect* analogy for her!

Across from me, Maddie froze, her teacup halfway to her lips. "What?"

I was too excited to notice the strange tone in her voice. Straightening in my armchair, I beamed at her over my iced coffee. "Yes! That is *exactly* what you are. A real-world fairy godmother!"

When Maddie just stared at me, I leaned forward. "Can't you see it?" I waved a hand, nearly sloshing my coffee all over myself in the process. "Zel needs babysitting. You provide it. I need help with Dave and—" I dropped my voice, "—Agnes, and you help me. Cedric—" I motioned in the general direction of the park, "—gets stranded in Starhaven without his memory and you figure out what he needs and help him too."

Maddie finally lowered her teacup, though I couldn't read her expression.

"Maddie, you have a knack, or a talent, or whatever you want to call it, for knowing what people need and getting it for them." I flourished a hand in her direction. "Hence, the reason you're a fairy godmother. Only a real-life one," I added, still smiling.

I was not prepared for her reaction.

Maddie drew in a sharp breath—almost like she was in pain— and then she squeezed her eyes shut as a shudder wracked her shoulders. Her teacup rattled on its saucer as her hands trembled.

I froze in mingled shock and alarm, dismay coursing through me. What was going on? Had I said something wrong? But why would that—

My breath caught in my throat. For a split-second, I'd have sworn Maddie *glittered*.

I blinked rapidly—I *couldn't* have actually seen that. In the space between one eye blink and the next, the silvery glitter vanished and Maddie sat in her armchair across from me looking perfectly normal, if a touch shaken.

"Maddie," I finally found my voice, "are you all right?" I leaned toward her, reaching out to pat her arm.

The older woman gave me a surprisingly bright smile. "I'm fine, dear. Just a little chill."

Just a little chill? I raised an eyebrow, but before I could question her, Maddie sailed on.

"That is very sweet of you to liken me to a fairy godmother, Celia." Her green eyes twinkled at me. "I must admit, no one has ever made that comparison before." She drank the last of her tea and rose from her seat in one smooth motion. "Now, if you'll excuse me, I've just remembered I have a rather important Foundation errand to run."

She didn't wait for me to answer, but offered me a blithe smile and hurried away, leaving me to stare after her in combined surprise and bewilderment.

I stared in the direction she'd departed for a long moment after she left the coffee shop, clutching my iced coffee. My fingers grew cold, but I barely noticed. What had just happened?

Was it something I'd said?

And why in the world would my brain decide to imagine that Maddie had *glittered?*

It didn't make any sense.

The icy sensation in my fingers finally registered. Setting my plastic coffee cup on the little wooden end table at my elbow, I tucked my fingers under my arms to warm them and tried to rationalize this morning's conversation. Maddie wasn't particularly good at giving straight answers, but she'd explained Cedric's situation more than I'd expected.

Also, she *was* past middle-aged—maybe she *did* get cold more easily now that the weather had started growing cooler.

But that doesn't explain the glitter, whispered a hesitant little voice in the back of my mind.

I rubbed my eyes. I'd imagined that. I must have. Human beings don't glitter on their own. Chalk that up to me being too excited to get much sleep last night.

Sighing, I picked up my coffee cup and stood. I'd hoped to talk to Maddie a little more, but it looked like that was all I was going to get today. At least I'd gotten some answers about Cedric.

Weaving through the smattering of early morning customers stationed at little tables or seated on the mismatched couches and armchairs, I made my way to the exit. I might as well get ready to open Celia's Craft Shop. With the weather turning cooler, there was a really good chance that people would start thinking about knitting and crocheting things like afghans, hats, and scarves now.

Better to think about *that* than consider the possibility that I was losing my grip on my sanity.

Starhaven might have some strange individuals here (and Agnes—let me not forget I have an actual *brownie* living in my apartment), but that didn't mean Maddie had actually *glittered*. It couldn't.

...right?

Monday morning, I'd barely unlocked the front door when my first customer of the day marched into my shop and approached the counter. He was a compact man in his fifties, not much taller than I was, dressed in khaki slacks and a sea green polo. He had short salt and pepper hair, a neatly-trimmed little mustache, and what looked like a perpetual tan.

"Good morning." I offered him a cheerful smile. "How can I help you?"

Jamming his hands into the pockets of his khaki slacks, the man bounced a little on his heels. His dark eyes swept around the interior of my shop with a kind of intensity that told me he hadn't missed a thing, and then he focused on me. His expression wavered somewhere between reluctant chagrin and grim determination.

"My wife says I need a new hobby or she's going to start locking me out of the kitchen." He had a deep, friendly voice that sounded vaguely familiar, though it currently bore traces of embarrassment, which matched the tense set of his shoulders.

I nodded, even as I tried to figure out where I'd heard his voice before. I don't think we'd ever met. "What kind of hobby are you considering?" I waved to my shelves, my smile turning conspiratorial. "You have lots of options."

"Counted cross-stitching." The man lifted his chin, as though daring me to comment.

That made me sad. Throughout the centuries around the world, men and women both have been masters at embroidering, sewing, and working with yarn. And yet, in parts of our country, at least, the pervasive idea that this kind of thing is only for women still holds strong.

"Oh, that'll be fun." I continued to smile. "My grandfather used to cross-stitch. He did a picture of the *Belle of Louisville* once that he framed and hung on the wall in his living room."

The man's shoulders relaxed a fraction. "Oh, yeah?"

"Yeah. He always said it helped him relax."

"Well," the man cracked a grin, "that's what my wife says I need." He held out a hand to me. "Rafe Levan. I own the Starhaven Grill."

Oh. *That* was why his voice sounded familiar. I'd heard it in the restaurant, even though I didn't remember seeing him.

"Celia O'Malley." We shook hands and I smiled at him again. "I've eaten at your restaurant a couple of times since I moved here. You have really good burgers."

"Thanks. I'd like to think so."

"The cross-stitching section is over here." I motioned to

the shelves. "I have a number of patterns, but if you don't see anything you like, I can order you something else."

Mr. Levan followed me over to the shelves. "I don't know what I want." He chuckled, a little ruefully. "But it probably ought to be good-sized. I love my restaurant, but it's stressful most days and Cindy thinks this would be good for me."

And he'd listened to his wife's advice. Internally, I swooned a little at this bit of everyday romance. Externally, I nodded professionally and pulled out several kits for him to look at. One of them was a stunning ocean view and another was a cabin in the mountains, the trees ablaze with fall colors.

"These already come with Aida cloth and embroidery thread, but if you like one of the patterns in these books better," I indicated a rack of themed cross-stitch pattern books, "we can do that, too."

"No ocean." Mr. Levan shook his head, wrinkling his nose. "Can't stand sand. Gets everywhere and then you track it home and can't get rid of it for months."

I laughed. "That's pretty accurate, actually." I'd been to Daytona Beach once, as a kid, and while I'd loved the sight of the Atlantic Ocean, I hadn't enjoyed dealing with the sand.

"This one." Mr. Levan tapped the kit featuring the cabin in the mountains. "My favorite time of the year, when all the trees change color."

"All right."

I made sure he had scissors, extra embroidery needles, and a wooden embroidery hoop, since the kit didn't come with one and then I checked him out at the front counter.

Halfway through, my phone chimed in my back pocket with an incoming text, but I ignored it.

"Have fun." I handed him a plastic bag with his purchases.

Mr. Levan just shook his head. "We'll see. Anyway." He raised a hand in farewell. "Thanks, Celia. Hope to see you at the Starhaven Grill sometime."

"Oh, I'm sure I'll be back."

Once the door closed behind him, I pulled out my phone and sank down into my chair behind the counter. I glanced at the screen and frowned.

Bianca had texted me, asking if I'd meet her around the back of Dave's antique shop at five that afternoon. *I need professional help and I can't wait until next week!*

I shook my head, wondering what she'd done. As far as I knew, she was still on a sock kick—had she dropped a needle or something? Oh, well, I'd find out later.

The bell jingled again to admit a group of older ladies, and I looked up with a smile, replacing my phone in my pocket. "Hi, ladies. How may I help you?"

At five o'clock, I slipped out of the back door of my craft shop and cut through the alley to the sidewalk. When I reached Black Forest Antiques, I ducked into the alley that separated Dave's shop from the one beside it and went around to the back to meet Bianca, just like she'd asked. I was fine with this arrangement—I didn't really want to deal with Dave today if I could avoid it.

Besides, I was nosy and this gave me a chance to see what the back of Black Forest Antiques looked like.

I don't know what I expected, but reality was mildly disappointing. The back of Dave's store didn't look much different than the back of my own shop, other than the fact that he had double doors to admit large pieces of furniture. Nothing special.

Bianca had been watching for me. As soon as I rounded the corner into the alley, she poked her head out of one of the double doors and greeted me with a bright smile.

"Come on in." She waved me over to the doors. "Dave's out front dealing with a customer interested in a special Edwardian settee." A mischievous grin lit her beautiful face. "He's going to be busy for a little while."

"Okay." I stepped through the door she held open for me and into a back room that was probably used as a loading room. It was half-full of furniture and other odds and ends.

Bianca waved a hand toward the far corner of the room. "I think you've met Cedric."

Startled, I blinked at Bianca. Cedric? Here?

Turning around, I looked in the direction she'd indicated. To my surprise, Cedric occupied a table in the corner. His sunglass-covered eyes stared sightlessly across the room while his fingers worked busily, sifting through the contents of a plastic box propped on a stack of similar boxes beside him. He seemed calmer, but that grief-stricken aura still hung around him.

I looked at questioningly at Bianca. "What is he doing?"

"Sorting antique marbles. They're mixed in with old rusty nails and a whole host of other miscellaneous junk." Bianca shook her head. "Dave bought that box because of the marbles. He said some of those are a hundred years old and made in different countries. Glass, you know, very collectible, but they were just thrown in with all of this other stuff."

"Oh."

"Yeah. Maddie talked Dave into hiring Cedric." Bianca's dark eyes twinkled merrily. "She's good at that."

"Yes." I smiled briefly. "Yes, she is." I tipped my head in Cedric's direction in a silent question.

Bianca just smiled and nodded.

A surreal feeling settled over me as I crossed the room to Cedric's table. It was oddly jarring to see him in this setting.

"Hi, Cedric." I stopped beside the table, trying not to be awkward. "It's Celia. We met in the park the other day?" I deliberately did not mention the clearing.

Cedric tilted his head to one side, listening to the sound of my voice, but his fingers did not stop their busy sorting. I had the distinct impression that he was very grateful to have something to do. "Yes," he said, in that rich, cultured voice. "Lady Celia. I recognized the sound of your voice."

I bit the inside of my lip. So, we were still on the Renaissance kick, apparently. Still, I was impressed he remembered me. "Wow. I didn't expect you to remember me."

Cedric lifted on shoulder in a shrug. "When one loses one's eyesight, apparently other senses sharpen a little." He shrugged again. "That and you have a friendly voice."

Well, that was good to know. I nodded, even though he couldn't see me. "How are you today?"

"I am...grateful to have something to occupy myself."

I couldn't restrain a smile at this admission. It made me

happy that my instincts had been correct. "We're shop neighbors. My craft shop is just down the street."

He inclined his head in a gracious nod, his fingers still sifting through the junk.

I took a moment to study the pile of marbles he had created on a soft gray towel laid out on the table. They really were quite beautiful. Some of them had colorful intricate swirls inside, while others were simply round spheres of colored glass.

Why someone had thought it a good idea to mix those in with a bunch of detritus was beyond me. I shook my head. Had they not known what the marbles were?

I said as much to Bianca, who came to stand next to me.

"Probably." The dark-haired young woman shrugged. "It happens all the time. Somebody dies, and the things that they prized go to the next generation, which doesn't care about them at all. Not always, but..." She shrugged again. "It's how we end up with some of the things we have."

"That makes sense, in a sad kind of way." I glanced back at Cedric. "Good to see you again, Cedric."

"And you, Lady Celia."

I gave a little shiver. *Lady Celia.* It still sounded so fancy when he said it.

Taking a deep breath, I turned to Bianca. "What's up?"

She sighed in frustration, some of the joy fading from her face. "I managed to drop an entire needle last night—don't ask how I managed it, because I don't know—and I lost a bunch of stitches. Do you think you could help me salvage them?"

"I can try."

Bianca led me over the other side of the room, where her black knitting tote sat on top of a glossy cherry credenza. She produced a nearly-finished sock on two double-pointed knitting needles from the tote and carefully handed me the entire thing.

"Ouch." I winced in sympathy as I examined it. Bianca had been knitting a complicated cable pattern in two different colors. I had to hand it to her. Cables were challenging for most people in one color, let alone two.

"Hmm." I gingerly checked the inside of the sock. It was difficult to see where some of the stitches were, and unfortunately a few of them looked like they might have worked their way down several rows, but...

I looked up at her. "I think I can fix it, but I'll have to take it home."

"That's fine." Bianca shrugged. "I have more needles. I'll just start the next one." She laughed ruefully. "And try not to drop another needle this time."

We both stilled as Dave's voice, surprisingly jovial, sounded from somewhere beyond the open door on the other side of the room. It was my turn to chuckle.

"I'd better go before Dave comes in here and has a conniption fit."

Bianca winced. "I'm sorry, Celia."

"Don't worry about it." I smiled at her, before nodding to her knitting project. "I should be able to fix this tonight."

"Thank you." Bianca abruptly brightened. "I'll bake you some more muffins."

My stomach rumbled at the thought and we both

laughed. I shook my head. "You don't have to, but I'll take them."

Bianca just winked at me.

Behind us, Dave's voice grew louder. Careful not to stab myself with her knitting needles, I cradled Bianca's nearly-finished sock and slipped out of the back door just as the little man came though the other door.

Relief flooded me as I hurried back to my own shop. That had been close.

FORTY-ONE

Bianca's project took me most of the evening to salvage, but I did manage to fix it. I sent her a text to say she could pick her sock up at her convenience the next morning and went to bed.

The next morning, I'd barely settled into my seat behind the front counter with my unfinished silvery shawl when the bell above the door jingled and Maddie glided into my shop. Apparently, this was the week for people to breeze through my door the moment I opened for the day.

I hadn't expected Maddie, though.

"Hi." I blinked at the older woman, slightly bemused. "How are you this morning?"

To my surprise, Maddie did not reply. Instead, she approached the counter and stood there in silence. There was something behind her expression I couldn't quite place.

If I'd known her better, I would have almost said she looked wary.

The upbeat music of my current playlist played in the background, keeping Maddie's silence from being so loud, but it did not prevent it from quickly becoming awkward. She stared at me, her green gaze piercing mine with an intensity that felt as though she was attempting to see straight through my eyes and into my head. I had the curious and rather unpleasant realization that she was taking my measure all over again, like I was an equation she had suddenly received a different variable to and now she had to make sense of me.

Uncomfortable with her scrutiny, I instinctively leaned back in my chair, clutching my knitting needles. "Can I...help you with something?"

All at once, Maddie propped a hand on her hips and scrunched her eyebrows into a puzzled frown. "Where did you say you were from?"

I blinked at the non-sequitur. What did *that* have to do with anything?

"Um...Louisville?" I tilted my head to one side, nonplussed. "I think I told you that when we were at the coffee shop the first day I was in Starhaven."

Maddie waved that reminder aside with a flick of her fingers. "Where is your family from?" She studied me as though she expected to find the answer written across my cheekbones. "Europe? Ireland?"

It was my turn to frown. What did my family's heritage have to do with anything here in Starhaven? "Maddie, what—"

"Answer the question, please, Celia. It's important."

I didn't see how that was possible, but... Maddie had been

kind to me so far. It probably wasn't the end of the world to humor her.

"My dad's family is from Ireland," I said slowly. "They immigrated to the United States in the 1800s. Why?"

Maddie did not answer, but nodded as though she had expected this. "What of your mother's family?"

I stared at her, downright baffled now. "I'm not really sure. France? Belgium?" I shook my head. "I don't know exactly. Family history is not exactly something my family used to sit around and talk about much."

I had friends growing up who loved to talk about their family lineage, but my parents had never been interested—at all. My grandparents had only been marginally more interested.

"I see." Maddie nodded again, pressing her lips into a thin line. She remained standing in front of the counter, but now she was practically vibrating with agitation.

Setting my knitting aside, I rose to my feet and faced her across the counter. "Maddie, what's wrong? Has something happened?"

For a moment, I didn't think the older woman would answer. Then, at last, she drew in a deep breath and shook her head. "I don't know how you did it, Celia. Clearly, there must be something about you, and yet..." She gestured toward me as though she couldn't pinpoint anything special about me in particular. "You're perfectly ordinary."

My eyebrows shot into my hairline. The agitation and confusion in her melodic voice kept her words from stinging the way they should have, but...good grief. What a thing to say to a person.

She's not wrong, said a voice inside my head. *You* are *quite ordinary.*

I bit the inside of my lip, forced to acknowledge the truth of those words. No, there wasn't anything particularly special about me. I didn't have a unique gifts or talents. I was just a girl with a dream of owning a craft shop and making people's lives a little brighter through creative craft options.

Still...

Folding my arms across my chest, I raised an eyebrow at her. "Maddie, I'm not sure whether I should be complimented or offended."

"Pish posh." Maddie waved my words away with a flick of her fingers, staring intently at me like I was a puzzle she was trying—and failing—to solve. "You *are* perfectly ordinary. And yet...there *is* something about you."

"Maddie—"

She ignored me. "How did you do it? It's amazing. I never dreamed—" She shook her head again, her gray curls bouncing with the motion. "I thought for certain we'd be stuck forever. But somehow you managed it."

This conversation made less and less sense the longer it went on. It was my turn to shake my head. "I'm lost, Maddie. What have I managed?"

Maddie opened her mouth and then shut it, a look of frustration filling her green eyes. I'm not sure if she was trying to choose her words carefully, or if she was having trouble stringing them in the correct order.

For the first time, I began to wonder if this wonderful lady had perhaps suffered a mental breakdown. Pouring all one's time and energy into people, I knew, could take a toll. Maybe Maddie had finally hit her limit.

I opened my mouth to suggest that maybe Maddie should go home and take a nap, or maybe even visit the hospital, but she started talking again.

"It'll have to be you," she said briskly, tapping a long, slender finger on the counter. "I don't think anybody else can do it. *I* certainly can't." A dark frown flitted across her usually cheerful face. "I've tried. But, no matter." She dismissed that thought with another flick of her fingers and smiled at me. "Celia O'Malley, I'm glad you came to Starhaven. We need you. More than you realize, and certainly more than we ever dreamed. Perhaps Old Man Moffat was onto something."

I took a deep breath, trying to maintain my sanity and keep a slightly panicky feeling at bay. I felt like Alice must have when she tumbled down the rabbit hole—lost in a sea of things that made zero sense. Sure, I thought Starhaven needed a craft shop, but I don't think that's what she was talking about.

"Maddie, what do you mean? Help you *how*?" I shrugged helplessly. "I don't understand any of this."

Maddie just laughed softly, the sound like tinkling bells. Her green eyes twinkled at me. "I think you'll figure it out, Celia. I have every faith in you. You're a smart girl with better intuition than most."

I barely managed to hold back an incredulous laugh. "Didn't you just say I was perfectly ordinary?"

Maddie ignored that too, in favor of tapping her finger on the counter again. "Just keep doing what you're doing, child. Talk to people. Be friendly." Her smile dimmed, just a touch.

"I'll help you as much as I can, but I'm afraid I'm a bit limited in this realm."

She turned toward the door, pausing long enough to say over her shoulder, "And, thank you." Her eyes twinkled at me again. "Although you won't know why yet."

On that enigmatic note, Starhaven's town facilitator sailed out of my shop, leaving me staring after her, wondering what in the world had just happened.

FORTY-TWO

Maddie's words lingered in my mind the rest of the day. *Keep doing what you're doing. Talk to people. Be friendly. You'll figure it out.*

What *exactly* was I supposed to be doing? Wasn't everybody supposed to be friendly? Wasn't that part of being a good neighbor?

In her roundabout way, she had made it sound like I had somehow managed to help her with something impossible—something she couldn't do herself. What was she talking about?

Surprisingly, I did brisk business the rest of the afternoon. A handful of teenagers came in looking for different projects, a couple of grandmothers, and another strange little wizened old lady. This one kept a dark red hood wrapped around her hair, as though she was afraid the wind would ruffle her silver curls.

When I finally returned to my apartment that night, I

stood in the center of the living room for a long moment, trying to process everything.

"*Meow.*" Sassy wound herself around my ankles, purring.

I glanced down. "Missed me, did you?" Cautiously, I bent and picked her up. Despite her fluffy fur, she was still quite slim.

"We'll get you fattened up eventually." I gently stroked her fur. "Not too fat, mind you. You want to be healthy. I'd be a little bit concerned if you were a tub like Garfield."

Sassy just blinked at me, as though she was offended I would compare her to Garfield. Which was ridiculous, because how would the cat even know who Garfield was? It was probably just a feline thing. I was out of practice—it had been a long time since I'd spent much time around a cat.

I walked to the kitchen, carrying Sassy, and she let me hold her until we crossed the threshold. Then she leaped from my arms to the floor and made a beeline for her food bowl, which was empty. She meowed up at me, but I was already reaching for the bag of cat food.

Once she was happily munching away, I opened the refrigerator and stared into its semi-empty depths. I needed to go grocery shopping again—I didn't have any leftovers worth eating. Or maybe I needed to have a grocery delivery. That might be easier. Less tempting to buy things I didn't need right now.

I cocked my head to one side, considering Did the grocery store deliver? I hadn't checked. Was Starhaven even big enough to have that service yet?

All at once, something else Maddie had said floated through my mind. *I'm afraid I'm a bit limited in this realm.*

I frowned at a jug of homemade iced coffee. Such an odd phraseology. Who talked like that?

Cedric, my mind supplied. He definitely talked like that. But it was an odd choice of words for Maddie.

Sighing, I pulled out the remnants of a block of cheddar cheese and a handful of pepperoni slices. I wasn't particularly hungry, though I probably should have been, after the day I'd had.

In the middle of slicing myself a piece of cheese, another question materialized in my brain. Where had *Maddie* come from?

I froze, staring down at the blade of my steak knife without actually seeing it. It had never occurred to me to wonder that before. Was Maddie a Starhaven native, or had she, too, moved here from someplace else?

Who could I even ask to find out? (Other than Maddie— and I wasn't sure I wanted to talk to her again tonight.)

I jolted with an idea. *Agnes.* I could ask her, couldn't I? It was a long shot, but she might know the answer.

Feeling a little silly, I called out, "Agnes?'"

I wasn't sure if she would listen to me or not. From the reading I'd done, I'd learned brownies were contrary, solitary little creatures who liked to be near people but not really around them. And they didn't like to show themselves, and they typically didn't answer summons either. That was usually grounds for them to depart and go someplace else.

Agnes was different in that she'd already told me she was lonely. And I liked to think we were on decent terms. If a human and a brownie could be on decent terms, that is.

Hence the reason why I thought she might answer.

Unfortunately, Agnes did not reply. Nor did she appear, though I glanced hopefully around the kitchen.

Ah, well. I shrugged mentally. It wasn't the end of the world. I'd just have to go about finding the answer another way.

In the meantime...I frowned down at my cheese and pepperoni. I probably needed to find something else to eat along with this oh-so-healthy supper.

Opening up my little pantry, I scanned the shelves. Crackers were the obvious choice, but I didn't feel like eating them tonight. I wanted something else. Something like—

My eyes lit on a box of microwave popcorn and I brightened. Popcorn! That was *exactly* what I wanted. I hadn't had any popcorn in a while and I was overdue for some.

A few moments later, I was just dumping my popcorn into a large bowl when Agnes appeared at my elbow. "What is that?" she asked in her reedy little voice, wrinkling her nose at my popcorn.

I startled, nearly spilling half the bowl on the counter. "Agnes! Don't *do* that." I pressed a hand to my chest, trying to get my heart rate under control. "I've *told* you. You scare me when you do that."

Agnes looked completely unrepentant, as though I should have expected her to appear when I least expected her. "What is that?" she repeated, raising a brown leathery hand to point at the popcorn.

I explained to her what popcorn was, though I wasn't sure it registered. "Try it." I offered her a couple of kernels. "It's one of my favorite snack foods."

The popcorn looked absurdly large in her small hands.

Agnes sniffed a kernel dubiously, and then licked it. Only then did she deign to take a small bite. Her expression remained inscrutable while she chewed.

She ate one kernel and then a second. I offered her another one, and she ate half of it before she finally shrugged. "It's passable." She tossed the rest of the kernel onto the floor for Sassy.

To my surprise, Sassy ate it, and then meowed as though she wanted more.

Agnes tossed two more pieces of popcorn down for the cat and then turned to me, cocking an eyebrow at me while she propped a hand on her hip. "Why did you call me? Don't you know you're not supposed to call brownies?"

"Do you know who Maddie is?" I sidestepped the question. "Do you know where she came from?" I paused, yet another thought occurring to me. "For that matter, where did *you* come from?"

I didn't really expect an answer...but I also didn't expect Agnes's reaction.

The little brownie did not freeze so much as her entire body just suddenly stopped moving. For a split second, as I stared at her, a wild corner of my mind wondered if she had stopped breathing.

"Agnes?" I reached out a hand to the brownie, but stopped shy of actually touching her. "Are you all right?"

It seemed to take an inordinately long amount of time before Agnes finally blinked and drew in a long, deep breath. "Oh," she said at last, completely bypassing last question. "I came from somewhere."

I bit my lip, unsure if I ought to ask her anything else, but my curiosity got the better of me. "Where is home?"

The little brownie shrugged.

"How long have you been in this apartment building?"

Another shrug.

Frowning, I leaned up against the counter and considered her. That...was interesting. I had no way of knowing how long Agnes had lived in this apartment, but my guess was that it had been years. Why couldn't she just tell me that?

Agnes helped herself to another kernel of popcorn and we munched in relatively companionable silence.

A thought niggled in the back of my mind. While she was here, I could ask Agnes about that clearing.

"Agnes," I said casually, "have you ever been to the park? Specifically, a clearing back in the woods?"

Agnes froze again, her popcorn kernel halfway to her mouth.

Watching her closely without trying to *appear* like I was watching her closely, I went on to describe the clearing in more detail. It was difficult to make it look like I didn't care about the answer when in fact I did care very much.

"Actually," I finished, taking another handful of popcorn. "That's where I found her." I nodded down at Sassy, who was weaving around my ankles and purring in the hopes that I would drop a few more pieces of popcorn. Which I did. (I love popcorn. It's one of my favorite foods. But I also think it's cool that the cat likes the popcorn, too.)

Agnes's head snapped in Sassy's direction so fast I half-expected to hear her neck crack. She stared at the cat, an expression of horror filling her large eyes, before she lifted her gaze to me. "Don't go there!" She shook her head and backed, still clutching her piece of popcorn. "No good, that clearing. No good!"

In the space between one blink and another, the little brownie disappeared.

Nonplussed, I stared at the spot on the counter Agnes had just occupied. *Well*, I thought. *That answers the question of whether or not there that clearing is important to whatever is going on here.*

Swallowing a sigh, I popped another piece of popcorn into my mouth. I'd have to figure out how to get my answers another way.

FORTY-THREE

I didn't sleep well that night. My strange conversation with Maddie and Agnes's terrified reaction to my question about the clearing chased each other around and around inside my head, blending into a strange amalgamation of a nonsensical scene set inside my craft shop. Maddie wandered around my shop, telling me to keep doing what I was doing while she blithely pulled things from shelves and tossed them onto the floor. Meanwhile, Agnes huddled in a corner clutching a bag of seed beads, warning me to stay away from the clearing.

I awoke bleary-eyed and tired, with a strange, itchy feeling that things were just...off. After fixing myself a cup of coffee with an extra splash of mocha creamer, I forced myself to eat a strawberry breakfast bar and dragged myself down to my shop to begin the day.

It'll be fine, I assured myself. *It's Wednesday. Probably won't be that busy, anyway. Besides, Zel and Bianca will be here for class later.*

The thought brightened my outlook on the day...at least until my phone vibrated with an apologetic text from Zel, informing me that she would have to miss our knitting class today. She'd gotten the job at Thornfire Books and Mr. Thornton wanted her to come in for orientation that afternoon.

I sighed. It figured. Next thing you know, Bianca would probably text to tell me something had come up as well. I just had that itchy feeling that today was going to go that way.

And I *still* couldn't shake that bizarre interaction with Maddie.

Shaking my head, I texted Zel back.

> t's no problem. Congratulations! I'm so happy for you! We'll work out a new schedule if we need to.

I slid my phone in my back pocket just as the bell jingled to admit my first customer of the morning. One of the moms I'd helped a couple of weeks ago, who had decided that she loved knitting soft, fuzzy hats and wanted to make more to donate to the local hospital. It took a little more effort than usual to smile, but I did manage to be friendly.

From then on, Celia's Craft Shop did steady business. I might be tired, but my customers kept me busy. At the same time, my brain refused to think of anything but that strange conversation with Maddie. I replayed her words over and over, searching for a way to make some kind of sense of them.

There was none, of course. At least none that I could determine.

After lunch, an older lady who had been referred to me by her daughter came in looking for yarn and knitting needles for a wavy afghan pattern she'd found on Pinterest. She was short and a little plump, with curly blond hair and wingtip glasses perched on her nose. She talked nonstop from the moment she set foot in the shop until the moment I rang up her skeins of metallic gold and emerald green yarn and brand-new knitting needles, introducing herself as Mrs. Spicer and telling me all about her newfound desire to knit and the beautiful creations she hoped to make.

I wasn't completely sure she ever even stopped to breathe between sentences.

"I'll be back of course," Mrs. Spicer said with a cheerful smile, as I handed her two plastic bags with her purchases. "This is the start of a wonderful new hobby, Celia. I just feel it in my bones."

"Hope you enjoy, Mrs. Spicer." I sent her on her way with a smile and rounded the counter to go check the yarn section.

Mrs. Spicer had bought enough of the emerald green and the metallic gold (which I particularly loved) that I needed to make sure she hadn't cleared the shelf. If she'd bought all of it, I needed to make a note to order more.

I found several sections of yarn in disarray, as though the older lady had pulled them out and put them up against each other to check for the right shades and whether they complemented each other, and then had carelessly thrust them back on the shelf every which way. It was a little annoying, but it wasn't a big deal—this was part of having a retail business. Customers touched things.

And, really, when it came to things like yarn and fabric, you *needed* to touch them. Some yarns were softer and silkier than others, and so were some fabrics.

I sorted the skeins of yarn automatically, my smile fading as my thoughts returned to Maddie. I couldn't put my finger on it, but there was something...*wrong* about that whole conversation, like when you scratch what you think is scab on the back of your leg only to discover you've actually been bitten by a little tick. She'd been genuinely frustrated by not being able to say what she wanted to say.

Unfortunately, that was probably because she was having some sort of mental issue, but... I frowned as something else occurred to me. The rest of Maddie's speech had been perfectly normal. It was just that one moment when it was almost like she *literally* could not tell me what she wanted to say.

If somebody's having a mental breakdown, doesn't that effect everything?

My thoughts flashed back to my conversation with Agnes the night before and a shiver went down my spine. Agnes had experienced that same thing.

Why? What was going on here?

I snorted, a bubble of amusement forming in my chest. *If this was a fairytale or one of those folk stories I've been reading,* I thought, *it would be because they were under a curse that* kept *them from saying certain things.*

The second the thought crossed my mind, I froze midway through replacing a skein of pine green wool yarn in its bin on the shelf. "No. That's ridiculous." My voice sounded too loud, even to my own ears. "It can't be that."

Shaking my head firmly, I replaced the skein of yarn and then stood back to survey the rows of shelving. Curses weren't real. Fairytales weren't real, for that matter.

The whole notion was ridiculous, wasn't it?

But what about Agnes? whispered a voice inside my mind. *She's a creature of folklore and she's real.*

I bit my lip. She *was* real—unless I'd been hallucinating her this entire time, which I definitely had not.

So... I drew in a shaky breath. What if there really *was* something like a curse preventing Maddie from telling me what was happening?

The thought was a little too overwhelming.

My ears started ringing and my knees wobbled—I had to hurry back over to the counter and collapse into my chair before I ended up on the floor. Propping my elbows on the counter, I rested my head in my hands and drew deep, bracing breaths. Once the ringing in my ears stopped, I wrestled with this new realization and whether or not it could possibly fit into the fabric of my reality.

Think logically, Celia.

Other than a curse, what else could physically keep Maddie from telling me specific information? And something had definitely impeded her—I'd watched as she tried and failed to speak. The same thing had happened to Agnes, though her reaction had been quite different. It was like the brownie had seized up at first, before she recovered and just completely sidestepped my questions.

But a *curse*? Really? I ran my fingers through the end of my ponytail, staring at my cheerful brown welcome mat.

Just because there's a brownie living in your apartment and you've noticed a few strange things about this town doesn't mean that there's a curse.

A weak laugh escaped me. This was *reality*, after all. It wasn't like I was living in a fairytale or some other fictional story.

But then I remembered our conversation at Starbright Café and how excited Maddie had been when I told her she was like a real-life fairy godmother. Too excited. Nobody got that excited over being compared to a fairy godmother, did they?

I bit the inside of my cheek. And, if I was honest with myself...she'd *glittered*. I hadn't imagined it.

That *definitely* wasn't normal.

I considered the situation for a few more minutes, letting my choice of music for the day (a massive playlist of every Loreena McKennitt album) wash over me. As the last strains of one of her old Irish ballads faded, I exhaled slowly and straightened in my chair. There was only one way I was going to get to the bottom of this craziness.

I would have to track Maddie down and figure out how to help her talk to me.

FORTY-FOUR

As it turned out, locating Maddie proved more complicated than I'd anticipated. I started by sending her text, asking if I could talk to her for a moment, but she never responded. That surprised me, given that she was Starhaven's oh-so-helpful town facilitator. But, in her defense, I had no real idea what she did in a day.

Next, I spent a few minutes poking around Google in search of the Starhaven Community Foundation's address. As far as I could tell, they did not have a website or any social media presence beyond an entry on Starhaven's community page with the Foundation's name and Maddie's name and number. Given that half of Starhaven wasn't online, that shouldn't have surprised me, but...

Leaning back in my chair, I frowned thoughtfully at my phone. If the nascent suspicions starting swirl around inside my head were any indication, there might be a really good reason why the Foundation wasn't online.

How did anybody find anyone in this town, though? I huffed in frustration. Did they issue old-fashioned phone-books in Starhaven? If so, nobody had delivered one to me.

Bianca, I thought suddenly. She knew Maddie fairly well —she might be my best bet on where to locate the Foundation's office. I texted her to ask and I also let her know that Zel was unable to meet this afternoon.

It took her a few minutes to respond, but Bianca texted me an address—a little hole-in-the-wall office two blocks from the Square.

I nodded to myself. An office within walking distance made sense, given that Maddie always seemed to pop up around the Square, and I never saw her in a vehicle.

My phone vibrated with another text.

BIANCA

I'm sorry, Celia, but I can't make our knitting class this afternoon either. Something's come up.

I sighed, but I couldn't say I was surprised—after all, I'd had that strange feeling all day. I brushed off the canceled class. It was fine; I wasn't sure I could focus on knitting and conversation anyway. It took all of my concentration just to deal with my customers.

At four-thirty, I wanted to call it quits for the day, but I forced myself to keep the shop open until five. I might own Celia's Craft Shop, but I had to be open to have business. And, sure enough, I had several more people trickle in at the last moment.

As soon as I'd ushered those last few customers out the

door with their purchases and smiles of thanks, I gratefully flipped my 'open' sign to 'closed'. Pulling out my phone, I stopped the music floating through my Bluetooth speakers. Blissful silence filled my shop. I stood for a moment on my welcome mat, trying to soak in the silence and quiet the noise in my head.

A frisson of unease washed over me, like ghostly fingers trailing over my skin. Quite inexplicably, I had the sense that I stood on the brink of a shadowy precipice leading down to some unknown drop. From this moment on, I would be entwined even deeper in this town and its goings on.

It was the strangest feeling, and yet I knew it was true. If I pursued this mystery, there would be no going back. I don't know how I knew that, but I knew it as clearly as I knew my own name.

I only hesitated a moment. I had no intentions of going anywhere. My future and my home were both here in Starhaven for the indeterminate future, if not forever.

What did it matter if I was entangled a little deeper in this town's goings on?

With that thought lodged firmly in mind, I grabbed my purse, locked the shop door behind me, and headed off down the sidewalk in search of Maddie. The early evening air was delightfully pleasant, but I barely noticed. I was a woman on a mission.

The Starhaven Community Foundation was tucked in between an accountant's office and a little print shop. I hastened my steps as I caught sight of the pale white lettering on the plate glass window by the front door. But when I reached it, I took one look at the 'closed' sign on the door and tasted disappointment.

Just to be certain, I tried the doorknob. Locked. Sighing, I leaned in and tried to peer through the glass. I realized I probably looked pretty silly, but...I had to be sure.

Unfortunately, that idea was a bust, too. As far as I could see, everything inside the office was dark and still. If Maddie *was* there, she was somewhere in the back.

A gut instinct, however, told me that Maddie wasn't here. My disappointment grew heavier. I had a theory and I really, really needed to talk to her. But—I checked my phone—she still hadn't texted me back and I didn't know what else to look for her.

Sighing again, I stepped away from the Foundation's door and stood to one side of the sidewalk while I determined my next move. If I knew where Maddie lived, I'd visit her house. But I didn't.

Worst case scenario, I supposed I could attempt to text her my questions, but... I wrinkled my nose at the thought. It just didn't have the same feel. There are some questions that should never be asked via text.

I'm pretty sure "Are you under a curse?" is one of them.

Hiking my purse up on my shoulder, I turned around and slowly retraced my steps across those two blocks to the Square. Well, now I'd have to figure out what else to do to keep myself occupied for the evening. Otherwise, I was going to drive myself crazy.

My feet took me toward the park without conscious input

from me. Mentally, I shrugged. I didn't want to visit the clearing right now, but the benches outside of it would be a pretty good place to sit and clear my head.

A few moments later, I passed the playground and took the path across the grassy field to the benches under the maples, oaks, and poplars at the edge of the woods. Halfway across the field, I caught sight of a lone figure with a riot of curly gray hair sitting on a bench, staring in the general direction of that clearing in the woods.

Maddie.

I stopped short in surprise, blinking in her direction. What was she doing out here?

The thought had barely finished crossing my mind before I knew the answer. The clearing. It had to be the clearing.

And, really, it didn't matter why she was here. The important thing was that I'd found her.

Eagerly, I set off again, but as I neared her bench, a wave of uncertainty and doubt overtook me. My footsteps slowed as I faltered, biting my lip. Maddie was under no obligation to text me back, and she certainly didn't have to tell me whatever was going on with her. Bothering her right now would be imposing on her.

I swallowed uncomfortably. The idea of *that* just about gave me a case of hives. But...she'd made it sound like I'd helped her. Further, she'd made it sound like Starhaven needed me. It was only fair to ask questions about that, wasn't it?

In that moment,

In that moment, as I considered the back of Maddie's head, I was struck by the almost wild sort of loneliness that seemed to surround her. It was the strangest thing. She was such a friendly, upbeat person that the aura she gave off right now was both jarring and incongruous.

No, something was *definitely* up with her.

Bolstering my courage, I marched up to her bench. "I'm sorry to bother you, Maddie," I said as I sat down on the other end and shifted toward her. "But we need to talk."

Maddie just continued to stare straight ahead. She could have been a million miles away for all the attention she paid me.

"I don't want to come across as pushy or imposing or anything," I said in the face of her silence. "But I am really confused right now. You came into my shop and said all those things, and then I started thinking and..." I waved a helpless hand through the air. "Now I have all these *theories*."

At long last, as though returning from some far distant place, Maddie turned her head toward me. The faintest hint of a smile twitched at the corners of her lips. "Theories?"

"Yes. *Yes.*" A shiver of excitement worked its way through me. I shifted on the bench again, angling myself more towards her. But just before I opened my mouth, I hesitated.

If I said this out loud, I was going to sound like I belonged in a mental institution. Maddie might even offer to escort me there.

But then I thought of Agnes and my resolve hardened. *It can't be* that *crazy. Not when there's a* brownie *living in your apartment.*

And Maddie knew about Agnes.

Taking a deep breath, I fixed her with a solemn look. "Maddie, are you under a curse?"

FORTY-FIVE

Whatever Maddie had expected me to say, it wasn't that. Her green eyes widened and her face went slack in visible shock.

Grimly, I barreled on. "Or are you under some kind of enchantment? Like in a fairytale or something? And you can't tell anybody about it?"

Now Maddie's eyebrows rose in surprise as well.

"I know, I know." I held up a hand. "It sounds crazy. *I* sound crazy." I shook my head. "I can't believe I'm saying this. And yet..." I shrugged helplessly. "It's the only thing that makes any sense."

Maddie finally found her voice. "What do you mean?"

"You *glittered*," I said flatly, meeting her gaze. "Saturday, when I called you a real-life fairy godmother, you *glittered*. I swear you did. I thought I was seeing things at first, but...I don't think I was." I shook my head again. "You rushed off, all excited, and then Monday morning you came into my shop, not as excited, and made a bunch of cryptic comments."

I smiled wryly, though my heart pounded madly in my chest. "If this was a story, I'd say you were under a curse."

When the older woman just continued to stare at me, I shrugged, a trifle self-consciously. "Like I said, it sounds crazy."

Maddie's gaze turned thoughtful, like she was turning my words around and around in her mind and trying to determine how best to answer them. "That," she said at last, "is an interesting theory."

"Is it true? Are you under a curse?" I raised my eyebrows in a silent challenge, but she just looked at me. My intuition prickled again. "Can you say *anything* about it?"

Maddie opened her mouth, but nothing came out. That look of frustration filled her eyes again, and then she canted her head to one side like a bird, her gaze sharpening. After a second, she said, "Ask me something else."

"Um..." I cast about for another relevant question. "Where are you from?"

"The Enchanted Realm."

The answer came so easily I was taken aback. "I beg your pardon?" I blinked. "Did you just say the *Enchanted Realm*?"

"Yes, I did." Maddie turned a small, enigmatic smile on me. "I would not have been able to tell you that to yesterday morning, you see. But today I can." Her green eyes twinkled at me. "Because of you, Celia."

I blinked at her again. "What do you mean, because of me?"

In lieu of answering, Maddie shook her head and turned

her attention back towards the patch of woods that held the clearing. In the distance we heard children laughing and playing on the playground and the distant sounds of traffic.

Impatience simmered in my gut. I yearned to ask all the questions and have all the answers *right now*. But I forced myself to fold my hands in my lap and wait patiently.

This was probably the strangest situation I'd ever been in. And it wasn't like I had anywhere to be. So... I waited. I waited for Maddie to gather her thoughts and return from whatever ethereal place her mind had flown off to.

At last, Maddie heaved a delicate little sigh. "You were right, Celia. I am a fairy godmother. Or was." She lifted one shoulder in a prosaic little shrug. "My powers don't work quite the same way here."

It was her turn to examine her hands, while I tried to keep my jaw from hitting the mossy ground beneath the bench.

"There was a point at which they did not work at all, but I found ways around *that*. And now..." Maddie turned her head, a gentle breeze ruffling her mass of wild gray hair curls, and smiled at me again. "Now I am free, at least in part." Her smile grew a little pinched. "It would seem there is still a hold on me."

"The curse?" I was proud of myself—my voice didn't squeak.

Maddie's smile grew even more pinched and I sank back against the bench, exhaling in a heady rush as the reality of that hit me. "Oh, my," I said weakly.

"Yes." Maddie chuckled gently. "The difference between theory and reality is quite something, isn't it?" Her voice grew thoughtful. "I told you Starhaven was special, Celia. And it is. A unique blend of your Realm and mine."

I took a couple of deep breaths—part of me couldn't believe we were actually sitting here having this conversation—and then roused myself. "Is the whole town under a curse? Where did it come from? How did it get here? What *happened*?"

My questions tumbled over themselves, but Maddie just held up a hand, shaking her head. "One day I hope to be able to tell you the story, but for now, suffice it to say that there are parts of the story that must remain untold."

Well. I wrinkled my nose at her. *That* sounded like fairy-tale nonsense if I'd ever heard any. "Is the whole town under a curse?" I asked again. I needed some clarification—I had no idea what I'd walked into. "Surely there are normal humans here, aren't there?"

"Oh, certainly." Maddie bestowed a kind smile on me. "A good deal of Starhaven's population is perfectly normal and human. But something about this place..." She shook her head again, her eyes drifting back to the trees that concealed the clearing. "When I first arrived, I found a number of Folk here who had migrated from other parts of the world. They didn't all come through the portal, you see."

"The portal?" I was proud of myself—my voice didn't squeak.

My expression must have been priceless, however, because Maddie chuckled. "Oh, yes. There's a portal in the clearing. One way only, I'm afraid, and it's not open all the time." She tapped a thoughtful finger against her lips. "But when it does open, there's always someone who comes through."

My mind instantly flashed to Cedric. "Like Cedric."

"Like Cedric." Maddie inclined her head in a long, slow nod.

I drew in a deep breath, trying to keep my head from spinning. My world wavered a little around the edges—I couldn't believe I was actually having this conversation. I took a second deep breath, followed by a third, and reality crystalized again.

"And you're from—and he's from—this...other realm?" I waved a hand, trying to remember what she'd called it.

"The Enchanted Realm, yes," Maddie confirmed with a smile. "Although I'm not entirely sure what part he's from." Her smile turned deprecating. "That's part of the curse, you see. When people appear here in your Realm, they don't remember who they are. And, unfortunately, I haven't been able to help them remember."

Her smile thinned around the edges. "In fact, most of the time, *I* don't even know who they are. I couldn't tell them if I wanted to."

I stared at Maddie. "What *is* this curse? It sounds absolutely horrible."

The older woman shrugged. "I don't remember all of it. I'm not sure I ever knew to begin with. The only thing I know for certain is that someone very powerful placed a curse on the inhabitants of the Enchanted Realm."

"All of them?" I shook my head. It sounded crazy—but also exactly like something you'd expect from a fairytale. "Why?"

Maddie shrugged again, spreading her hands in a help-less gesture. "I don't know. But—" Her forehead abruptly scrunched into a frown. She closed her eyes, raising her hands to massage her temples as though she was in pain.

I waited, caught between hopeful curiosity and a slightly guilty feeling that I'd caused this by asking too many questions.

"I think I've remembered." Maddie opened her eyes, a short-lived expression of triumph flashing across her face. "When someone reaches their happy ending, instead of getting to live it out, they're brought here to this Realm with no memory of who they are."

"That's terrible." I shook my head, sympathy knotting my stomach. "That would be terrible for anyone, let alone—" I broke off, a delayed thought finally dawning on me, arriving like the lag on a video chat when the internet was particu-larly slow.

I stared at Maddie, a shiver of excitement and wondering running through me. "You're a fairy godmother from the Enchanted Realm. And these people are losing their happy endings?"

Maddie lifted a patient eyebrow. "I believe we have already covered this, Celia."

Her tone said she was humoring me, but I didn't notice. Straightening on the bench, I stared at her with wide eyes. "You mean, like in fairytales? A *fairy godmother* and *happy endings* from *fairytales*?" My voice cracked on the last part.

"Yes, dear." Maddie gave me a chiding look that said this should have been patently obvious. "Fairytales. That's what your Realm calls the stories of our peoples' lives."

The world spun around me again. Agnes was one thing, but...people from *fairytales*? I sank back against the park bench and buried my face in my hands. *There are* actual *fairytale creatures living here in Starhaven.*

A gentle hand touched my shoulder. "I know it's a lot to take in, dear," Maddie said kindly. "And I truly don't know what it is about you."

Dropping my hands, I turned my head to find her considering me again, those green eyes filled with something ancient and scrutinizing all at once.

"But I think you came here for a reason, Celia."

"Maddie, I'm not—"

"I think you can help us."

"What?" A weak, borderline hysterical chuckle escaped me. "Are you thinking I should just march around town and ask everybody what character in fairytale they are?"

"Oh, no, dear." Maddie dismissed that idiotic statement with a flick of her fingers. "It's not that simple. Random questions won't break the curse. You'll have to be intentional about it."

I drew in another deep breath, staring hard in the direction of the clearing while I tried to make sense of the maddening jumble of thoughts swirling through my head. Part of me screamed that this entire conversation was insane. But the other part of me recalled Agnes...and Cedric...and some of the *other* strange things I'd noticed about this town.

Slowly, the world shifted into a new paradigm around me, settling like the invisible folds of a beautiful ballgown.

"Okay." I blew out a breath and straightened up on the bench. "Say I believe you. And there really are a bunch of—" I fluttered a hand, "—fairytale characters living here in Starhaven. Say I broke your curse." I drilled Maddie with steady look. "Why can't you break other people's curses?"

An air of misery washed over Maddie, before she clamped down on it. "I tried. But apparently the curse thought of that too. There's no loophole, as far as I'm concerned." She frowned, shaking her head. "No, the curse has to be broken by a human from this Realm."

Her frown faded, to be replaced by a beautiful smile. "By you, Celia."

FORTY-SIX

I don't really remember much of what happened after that. Maddie and I talked for a few minutes more before she sent me home with a pat on the back and an almost grandmotherly smile. Somehow, I made it back to my apartment and managed to fix myself dinner and clean up before I crawled straight into bed.

My bed felt like the best place to be right now. A cozy little oasis from the crazy that had inexplicably taken over my life.

Frowning, I stared up at the ceiling through the darkness that filled my bedroom. I'd hung room-darkening curtains to block the lights from the streetlights outside, so it didn't matter that the last of the evening light hadn't quite faded.

Once again, Maddie's words kept ringing in my ears, mixed with a montage of all the strange little things I'd noticed since I moved to Starhaven. Actual fairytale characters from *fairytales*, here in our world. And I was supposed to help them.

I rubbed my forehead. How was it possible that someone like me was capable of breaking a curse from a place called the *Enchanted Realm*?

It sounded like some crazy science fiction thing—portals opening between dimensions, or realms, or whatever you wanted to call them, and stranding people here.

I rolled over to punch my pillow into a more comfortable shape, but paused as that thought really struck home. Portals opening between dimensions. It wasn't the craziest thing I've ever heard—at least not when it came to the storylines in movies, video games, or books.

But in the real world? Yeah, that was totally nuts.

I stifled a slightly hysterical laugh. Of course, in the real world, people didn't have *brownies* living in their apartment, either. Maybe *I* was the one who'd stepped through a portal into some strange new dimension.

My mind racing, I lay back against my pillow. No, I had to accept that there was some element of truth to what Maddie said. I mean, she *did* glitter. And there *was* a brownie living in my apartment.

And that man, Cedric, *had* appeared in the clearing from nowhere.

So... I bit my lip. That meant that I had to admit it *was* possible that clearing contained a portal leading to another Realm.

A portal leading to a fictional Realm, yes, but...still.
Another Realm.
And the way Maddie explained it, most of these new

arrivals in Starhaven had no idea who they were or where they were from. That made my heart hurt. I thought of Cedric again.

A shudder wracked my shoulders. I could only imagine how terrible it would be to wind up somewhere strange and have no memory of who I was.

Somehow, Maddie was an exception to that part of the curse, but she hadn't explained why. That was curious, too. I'd have to ask her about it.

But, never mind. I waved my hand through the darkness, mentally telling myself to carry on. I could circle around to that later. Back to the notion of fairytale characters being citizens of Starhaven.

Maddie believed that I could help break their curse. She'd also implied that that meant I had to know who a particular character was—or at least have a good idea.

An unladylike snort escaped me. How was I supposed to pull *that* off? I'd gone through a fairytale stage when I was a child, reading everything I could get my hands on, but there were dozens, if not hundreds, of fairytales from all over the world.

I ticked them off on my fingers in the dark. There were well-known stories like Sleeping Beauty and Snow White, Beauty and the Beast, and lesser-known stories like the Twelve Dancing Princesses. There were stories specific to Africa and Asia and other countries, and...

The list just went on.

It was an impossible task—how in the world was *I* supposed to figure out who these people were?

I thumped a fist on my bedspread. And *that* was

supposing that they were major characters in these fairytales, and not minor characters.

A second later, I had to amend that thought—I'd remembered something else Maddie said. The curse prevented characters from getting their happy endings.

All at once, I sat up in bed and ran my fingers through my hair, thinking furiously. If the curse had to do with preventing happy endings, then maybe the people showing up in Starhaven *were* main characters after all. Minor characters didn't typically get happy endings in fairytales— unless one counted living in a kingdom at peace as a happy ending.

But really, most characters would never rate high enough for someone to bother cursing them. Not on this scale—and this did sound like a curse on a *massive* scale.

The faces of everyone I'd met so far in Starhaven filtered through my head. It would be impossible to determine who might have come from this Realm, and who was just an ordinary human being. How was I supposed to tell the difference?

Frowning, I drummed my fingers on my mattress. I'd just have to ask Maddie who had come through the portal. Frankly, I was surprised she didn't already have a list of names ready for me.

And then a thought occurred to me, like a lightning bolt piercing the darkness of my room with vivid intensity. I might not know right now which other Starhaven citizens had come through the portal, but I *did* know at least one person.

Cedric.

Poor, confused, blind Cedric. A man with no memory of

he was and who talked like he had escaped from a Renaissance fair.

My eyes narrowed as I stared through the darkness at my oak dresser. Since he was the only person I knew for a fact had probably come through that portal, I would start with him. What fairytale might a blind nobleman or prince belong to?

A vague memory fluttered in the corner of my mind. I had read something like that once, I thought. Fortunately, I didn't have to rely on my memory.

Reaching over to my nightstand, I snagged my phone and brought up a browser. Typing in 'fairytale with blind prince', I hit search. I expected to filter through half a dozen stories at least, but to my surprise, there was only one major story in which the prince was blinded.

The fairytale about Rapunzel.

Specifically, the Grimm's version of Rapunzel.

I wrinkled my nose as I skimmed through the outline. Well, parts of this didn't seem quite that romantic. Perhaps there was more to the story.

But anyway, Cedric *had* to be the prince from Rapunzel's fairytale. If he wasn't...well, I wasn't sure who else he could be.

I spent a few more minutes poking around the internet, asking different questions and trying to see if I could bring up anything else. But everything boiled down to Rapunzel's story and Rapunzel's story alone.

No, Cedric had to be Rapunzel's prince.

Excitement fluttered in the pit of my stomach. Now, all I had to do was somehow get *him* to realize that.

In all the excitement of curling back up under my blankets and plotting ways to possibly break Cedric's curse, I forgot to ask myself another question: if Rapunzel's prince was here, where was Rapunzel?

FORTY-SEVEN

The realization that I had forgotten about Rapunzel dawned on me at breakfast the next morning. I'd woken up early, too excited to sleep. Halfway through a piece of buttered toast and a fried egg, it occurred to me that I had no idea if Rapunzel was here or not.

My fork froze on its way to my mouth. Would I break Cedric's curse only for him to remain here in Starhaven without the love of his life?

Well. I blinked down at my half-finished piece of toast. I *assumed* Rapunzel was the love of his life. Fairytales are, after all, a little short on depth and true feelings and long on hormonal love at first sight.

Grabbing my phone, I pulled up the fairytale again and read through it again, a little slower than I had at two AM this morning. If the Grimms' version was the right fairytale, his Rapunzel would have twins.

Twins. I jolted in shock, nearly knocking my coffee mug

over. The *only* person in Starhaven I had met so far who had twins was Zel. Was it possible? She *was* a single mom with twins.

Even as the thought crossed my mind, I realized how insane I sounded.

"Just because she's a single mom with twins does not mean she's Rapunzel under a curse," I told myself out loud. "Plus, she doesn't have super long hair."

But she wouldn't, whispered a voice in my mind. *Not now.*

My eyes dropped back to my phone screen. I read through the rest of the fairytale, even more slowly, and then leaned back in my chair, the rest of my breakfast completely forgotten. No, Rapunzel didn't have long hair at the end of the story. The old witch chopped her hair off before she cast Rapunzel out into the wilderness—and then she used Rapunzel's hair to set a trap for the prince.

Zel had short golden blonde hair—but that still didn't mean anything...did it?

I bit my lip. *Oh, boy.* I could picture it now—if I started asking Zel questions about Rapunzel and indicated I thought she was a character from a fairytale, she would think I had absolutely lost my mind.

The worst part was that if was wrong...she'd be right.

I took a deep, bracing breath. What was I going to do? All I had was speculation. *Crazy* speculation. Surely there were other young women in this town who had blonde hair and twins.

Absently, I tapped my leg. *Where do I start?* According to the fairytale, the prince never knew he had children until after he found Rapunzel again. *Do I try to find Rapunzel first? Or do I see if Cedric is the prince?*

Another, far more dire, thought occurred to me. Say Zel really was Rapunzel and Cedric really was her prince. If they were both cursed, would they even recognize each other if they *did* see each other again?

I blew out a frustrated breath. There really wasn't a safe way to get them together, either. I mean, I couldn't just drag Zel and her children to meet up with a strange man without any explanation. That wouldn't be right.

I tried to brainstorm other options. Could I casually take her into the antique store with me? (I completely dismissed the fact that I wasn't welcome there, as far as Dave was concerned) That was a possibility, wasn't it?

All at once, it hit me what I was doing. Propping my elbows on the table, I buried my head in my hands. *You're losing it, Celia.* I told myself. *Absolutely losing it.*

This was bonkers. Here I was, contemplating running around Starhaven and asking people if they were *characters* from a *fairytale*. On the word of an old lady I hadn't known very long.

On paper, it did sound bonkers. But... I blew out another breath. Call me a romantic, but if there was a cursed, amnesiac Rapunzel living in Starhaven, the idea of breaking the curse and reuniting her with her prince was really appealing.

And not just reuniting them, but reuniting their family. Didn't their children deserve to have both parents in their lives, if at all possible?

Swallowing, I fixed a few strands of hair that had slipped out of my ponytail. Well, when you came right down to it, most of the town already thought I was nuts. And I didn't know most people here anyway.

What did it matter if half of Starhaven decided I was a little crazier than they'd expected? I thought about Dave and his perpetually sour expression. At least I was the nice kind of crazy.

Somehow, that thought did not comfort me as much as I thought it should have.

FORTY-EIGHT

The idea of whether I should approach Cedric or Zel first tortured me for the rest of the day, overnight, and well into the following morning. Finally, I made up my mind. I'd start with trying to find Rapunzel.

And that meant starting with Zel.

Because she was *still* the only young, short-haired, blonde, single mom of twins that I knew in this town.

To that end, I sent Zel a text, inviting her to have pizza from Tam's and a picnic in the park after work that evening. I even brought a sheet for the children to play on. It hadn't taken much convincing. Tam's pizza was that good—and Zel needed some conversation with another adult who wasn't her new boss.

So, here I was on a Friday evening, sitting cross-legged on a cheerful watermelon print sheet I'd spread out on the park grass. It was an absolutely perfect evening—warm and breezy without being either overly hot or humid. A boxed pizza waited temptingly to one side of the sheet. I'd brought a couple paper plates and a few napkins, as well as several cold cans of Dr. Pepper. Zel and I both liked that soft drink.

When I caught sight of Zel pushing her stroller up the sidewalk towards the park, I waved. She was wearing another of her favorite flowery skirts, and her shoulder-length blonde hair fluttered in the breeze. Rowan and Rosalie smiled and clapped in their stroller as Zel pushed it toward the grass where I sat.

I had positioned myself so I could keep the clearing in view. I don't know why, I just felt like I needed to keep an eye on it. That meant I was in the perfect position to see Zel freeze for a second as she came across the grass and her gaze caught the trees concealing the clearing.

A very peculiar kind of shudder traveled over her body, but it was over in an instant and then she carried on as though nothing that happened. Had Maddie not completely piqued my curiosity, I wouldn't have been paying close enough attention to her to have even noticed.

Now, I thought ruefully, *I'm probably in danger of reading too much into everything.*

"Hi," Zel said a little breathlessly, as she maneuvered the stroller up to the watermelon sheet and stopped.

"Hey." I smiled at her and nodded toward the stroller. "Can I help you?"

"Oh, no. I've got this." She pulled a selection of baby toys out of a basket underneath the stroller and laid them on the sheet. A moment later, she had taken both children out of the stroller and settled them comfortably in the middle of the sheet. She sat down on the side opposite me, her back to the clearing.

I couldn't help but wonder if that was a subconscious move on her part.

"Oh, that smells so good." Zel beamed at me before reaching for a plate and a napkin. "I love Tam's pizza."

"Me too." I shook my head as I did the same. "I don't think there's a pizza place in Louisville that can rival it."

Zel opened the box and we shared a grin as the delicious smell of garlic and pepperoni wafted out and met our noses. My stomach growled, hunger temporarily overriding the anxiety that had been tying me into knots all day. In between bites, we exchanged conversation about our respective weeks.

I tried to pay attention to Zel's description of working at Thornfire Books and her interactions with her new boss, but I was having trouble focusing. All I could think about was whether or not she was Rapunzel—and how in the world I was supposed to figure that out.

By the time we'd both had two slices, I'd decided it was now or never. I couldn't take the suspense any longer.

My heart started pounding in my chest as I dropped my used napkin onto my plate and pushed it aside. It was just as well I was done eating—there was an uncomfortable knot in the back of my throat. I don't think I could have taken another bite anyway.

I was going to sound crazy—I knew that—but it had to be done. I don't know how I knew that, but I knew that with the same sort of certainty I knew the sun was going to rise over the eastern horizon in the morning.

Taking a bracing sip of my Dr. Pepper (and nearly choking when it fizzed down the back of my throat), I swallowed and said lightly, "I can't remember, Zel—where did you say you were from?" I flashed her an apologetic smile over my can of soft drink. "Sorry, I forgot. Didn't you say it was somewhere in Tennessee?"

Zel blinked at me, her expression turning quizzical, before she smiled and shrugged. "Yes, I'm from Tennessee." She lunged into her story, which I really didn't remember at all, and I listened carefully.

The more she talked, the more I realized that everything she told me about herself came down to a list of facts. No personal anecdotes, no mentions of memories of certain places or things. Just a list of facts, like she was reciting her bio.

A bio she'd memorized, but had no real connection to—except for some emotion where her missing husband was concerned.

I was hard-pressed to keep from bouncing on the sheet in excitement—I had forgotten she didn't know where he was. That was another point in favor of my Rapunzel theory, wasn't it?

"Thank you," I said when Zel finished. "That sounds like a lovely town." Heart pounding, I took a more careful sip of my Dr. Pepper and then settled the can in the grass beside the edge of the sheet. "Not to change the subject or anything, but do you read stories to your children?"

"I do." Zel's face softened in a smile. "I think it's important to read to them."

"What kind of stories do you like?" My heart continued to

pound in my chest as though I was running a marathon. "Do you ever read them fairytales?"

"Fairytales?" Zel blinked, and then her forehead scrunched in a confused frown. "I don't think I'm familiar with those."

"Really?" I sat up a little straighter on the sheet. Regardless of everything else, that surprised me. Fairytales were such an intrinsic part of pop culture that it was hard to fathom she hadn't been exposed to any of them. "You've never read the story of Snow White or Sleeping Beauty or Cinderella?"

"Cinderella?" Zel's frown deepened. "Sleeping...Beauty? What did you say they were?"

"Fairytales."

"Fairytales?" Zel shook her head. "I don't think I've ever heard of those." She tucked a lock of blonde hair behind her ear with a self-deprecating laugh. "No, I've been reading the children storybooks Maddie brought me. And a few I've bought at Thornfire Books since I started working there."

Hmm. That was interesting. So much for my potentially easy way into this subject.

I offered Zel a friendly smile. "Well, when they're older, they might like fairytales. There are quite a lot of them. Some of them are a little dark," I admitted, "but all of them are quite interesting."

Over the next few minutes, I gave her an introduction to Cinderella and Sleeping Beauty...and then I seized the moment to segue into the fairytale I really wanted to discuss.

"One of the ones I've always found most interesting," I said casually, though my heart hammered in my chest like it was trying to beat its way out, "is the story of Rapunzel." I paused and held my breath, waiting to see if anything would happen at the mention of her name.

Nothing did.

"Oh, really?" Zel just raised a polite eyebrow at me.

"Yeah." I paused again, uncertain how to proceed. Obviously, she was completely ignorant of the story. Where did I—

The sound of a car backfiring on its way down the street beside the park startled us both—and frightened Rowan and Rosalie. They both began to cry. Zel scooped them both up and cradled them to her chest, making soothing sounds.

I took a hasty sip of my Dr. Pepper. *Get it together, Celia*, I scolded myself. *This is not that hard.*

Once Zel had calmed her children and was able to set them back down on the sheet, she snagged another piece of pizza and a banana pepper. "Okay, sorry. You were saying?"

I almost told her I was grateful for the interruption, but stopped myself just in time. Instead, I flashed her a smile and hoped she couldn't see how nervous I was.

"Well, there are actually several versions of the story of Rapunzel. But in all of them, an old witch takes a baby girl in payment for vegetables stolen from her garden and keeps her locked up in a tower."

Zel listened, eying me while she alternated between bites of pizza and bites of the banana pepper.

"Over the years, the girl grows really, *really* long hair." I spread my hands apart in exaggeration.

"Really long hair?" Zel raised a skeptical eyebrow, before

darting a glance at her babies to make sure they were still happily entertained by their toys. "Like, how long?"

"Long enough for the old witch to use her braid to climb up into the tower."

Zel's gaze snapped to mine, her green eyes wide with astonishment. For a split-second, I dared to hope that she'd perhaps remembered something...and then the small blonde shook her head. "That would be a terrible pain to take care of. Can you imagine having hair that long?"

We shared a commiserating glance. I lifted a hand to my own medium-length brown ponytail. "No, I can't imagine having hair that long. Anyway..." I went on to explain the rest of the story. "A handsome prince finds the girl one day and they fall in love. And then, depending on which version you read, the witch finds out and causes trouble, but Rapunzel and the prince are eventually reunited."

I deliberately left out the part about Rapunzel having twins and the prince getting blinded. That *was* the Grimm version, after all.

Dead silence fell between us while Zel processed this. "Well..." she said at last. "That's an interesting story, Celia." Her eyebrows scrunched into a frown again. "And what do people find so fascinating about it?"

Oddly enough, I'd been wondering that same thing myself ever since I'd gone back and read the story again.

"Um, well..." I shrugged, a little helplessly. "I guess it's the romance of it? People like the idea of a prince coming to save a girl locked up in a tower."

"But he didn't save her." Zel shook her head sharply. "You

just told me that this girl stays locked in the tower until the witch finds out about the prince."

"I know." I smiled ruefully at Zel. "I don't understand it either. If they were so in love, why didn't he just bring her some rope and take her away to his castle?"

Zel's frown deepened, as though she was attempting to puzzle this out. "Maybe he—" She broke off, putting a hand to her temple.

Alarm coursed through me. "Zel?" I leaned toward her. "Are you all right?"

"Just a sudden headache." Zel braved a smile, rubbing her temple. "I get them sometimes. I don't know why." She shifted her position on the sheet, inching closer to her children, and turned her back on the clearing even more solidly.

I chewed on the inside of my lip, debating my next move. If her sudden headache *didn't* have anything to do with my story...well, it was an awfully big coincidence.

And, as a character from a Navy police procedural show I've always loved was fond of saying, there were no such things as coincidences.

Throwing caution to the wind, I decided to go straight to the point. *Here's nothing.*

"There's another version of Rapunzel's story." I kept my voice deliberately casual, though I couldn't keep an anxious flush from rising in my cheeks. Hopefully Zel wouldn't take offense, when this was all said and done. "Only this version isn't quite as fluffy as the other one."

Taking a breath, I plunged ahead. "In this story, the prince and Rapunzel marry secretly...and then Rapunzel has twins."

FORTY-NINE

"She has twins?" A bright smile suffused Zel's face, smoothing away the lines of pain in her forehead.

"Yeah." I swallowed—my mouth had suddenly gone bone dry. "But when the witch finds out, she kicks Rapunzel out of the tower and lays a trap for the prince."

"Oh, dear." Zel's green eyes widened in alarm. "That does sound different."

"When the prince comes back, the witch tries to hurt him, but he manages to escape by jumping from the tower." I swallowed again. "The only problem is that he lands in some thornbushes and is blinded. Then he spends a long time wandering around grieving Rapunzel, because he doesn't know what's happened to her."

"That's awful," Zel said, even as she winced and pressed the tips of her fingers to her temples again. "Why would anyone want to read a story like that?"

"Well, if the story ended there, I'd agreed with you, but it *does* have a happy ending. Rapunzel and the prince eventually reunite and somehow Rapunzel manages to heal him."

Something flashed through Zel's eyes—was that *alarm?* "That," she said, her voice sharpening, "sounds very much like magic."

"It was magic." I shrugged, a peculiar shudder working its way down my spine. Why was she reacting that way? "Most of the fairytales involve that sort of thing."

Zel shook her head. "I'm not sure I want my children reading those—fairytales, did you call them?—any time soon. They sound quite gruesome."

I had to press my lips together to hold back a sudden burst of laughter. If Zel thought *fairytales* were too gruesome for her children, I don't know *what* she would think of the wide variety of literature available for children these days.

"And you said this was your favorite story?" Zel regarded me as though I had suddenly sprouted another head, her expression astonished and slightly wary.

"No, no." I waved both hands in protest. "I've just been studying it lately. I've...recently taken up an interest in fairytales again."

When Zel just continued to stare at me, I felt compelled to explain. "I used to read them when I was a child, but I'm learning that there are way more fairytales than I ever realized there were."

Zel nodded slowly, and then glanced down at her little ones again. Despite the peaceful atmosphere permeating the park, an uncomfortable silence fell over us.

Well, *I* thought it was uncomfortable. Maybe it didn't bother Zel at all. Frustration vied with embarrassment for chief position in my mind as I clenched one hand into a fist, my fingernails biting into my palm.

This was not going well at all. It *definitely* wasn't going the way I had hoped.

And I *still* didn't know what to do. I bit the inside of my cheek, almost hard enough to draw blood. Telling Zel the story of Rapunzel hadn't worked. Was it too subtle?

Probably, said a wise voice inside my mind. *You were much more direct with Maddie, after all.*

I held back a frustrated sigh. That had been an accident, but...okay. Time for a new approach—all cards on the table.

"Zel," I said, so abruptly that she looked at me in some alarm. "The reason I'm talking to you about fairytales is that—" my chest tightened, my face growing hot, "—I think you're a fairytale character. In fact, I think you're Rapunzel."

The words hung between us in the hazy evening air.

I don't know what I expected. Maybe for her to glitter, or swoon, or gasp. *Something.* A least a *little* indication that I had hit the mark.

Zel did none of those things. She just sat there on my watermelon-print sheet, blinking at me in astonishment and confusion. "You...think *I* am Rapunzel?"

I nodded, my throat too tight for any more words.

"A character from these *fairytales* you just told me about?" The look on her face told me she was contemplating picking up Rowan and Rosalie and running for dear life.

I swallowed dust. No, this was definitely *not* going the way I had planned. And, even more obviously, I had clearly not broken her curse.

Or I was completely wrong about her being Rapunzel. But I wasn't even going to entertain that possibility. Not yet.

Gathering up my courage, I managed to find my voice. Because if you looked at it from a certain (albeit crazy, I'll admit) angle, it *did* make sense.

"You *are* Rapunzel, aren't you? The Rapunzel from the Grimm's version." I gestured to her children. "The Rapunzel who fell in love with the prince and married him and had twins."

Zel's gaze dropped first to her children, and then to the thin vine band on the ring finger of her left hand. "I..." she began, but stopped short.

A thin thread of hope unfurled in my chest. *I'm not crazy*, I told myself—and latched onto that thin thread. "Zel, I've noticed you don't talk much about your husband."

"I—" Zel continued to stammer, apparently unable to string words together. "He... he's gone. I *told* you that."

"Who was he?" I asked gently. "How did you fall in love?" I nodded to her ring. "How did he propose?"

"I—I—" Her voice grew more anxious and stressed, hitting a higher pitch. "I—I don't know. I—" she broke off with a small cry, pressing both hands to her head.

Well, I thought grimly. *Either she's Rapunzel, or she's having some sort of emotional breakdown, and I'm responsible for it.*

Cautiously, I laid a hand on her wrist. "Zel, you're Rapunzel."

And in that moment, I really believed it.

It all fit. The way she touched her hair, as though it used to be longer. It was a subconscious gesture—I don't think she even realized she was doing it. The twins. The ring. The fact that she couldn't really tell me anything about her husband.

The fact that, every so often, something about the world around us that I took for granted still surprised her.

"Zel..." I smiled at her, even though she couldn't see me. "You're Rapunzel."

Zel screwed her eyes shut, her fingers digging into her scalp as though that would help stop the pain. She let out a low, keening cry, slumping over as a shudder wracked her small frame. On the sheet, both Rowan and Rosalie whimpered, picking up on their mother's distress.

I winced in sympathy. This experience was nothing like what happened to Maddie. Was it because Maddie had known who she was and Zel didn't? I could only imagine how jarring it must feel to have two sets of memories jostling for place and trying to merge together.

At least, that's what I *hoped* was happening right now.

All at once, Zel froze. In fact, she froze so completely and so thoroughly that for a second, I thought I had done something terribly wrong and she'd just stopped breathing.

My heart leaped into my throat. "Zel?" I patted her arm. "Are you okay?"

Very slowly, Zel drew in a deep breath and straightened up, lowering her trembling hands from her face. She looked at me with clear green eyes. "I remember now." Her tone was soft and wondering, as though she couldn't quite believe it herself. "My name *is* Rapunzel."

CHAPTER

FIFTY

Despite the fact that I'd approached this entire conversation with the hope that she'd prove to be Rapunzel, Zel's admission still shocked me enough that I nearly toppled off the sheet onto the grass. I had to swallow a bubble of hysterical, slightly maniacal laughter.

It had *worked*. It had *actually* worked.

Zel—Rapunzel—touched her fingers to her temple again, and then to the ends of her hair. "I am not entirely sure what just happened, but..." She looked around the park and at Starhaven beyond us with new eyes. "I've been under a curse, haven't I"

The forthrightness of that statement made me smile. From where I was sitting, if something like that had happened to me, a *curse* was *not* the first thing that would have come to mind. But, given where Rapunzel was from, it made perfect sense.

"I think so." I had to clear my throat before I could speak. "Apparently, when people from your Realm—" I gestured to her, "—appear here, you have no memory of your past, or who you were."

Rapunzel was silent for a long moment, digesting this, before she considered me with new eyes as well. "And you broke this curse." She tilted her head to one side. "Are you a fairy? Or a witch?"

"Oh, no." I shook my head. "I'm not any of those things. Just a girl with a craft shop." I shrugged, a little apologetically.

"But...then...how?" Rapunzel looked confused.

I shrugged again. "I have no idea how. I'm sorry. Maddie told me to try, so I did."

"Maddie." Rapunzel's green eyes widened. She leaned forward and lowered her voice conspiratorially. "I think there's something special about her."

I couldn't help but smile. "I think you're right."

Sitting back, Rapunzel touched a hand to her temple again before she placed a hand on both of her children's heads. Her gaze grew distant, and then her head snapped up, anguish suffusing her features. "Where is—" she tried to say his name, but nothing came out.

"Your prince?"

She nodded. The aching hope threading through the pain on her face made my heart clench.

"Uh..." I stared at Rapunzel, uncertain how best to answer that. "I don't know for sure," I said cautiously.

Rapunzel's eyes turned pleading "Can you tell me anything more about this curse, then?"

I opened my mouth—but hesitated. This was like facing a giant jumble of pieces belonging to a massive puzzle. I had a few pieces in Rapunzel, and a few in Maddie, and a whole handful of pieces that I had no idea how they fit together.

Pressing my lips into a thin line, I tilted my head to one side in consideration. "Maybe it would be best if we started with *your* story, Zel—I mean, Rapunzel. Can you tell me what happened? Do you remember anything?"

In lieu of answering, Rapunzel picked up her little girl and snuggled her against her chest. Closing her eyes, she breathed in the scent of Rosalie's hair. Beside her, on the sheet, Rowan continued to play happily, cooing.

Around us, the early evening sun spilled over the park, gilding everything with gold. Children played in the distance, and on the other side of the field, a handful of boys and girls laughed and hollered while playing frisbee. It would have been peaceful, were it not for the tangle of emotions practically rolling off of Rapunzel as she tried to put her newly-returned memories into some sort of order.

After a long moment, she opened her eyes, laid her little girl down, and picked up her son. She nestled her cheek against his before she pressed a kiss to the top of his head and laid him back down beside his sister. She then picked up her can of warming Dr. Pepper and took a sip, staring out across the park.

Questions burned on the tip of my tongue, but I held them back. Zel—it would take some time to get used to calling her Rapunzel—was still processing everything. The wisest course of action now was for me to be quiet for a few minutes.

Eventually, Rapunzel looked over at me. "I don't even know where to begin, Celia. It all seems like such a long time ago, and yet..." She waved her can of Dr. Pepper toward her children. "I know it can't be that long ago."

l bit my lip, my gaze dropping to her children as well. No, it hadn't been that long ago.

"This Realm—your Realm—is so very different from mine." Rapunzel shook her head in wonder. "I've learned so many new things since I've been here." She gave me a wry look, old pain in her eyes. "Do you remember when we first met, how I told you I couldn't stand embroidery?" She laughed softly, though it held a bitter note. "Now I remember *why*."

"I'm sorry, Zel—I mean, Rapunzel."

Rapunzel drew in a deep breath, tucking a lock of blonde hair behind her ear again. "I suppose I should start my story with the fact that I didn't know that my mother wasn't my mother." A pained smile twisted her lips. "At least until she threw me out of the tower."

She pressed her lips together, her eyes glistening with a sudden sheen of tears, and sympathetic tears pricked the back of my own eyes.

"Oh, Zel." I leaned forward to rest a comforting hand on her shoulder for a moment.

Rapunzel swallowed and then found her voice again. "I grew up as only a child, in a tower hidden away in a forest." She snorted softly. "I didn't know this was unusual until much later. I was a child. What did I know of the way things should be?"

"You wouldn't." I shook my head.

"My mother was my whole world. She taught me how to cook and bake and sew and embroider." A shadow passed over Rapunzel's face. "And she taught me to read, which I also did not know was unusual at that time." She spread her hands. "I lived and worked in the tower, and I read books that my mother brought home for me. Later, I learned she had a great number of books for a woman at that time."

Another shadow passed over her face. "But I'm getting ahead of myself." She sighed, looking down at her twins. "I knew there were other people in the world, of course. I read books, and Mother told me stories. She made it quite clear, however, that I was never to leave the tower."

"Did *she* leave?" I asked, although I already knew the answer.

"Oh, of course she did. Someone had to go buy food." Rapunzel shrugged unhappily. "You don't question these things when you're a child."

"How did your mother leave the tower?"

Rapunzel went very still, and then offered me a pained smile. "It's going to sound daft. I can scarcely believe it myself, now that I think back to it."

In that moment, I knew Rapunzel did not remember the conversation we'd had while we were eating. I couldn't blame her—I'm not sure I would remember our conversation about fairytales either, if a tsunami of memories had bowled me over a moment later. *Ah, well.*

Instead of trying to explain that I already knew her story, I offered her a gentle smile of encouragement. "Try me."

"Well..." Rapunzel's fingers absently reached up to touch

the ends of her hair. "I had very long hair, you see. *Very* long hair." She cast a glance at me from under her eyelashes. "Long enough that I braided it and looped it over a hook in the side of the tower and used it like a rope to lower my mother down and then help her climb back up."

Even though I *knew* how long her hair had to be, the sheer logistics of it were still mindboggling. "That is amazing, Zel." I fluffed the ends of my ponytail. "I've always wanted really long hair, but it just won't grow past about this length. The fact that you had hair long enough to do *that is* just incredible."

Rapunzel touched the ends of her hair again and then deliberately dropped her hand back to her lap. "Well, I don't ever want hair that long again." She shook her head, her mouth firming. "Taking care of my hair was a chore. I can't believe it grew that long—or that Mother let it." She shot me a questioning look. "No one in this Realm has hair that long, do they?"

"Not that I know of."

Rapunzel nodded, as though that settled it, before she waved a hand. "Anyway, as I grew older, Mother often left for longer stretches of time, leaving me with work to do." A wry smile curved her lips. "I was quite good at embroidery, you see, and she often set me to work far longer than I wanted."

"And that's why you can't stand it." It was my turn to smile wryly. "I would, too, after that."

Rapunzel nodded, twisting a section of her flowery skirt between her fingers. "I know Mother sold the things I embroidered for her and picked up more commissions on those journeys, but I don't know where she went or what else she did. And..." She blew out a sigh. "I suppose it doesn't matter, now."

I listened, fascinated. There were so many more details to Rapunzel's story than the fairytales had ever recorded. "Did your mother ever tell you why she wouldn't let you go with her?"

"No." Rapunzel shook her head. "She just said the world was a dangerous place and I was better off tucked safely away where I couldn't be hurt. I was always delighted to see her whenever she returned, but...as I grew up, I began to despair of ever meeting another human being."

I grimaced—that sounded awful. "Did you ever think about leaving the tower?"

"Oh, heavens, yes. All the time. But it was a long way down. And once I got down, I wasn't sure how I would climb back up. And—" Rapunzel shuddered slightly. "I did not want to make Mother angry. She was very cold when she was angry, and she was, after all, the only person I knew."

My heart wrenched at the idea of Rapunzel, trapped alone in that tower at the whim of an old crazy lady who had controlled every aspect of her life so thoroughly that she had never even interacted with another human being. *No wonder she fell in love with the prince.*

I couldn't wait to hear how *that* played out.

A softer smile lit Rapunzel's face. "I've always liked to sing. When I was quite little, I discovered that my voice echoed marvelously out of the window on the west side of the tower. We were deep in a forest, but there was a mountain behind the trees on that side. And so I used to make up songs and I would serenade the birds and the trees, especially when Mother was gone."

A faint flush suffused her cheeks. "And then one day I was singing and someone spoke to me."

FIFTY-ONE

The romantic idea of the Prince hearing Rapunzel sing and being drawn to her made me swoon...and then I promptly chided myself. This was the first man Rapunzel had ever met—she had absolutely no basis for comparison.

Rapunzel's next words drove that point home. "I'd never met a man before, you see, only read about them in books." Her rosy blush deepened. "It was amazing to see someone who was like me and yet completely different."

"I can imagine." I nodded encouragingly, but part of me wanted to weep for Rapunzel. The poor girl had married the first man she'd ever met. Literally.

Her next words, however, astonished me.

"After a few miscommunications, we became friends." Rapunzel smiled, though her blush continued to deepen. "He would visit quite regularly, and it didn't take long for him to convince me to visit the outside world."

"Outside world?" I blinked, amazed. That was *not* what I had expected to hear her say. I leaned forward, my interest even more piqued. "You mean, you actually left the tower?"

"Yes. We didn't venture very far away, those first few times." A touch of bitterness colored her voice. "I was afraid of disobeying my mother, you see. But, eventually..."

"You got used to it." I nodded sagely. Sounded like normal teenage rebellion: the forbidden eventually becomes normal and loses its fearful, heart-pounding element.

"Yes." Rapunzel nodded, absently smoothing a hand over her son's head. She tried and failed to say her prince's name, and shook her head in frustration. "*He* thought it was terrible I'd been locked away from the world and wanted me to experience life." She smiled faintly. "Actually, he wanted me to leave the tower and come stay with his family, but I couldn't leave my mother." That dark shadow flitted over her face again. "She needed me."

I shook my head in wonder. This was so not the tale I had expected to hear. "Did you know he was a prince?"

"No, not at first." Rapunzel laughed, a beautiful tinkling sound. "He is third in line, so it is very unlikely he'll ever take the throne."

I nodded. *Which means he might have had a little more leeway in his choice of a bride.* Aloud, I said, "Did your mother ever suspect anything?"

Rapunzel snorted. "It never occurred to her that I would ever have the courage to leave the tower, and so she saw what she wanted to see. Besides," she shrugged, "we were always very careful."

"But you were falling in love, weren't you?" Memories

of my own teenage years returned to me, memories of teenage crushes and all the hormones involved. And that wasn't even counting when I was an adult and I'd really and truly believed I was in love with a man I'd planned to spend the rest of my life with. "How did your mother not notice *that*?"

"I don't know." Rapunzel turned both hands palm up. "I sang more and daydreamed more, and..." She shook her head. "Maybe she did not see it because, in her mind, there was no way I could possibly have met anyone."

"That's certainly a possibility."

Rapunzel looked down at the twins, who were starting to fuss. She scooped both children up and cradled them in her arms, shushing them gently. "To make a long story much shorter, he visited me all summer. And by the end of that time, we were very much in love."

I bit my lip again, dreadful anticipation filling me at the direction we were now headed.

A bittersweet smile curved Rapunzel's lips. "He asked me to marry him." Her green eyes took on a faraway cast. "While we were standing on the grass at the foot of the tower."

Under different circumstances, I thought that would have been quite romantic.

"I said, no, of course."

Rapunzel said those words so matter-of-factly that it took me a second to register them. "What?" I stared at her in shock. "You turned him down?"

"I did." She nodded serenely. "I told him he was a prince, and he could certainly do better than a girl who'd spent her whole life confined to a tower."

I gaped at her. This had *definitely* not been in the fairytales I'd read. "What did he *say*?"

"He told me I was perfect for him and that he would never ever love anyone else." Rapunzel held out her hand. "He gave me a ring he'd woven himself from the grass that grew around the tower."

Realization dawned on me as I stared down at that ring made of vines. Somehow, Rapunzel's ring had survived the curse that brought her here. Happiness swelled in my chest— I was so glad she remembered where she'd gotten it.

"He told me to keep the ring and think about it." Rapunzel pressed her lips into a thin line. "He doubted that my mother would even notice."

My eyes widened and my heart started pounding at the sheer boldness of that idea. One hand crept up to flatten itself over my chest, as though it might keep my heart inside. "And did she?"

Rapunzel shook her head. "I wore it for two weeks, and she never noticed a thing, even when she critiqued my embroidery."

We shared a look, and I saw reflected in her gaze the same thought running through my mind. Her mother might not have noticed initially, but eventually all those bits of information she'd overlooked had come together to paint a picture she did not approve of at all.

"What did you decide?" I knew the outcome of this story, but not the details—and as I'd just learned, the devil was *definitely* in the details.

"I didn't know what to do. Mother was all the family I had, all the family I knew, and I—I loved her." Tears glistened in Rapunzel's green eyes. She dashed them away on her shoulder, her arms still full of her babies. "I wanted to leave, wanted to marry—marry my prince, but I didn't want her to be angry with me."

A cold knot formed in the pit of my stomach. I knew that feeling, and even if I hadn't already read Rapunzel's fairytale, I knew where this story led.

"I spent a week carefully sounding Mother out, asking her if we could ever leave the tower and live somewhere else." A fine shudder ran through Rapunzel. "She made it quite clear that she would never allow me to leave—the world was far too dangerous, she loved me too far too much, and—" she gave a bitter little laugh, "—I was too fine an embroideress to waste my talents on an average life."

Something clicked into place inside my head. *That* was the real reason the old woman wouldn't let Rapunzel leave. She was far too valuable. Oh, she might have really loved Rapunzel, but she'd become far too valuable to give up because of her skills.

A soft, quiet sigh escaped Rapunzel. "I realized then that Mother was never going to let me go."

I pressed my lips into a thin line, a lump clogging my throat. I could well imagine how Rapunzel must have felt— hollow and empty, unwanted for anything other than the services she provided. Silently, I reached out and rested my hand on her shoulder again.

It was a long moment before Rapunzel said anything else. By now, birds had begun their evening songs, while the sun slowly sank behind the horizon, the golden rays of light bathing Starhaven gradually fading away. Rowan and Rosalie grew increasingly fussy in Rapunzel's arms.

"Do you mind if we walk around?" she asked hesitantly. "They do better when they're in motion, sometimes."

"Sure." I offered her a cheerful smile. "That's not a problem at all."

Rapunzel spent a moment getting her children settled in the stroller again, tucking their muslin blankets around them, while I cleaned up the pizza box and remnants of our picnic. After a moment's consideration, I stowed our unopened soft drinks in the basket beneath her stroller. Then we set off along the path, heading back toward the playground.

"Thank you for being patient with me." Rapunzel sent me a grateful smile. "And thank you again for breaking my curse."

"You're welcome. I'm just glad you remember who you are now." I glanced down at her children. "I know they're going to need to go to bed soon, but may I hear the rest of your story?"

I *needed* to hear the rest—both for my own curiosity and because I really, really hoped that Cedric would turn out to be her prince.

Rapunzel looked away, staring at the path ahead while she gathered her thoughts. "Well, the next time—" that look of frustration filled her face again at her inability to say his name, "—the next time my prince visited, I told him I had decided I'd marry him after all. If he was sure his family would approve." Her lips curved in a slow, tender smile. "I'll never forget the way he looked at me. He was so happy."

"I'm sure he was." I couldn't help but smile too. The joy on her face at the memory was contagious.

"But I told him I couldn't leave until I finished one last piece of embroidery for Mother. I knew this tapestry would bring her a great deal of money. He had explained all that to me, you see," Rapunzel added as an aside. "I could at least leave her that, as a thank you for everything she'd done for me."

I frowned. It didn't sound to me like her so-called mother had done much of anything beyond the bare minimum. I bit my tongue, however, and did not voice these thoughts. Rapunzel was a mother herself now—she probably had an even better understanding of her mother's shortcomings.

Instead, I thought of the prince—who had turned out to be much more of a gentleman than I'd expected after re-reading this fairytale. "What did your prince think of your idea?"

Rapunzel sighed. "He did not like it. He wanted to take me away immediately, but I persuaded him. He understood for my sake, even if he didn't agree." A slightly impish smile curved her mouth again. "I think he was afraid I might change my mind about marrying him."

"Really?" That made me laugh. "The prince who could have any girl he wished was afraid *you* would change *your* mind?"

"I know, it sounds daft, doesn't it?" Rapunzel laughed too, before she twitched one shoulder in a shrug. "He was convinced that some other handsome young prince might come along and snatch me up." Her gaze fell to the ring on her finger again. "He was so serious about not losing me that he asked me to pledge our marriage vows."

FIFTY-TWO

"Really?" My eyebrows climbed into my hairline, even as my stomach dropped. Now we were getting to the sticky bits of the story.

Rapunzel nodded. "He was very serious. He said he had a bad feeling and that he did not wish to leave me unless we were bound together forever." She smiled again. "What else could I say but yes? I had told him I would marry him, I only needed a little more time to finish Mother's embroidery. And so we said our vows there on the grass. And then he kissed me and went back to the palace."

I almost missed a step in surprise. Oh, this story was not what I'd expected. "He went back to the palace? After you said your vows?"

"Oh, yes. He had duties to attend to. He was gone for several days, and the next time he returned, Mother was there, so I had to wave him off." Rapunzel shook her head. "I hated to do it, but at the same time, I wasn't ready to tell

Mother about him yet. I still hadn't quite finished the tapestry, you see."

I blinked, processing this turn of events. *Looks like the fairytales leave a* lot *out of the story.*

We turned right at the playground, taking a paved path that would loop us around the park again. The twins had settled down and were contentedly chewing on teething rings. A gentle, balmy breeze rustled the leaves of the trees and kissed both our cheeks.

"Mother was gone the next time he visited, thankfully. He brought me chocolate—I'd never tasted such an amazing thing before—as well as a new gown." Rapunzel sighed. "It was beautiful. Leaf green, with gold embroidery. But of course I couldn't wear it yet. He just told me to put it away for the day he came to get me."

She bit her lip. "By this time, I was nearly finished with the tapestry. I'd made such good progress that Mother had even commented several times she couldn't believe how industrious I'd been lately." A wry, bitter laugh escaped her. "If only she'd known the reason why."

Sympathy swelled in my chest. We walked in silence for a moment, and then Rapunzel shook her head.

"That evening, it was so hard to say goodbye to him when I wanted so badly to go with him. And he did not want to leave me. He kissed me and, well..." A deep blush stained her porcelain cheeks. "We *were* married."

A blush stained my own cheeks. Fortunately, the fairytales glossed over that part.

Around us, the light was slowly fading and the street lights began to come on one by one. The smell of charcoal drifted through the air—someone was having a late-night cookout.

Rapunzel sighed, the sound nearly as soft as the whisper of the wind. "He had to leave the next morning, but I'll never forget the look on his face when he kissed me goodbye. He was so happy. He told me he would be back as soon as he could and we would tell my mother."

I bit the inside of my cheek, knowing—and dreading—what came next.

"I let him out the window...and that was the last time I saw him." Rapunzel's voice almost broke, despite her best efforts to hold it together.

"What happened?" I asked gently. I wondered what his parents had thought when he did not return to the palace that night—or if they had even known.

"I don't know." Rapunzel shook her head. "I didn't think anything of it the first few days, but when the days turned into weeks, I began to fear that something had happened to him. Something terrible."

The bleak despair in her voice hurt my heart—and realization washed over me again. Out of the corner of my eye, I studied Rapunzel. I knew from the fairytale what had happened—or what I *thought* had happened.

But, for the first time, it dawned on me that in the story *Rapunzel* never knew what had happened to her prince. Not until the end, when the two of them reunited.

Silence fell between us, seeping into the cracks like a foreboding invisible mist. My heart started pounding again. I knew what came next.

This was the dark night of the soul part of the story.

Rapunzel sighed. "I fell ill not long after that. And when I did not improve, my mother grew suspicious." She did not look at me, but hunched her shoulders. "I was...well...not *entirely* ignorant of these things, but...mostly. I didn't realize what was wrong, at first."

A shudder wracked her body. "I'll never forget the look on her face when she asked me if a man had been in the tower while she was gone. The way her eyes blazed, she looked like a stranger, not the woman I'd called Mother my entire life."

The hair on the back of my neck prickled as I imagined what that scene must have looked like.

"I couldn't lie to her." Rapunzel shook her head, her shoulders hunching further. "I told her the whole story. How we'd met and fallen in love. How he'd asked me to marry him, and I'd said yes. How I'd finished that last tapestry for her. I thought that part might make her happy, but if anything, it just made her angrier."

Her face went very white as she relived those horrible moments. "And then...then Mother told me I wasn't her daughter, not really. She told me she'd taken me as payment, that my real parents had stolen from her and she had demanded me in exchange."

Rapunzel looked at me then, her eyes full of pain. "She didn't know I'd be any good at embroidery until I was older. Why did she want a child if she was only going to lock me away in a tower?"

Tears pricked the back of my own eyelids at the anguish in her voice. I didn't know how to answer that.

"Well," Rapunzel swallowed hard, "after all that, she told me that if I wanted my prince so much, I could leave and have him. But she doubted he was ever coming back. She told me I was a foolish girl whose children would bear the price for my foolishness. And then..."

Her fingers traveled up to her hair again. "She snatched up a knife, and I thought—I thought—" her voice hitched, "—but all she did was cut off my braid." She shook her head. "I didn't know my head could feel so light. She tied my braid up and ordered me to get out of the tower to leave. So I did. And then she pulled my braid up and closed the shutters." Her voice broke on a sob.

Tears leaked down my cheeks. I might have grown up knowing Rapunzel's story, but I couldn't say I had ever really considered the depths of the pain and despair she must have experienced being rejected by the only mother she'd ever known.

Rapunzel dashed tears away. "To my shame, I tried to plead with her and apologize, but she ignored me. After that, I thought I would return to the village where—where *he* used to take me, but I got lost in the forest."

"I'm sure that was frightening." I shook my head, slowing my steps and moving to the side of the path behind Rapunzel long enough to let an evening jogger pass us. "I can only imagine."

"My memories of what happened after that are...hazy." Rapunzel's forehead creased in a frown. "I think I found the village eventually..." The crease between her eyebrows deepened. "And then...somehow...I was here in Starhaven."

She looked at me. "Only I didn't remember anything about who I was or where I'd come from until you broke my curse." Her stare was so straightforward and relentless that I felt a little unnerved. "Are you *sure* you're not a fairy?"

I laughed, raising one hand to rub the back of my neck. "Yes, Zel. I'm sure."

Silence fell between us again, broken only by the occasional tiny yawn from one of the twins. I bit my lip, my thoughts whirling and racing around inside my head as another crazy thought occurred to me. If Cedric *was* Rapunzel's blind prince, maybe we could break his curse tonight as well.

It's not any crazier than what you've already done today, said a dry voice inside my head. *And that crazy idea just paid off.*

"Zel." I increased my pace so I could get in front of Rapunzel and then stopped walking, forcing her to halt pushing the stroller so she didn't run me over. "I know we haven't known each other very long, but do you trust me?"

For a second, Rapunzel stared at me in surprised confusion...and then she started laughing. "Trust you? Celia, not only have you been a friend to me, but you broke my curse. How could I *not* trust you?"

"Okay." I nodded once, and then again, my palms growing sweaty. I rubbed them on my jeans. "Okay. Because I have a really crazy idea. Are you done walking?"

Rapunzel looked down at her sleepy children in the stroller. "Yes?"

It came out as a question, but I didn't care. "Good. Because I need you to call Maddie."

That was not what Rapunzel expected to hear. She frowned at me. "Why?"

I bit the inside of my cheek, almost hard enough to draw

blood. *Do I tell her and get her hopes up? Or do I hold off a little while?*

I only debated with myself for a second before I took a deep breath and met her confused green gaze. "Zel, I think I might know where your prince is."

Rapunzel drew in a sharp breath, her green eyes going impossibly wide.

"I can't *promise* he's your prince," I said hastily, holding up a hand. "But... he kind of matches the prince from your fairytale."

"Fairytale?" Rapunzel blinked. The blank look on her face told me she still didn't remember our conversation from earlier.

"Yeah. I figured out who you were because of a story." I brushed that away with a flick of my fingers. "It's okay—we can talk about it later. For now..." I offered her an encouraging smile. "Do you remember what your prince looks like?"

It was probably a dumb question, but who knew? The curse kept her from saying his name. It was possible it had other effects as well.

Rapunzel blinked again. "I would certainly hope so. It hasn't been *that* long, has it?"

The uncertainty in her voice made my heart hurt. I nodded, still smiling. "Okay, that's good. Now, will you call Maddie?"

It was Rapunzel's turn to nod, a little shakily. Bending down, she withdrew her phone from the diaper bag stowed in the bottom of the stroller and called Maddie. As soon as the older woman answered, she handed the phone to me.

"Maddie, it's Celia," I said, without preamble. "Zel is

Rapunzel, and I think I might know who Cedric is. Can you bring him to my craft shop right now?"

"Celia?" Maddie sounded thunderstruck, but then she laughed—the sound bright and tinkling and full of joy. "All right. We'll be there."

The line went dead. I returned Rapunzel's phone to her, anticipation and excitement fluttering wings inside my stomach. "Did you hear that?"

Rapunzel nodded, before tucking a lock of gold hair behind her ear with trembling fingers. Hope swirled in her eyes, but then she went a little green around the edges, like she was about to throw up.

"Hey." I put my arm around her and gave her a gentle hug. "It's going to be all right."

If Cedric was her husband—and I was pretty sure he was—they were about to have a wonderful reunion.

"Let's go." I smiled brightly down at her. "We have a prince to find."

FIFTY-THREE

Ten minutes later found us sitting on the black folding chairs in the back of my craft shop, waiting for Maddie to arrive with Cedric. I hadn't been in here this late in a while, and with the days growing shorter, it was downright odd not to have light pouring in from the large plate glass window. Rapunzel cradled Rosalie while I held Rowan. The twins had woken up and were a little fussy at having their usual routine interrupted.

Resting my head against the top of the little boy's head, I closed my eyes briefly, soaking in the warm, cuddly, soft weight of him in my arms. There was something so calming about holding a baby. For an instant, my mind flashed to what could have been, if I'd made different choices. I had a sudden vision of myself holding a little one, but then I remembered that meant my child's father would have been my ex-fiancé.

The very idea popped *that* mental image like a soap

bubble. Having a kid with Darren would have been a disaster. No child deserved that kind of chaos.

After a moment, Rowan calmed down, and I laid him back in his stroller and covered him up with his blanket. He blinked sleepily at me before his eyes slid shut.

Rapunzel still cuddled Rosalie, but she placed a hand on her stomach. "I feel like I just swallowed a million butter-flies." She turned anxious, pleading eyes on me. "What if it's not him? What if he doesn't recognize me?" Her face blanched. "What if *I* don't recognize *him*?"

I just offered her a tentative smile, trying to convey all the comfort and positivity I could. I had ideas, but no real way of knowing how this was going to go down. I almost opened my mouth and told her again that I didn't want to get her hopes up, but stopped myself just in time.

It's a little late for that, Celia.

"I don't think I'm wrong," I said at last, "but I'll admit I have no idea how this is going to work." A flush rose in my cheeks as I shot her a self-deprecating smile. "I'm new to this, curse-breaking business, remember?"

It was Rapunzel's turn to offer me a comforting smile. "I know, I know. I'm sorry, Celia. I'm just—" she flattened a hand over her stomach again, "—*so* nervous. I feel like I've traveled back through time to those early days when we'd just fallen in love and I was waiting for him to arrive after Mother left on a journey."

I nodded sympathetically.

The bell above the front door jingled. We both looked sharply in that direction as Maddie sailed into my shop, Cedric trailing in her wake with his walking stick. Beneath his ever-present sunglasses, his demeanor held an air of mild curiosity, though it couldn't quite dispel the somber loss and grief that still permeated everything about him.

My heart gave a little wrench as I was reminded once again that Cedric might not remember exactly *who* he'd lost, but he *knew* he'd lost *someone*. I drew in a deep breath. Hopefully he and Zel would both be *much* happier in a few moments.

"Celia." Maddie caught sight of me and flourished a hand toward the blind man.

"Thanks, Maddie," I began, but before I could say anything else, Rapunzel shot to her feet, still holding her daughter. She was trembling, and her green eyes had gone impossibly wide.

Well. That was a good sign. Clearly, she recognized him.

Anticipation prickling my skin, I rubbed my hands together and approached Cedric. "Hi, Cedric." I infused as much warmth in my voice as I could. "Thank you so much for coming here tonight."

"Lady Celia." The blind man shifted towards the sound of my voice. "Maddie informed me that you had something most urgent to impart to me, but she refused to give me any indication of what that might be." His tone held a touch of impatience, colored by something that sounded a lot like hope.

"Yes." I took a deep breath. "I have someone I'd like you to meet."

Before Cedric could respond, I motioned to Rapunzel, who set her daughter into the stroller next to her son and took a half-step forward. The look in her eyes said she wanted to run to Cedric, but that appeared to be about as far as she was going to get at the moment.

"Hey, Zel," I said gently. "Can you sing something? Maybe one of your old songs?"

After all, in the fairytale that was what had originally drawn the prince to her. It was also how he had found her again. I thought there was a pretty good chance the sound of her singing might break his curse.

Understanding lit Rapunzel's eyes. She drew in a breath and opened her mouth...but nothing came out. She tried once, twice, and then tears of frustration filled her eyes. "I can't do it." Her chest heaved with emotion. "I don't know why."

Maddie looked thoughtful. "Do you not remember? Or can you simply not sing?"

Rapunzel shook her head. "I can't sing in here. Something's wrong."

"Lady Celia." Cedric instinctively drew himself up to his full height, despite the fact that he was stone blind. "What is the meaning of this? Who is this person?"

All three of us women ignored him. It sounded bad, but we had far more important things to consider than the fact that he couldn't see Rapunzel and didn't know what was going on.

A frown crinkled my forehead. What *was* going on here? I looked back and forth between Rapunzel and Cedric, trying to parse through this new wrinkle.

Rapunzel obviously recognized her husband, but it seemed the curse was far more extensive than we'd realized. I bit my lip. *She can't even speak—or sing—to him directly.*

For his part, Cedric couldn't see her because he was blind, but I had the sudden and distinct impression that he wouldn't recognize her even if he had his sight back. I don't know how I knew this, but I did.

At that moment, several more puzzle pieces slotted into place inside my head. I sighed, realization mixing with resignation. So it *did* have to be me.

Turning to Maddie, I arched a wry eyebrow. "This is what you meant when you said that you couldn't do it, isn't it?"

"Yes." The fairy godmother nodded solemnly, and then her gaze swung went back to Rapunzel and Cedric, concern written all over her face.

Hmm. I nodded sharply to myself. *All right, then on to Plan B.*

...as soon as I figured out what, exactly, Plan B entailed.

A loud *crack* echoed through my shop, startling all of us. My heart leaped into my throat as I spun around to find the source of that sound. In their stroller by the wall, the twins startled awake, letting out matching small cries. Rapunzel hastened to comfort them before they started crying.

Cedric, frustrated by our lack of response, had thumped the butt of his walking stick on my hardwood floor.

"Cedric," Maddie said sternly, but he ignored her.

"Lady Celia." His voice could have been forged from iron. "I demand to know what is going on here."

Relieved that it wasn't something worse, I almost laughed, but managed to restrain myself at the last second. He *definitely* sounded like a prince just now. Instead, I cleared my throat. "Yes. My apologies, Cedric. We are...working a few things out."

Above his sunglasses, his dark eyebrows knit in a thunderous frown, but before he could demand further answers, I said, "Tell me, Cedric. Do you remember anything about your previous life before you ended up here in Starhaven?"

Just as I'd hoped, my abrupt question caught him off-guard. "My...previous life?" He drew back, confused. "I'm afraid I do not know what you're referring to."

I nodded silently. Starhaven's finest had already confirmed the extent of his amnesia, but at least I'd distracted him enough to buy myself a moment or two to think. I bit my lip, my mind racing frantically to put together Plan B.

Rapunzel and Maddie stood to one side, watching us both.

No pressure here, I thought wryly, as a wave of frustration coursed through me. I'd broken Rapunzel's curse by telling her who she was. How was I supposed to do that for Cedric if I didn't know his real name?

I cast my thoughts back to the research I'd done. None of the stories mentioned Rapunzel's prince by name. He was always referred to as the prince. I scrunched my forehead into a frown. Maybe...just maybe...that would be good enough.

Well, I thought grimly. *It* has *to be good enough. Doesn't look like there are any other options.*

Facing Cedric again, I cleared my throat. "Cedric," I said loudly, in as clear and steady a voice as I could manage, "I know who you are. You are the prince who saved Rapunzel from her tower. You fell in love with her and married her. You —" I paused, uncertain what else to add. *Was* there anything else to add?

"—you were blinded by thornbushes when you escaped the witch," I finished, a little weakly. That just didn't seem like a great note to end on, but I didn't know what else to say. The curse had interrupted their happy ending, so I couldn't exactly announce he'd been reunited with Rapunzel.

Dead silence greeted these words. The prince froze. He could have been made from stone, he was standing so silently and motionless. (A dim corner of my mind wondered if this reaction would happen *every* time I broke somebody's curse.) For their part, Maddie and Rapunzel both seemed to be holding their breath.

The tension in my shop mounted until the very molecules of the air seemed to form into strings drawn so tight that it felt as though they would snap at the slightest provocation. My gaze traveled to Maddie for a second, and the look on her face told me that this was *not* normal silence. Her green eyes were wide and a filled with an almost ancient wariness.

Cedric touched a hand to his temple, wincing at a sudden pain in his head. A muscle in his jaw clenched, and then a fine shudder worked through his body. "Rapunzel..." His voice sounded as dry and unused as though he had been mute since he arrived in Starhaven as well as blind. "*Rapunzel.*"

"Yes," I said, a little louder. "You are Rapunzel's prince, the prince who—" I broke off as Cedric abruptly staggered sideways, as though the world had suddenly tilted beneath his feet.

"Rapunzel!" he cried, clutching his walking stick for balance. "Where is she? Have you seen her? Does she live?"

My heart ached at the grief in his voice.

Beside me, Rapunzel gave a little cry. "Oh, Alan!"

At the sound of her voice, Cedric—no, Prince Alan—whipped around so quickly that I was afraid he'd overbalance completely and fall into my shelving. (I had a sudden vision of all the shelves falling over like dominos.) "Rapunzel?"

The sheer *hope* threaded through his voice caused my eyes to fill with tears. Unconsciously, I held my breath and clasped my hands beneath my chin.

"Rapunzel?" Alan's hands clenched and unclenched, as though he wished he could rip his sunglasses off and *see* her.

It wasn't necessary.

Rapunzel launched herself towards him. "Alan!"

FIFTY-FOUR

I don't know how Alan managed to catch Rapunzel, given that he couldn't *see* she was coming. But the romantic part of me liked to think that it was an instinctive thing—their two hearts recognizing each other. The prince's arms folded around Rapunzel, her arms looped around his neck, and they clung to each other. Their lips met in a series of kisses, disbelieving at first, and then increasingly joyful.

Maddie and I stood to one side, watching them reunite, both of us fascinated and at the same time not wanting to intrude. But I couldn't look away. Tears leaked down my cheeks and I kept brushing them away.

"I thought you were dead," Alan repeated over and over, holding Rapunzel so tightly against him that I was afraid she might be squished. "I thought you were dead. She made it sound like you were."

"No," Rapunzel managed to say, half-laughing and half-sobbing.

One of his hands trailed over her golden hair, stopping at the short ends. "She cut your hair."

"Yes."

"I thought it was you, Rapunzel. I called for you, and she threw down your hair, and I climbed up, but it wasn't you."

"No," Rapunzel said breathlessly. "No, it wasn't me. She found out about us."

"How?"

Rapunzel sidestepped the question. Removing his sunglasses, she brushed gentle fingertips over his eyes. "What happened?"

"She told me you were dead. I was so overcome by grief that I could not see. I jumped from the tower—" his face twisted into a wry grimace, "—on the wrong side."

Rapunzel gasped. "You fell into the thorns."

"Yes."

I winced. I'd always thought that the thorn bushes from Rapunzel's story just had little thorns, maybe similar to the thorns you'd find on roses. Looking at the princess's scarred face, I realized now that those thorns were not as little as I had thought.

"I escaped," Alan continued, "and wandered the Forest in my grief. And then one day..." He paused, his face going slack in that same way Rapunzel's had, which told me he was sorting through his newly-returned memories. "One day I heard you singing. I heard your voice. But it vanished before I could get to you. And then..." His thorn-scarred face scrunched again. "Then somehow I ended up somewhere else... where Lady Celia found me."

His head turned in my direction, his sightless eyes searching for me out of habit. I debated whether or not to answer, but decided against it. I didn't want to interrupt the flow of his story.

"I'm sorry." Rapunzel brushed gentle fingers across his scars again.

"I was coming back for you, Rapunzel. What happened?"

Rapunzel sighed. "You had been gone so long. I didn't know what to do. I didn't know what had happened to you. Where did you go? Why didn't you return?"

It was Alan's turn to sigh. He shook his head, frowning. "My father decided at the last minute to send me instead of my brother on a diplomatic mission to another kingdom. We were gone much too long." He crushed Rapunzel to him again. "I swear I'd meant to be back to you, back to your side in three days. I was going to present you to my family. Present you to the whole kingdom."

My breath caught in my throat. Oh, the old witch had thoroughly scuttled that plan.

"Then when I came back to the tower..." He trailed off, the grim tale hanging between them. "How did she find out about us? We were so careful."

Rapunzel laughed, though it ended in a hiccup. "Well... She found out because I learned I was with child."

It took a second for the meaning of those words to take shape in his mind...and then the prince went rigid in surprise. His fingers found Rapunzel's shoulders. "What?"

"Two of them actually," she said, half-laughing, half-sobbing. "A boy and a girl."

Alan's scarred face grew pale. "I'm a father?"

Rapunzel nodded, before remembering he couldn't see her. "Yes."

"Where are they? Are they here? Are they alright?" His fingers tightened on her shoulders again before he patted her as though he could ascertain whether or not she was in one piece. "Are *you* all right?"

"We're fine, Alan." Rapunzel breathed a laugh. "We're all fine. They're right here." Taking him by the hand, she drew him over to the stroller where the babies had fallen asleep. "Rowan and Rosalie."

Alan knelt beside them and carefully, gently, as though he was half afraid to touch them, swooped his hand over the tops of their little heads, tracing their features. Tears leaked from behind his ruined eyes. "I'm a father." His voice choked. "Oh, Rapunzel, I'm so sorry you had to endure that by yourself."

"We survived. And then we ended up here and Maddie has been a hero." Rapunzel smiled at the older woman, before turning to me. "So has Celia. She's become a good friend." Her smile widened, even as tears dripped down her cheeks.

I did my best to return her smile, but stayed silent. I couldn't speak even if I wanted to. A lump the size of the Ohio River clogged my throat.

Out of the corner of my eye, I noticed Maddie discreetly lift a delicate little handkerchief to her eyes and dab lightly into the corners.

"Oh, Rapunzel." The prince rose to his feet and reached

out his hands for Rapunzel again. She went willingly and he folded her into his arms, holding her tightly. "I missed you so much," he whispered into her hair.

"I missed you too." Rapunzel buried her face into his chest and the two of them just stood there, entwined, for a long moment.

Eventually, Rapunzel drew back far enough to study Alan's face again. "I'm so sorry about your eyes, my love." She brushed gentle fingertips over his eyes again. "I'm so sorry."

"It's not your fault." Alan nuzzled into her touch, a man starved for his wife. "I should have waited until you were safely away from her to marry you."

Tears still tracking down her cheeks, Rapunzel took his face in her hands and pressed a gentle kiss to his forehead. She then pressed kisses to his cheeks before moving on to his ruined eyes.

I caught my breath, jolting with realization. *Her tears!* In the story, Rapunzel's *tears* had healed the prince's eyesight.

Before I could open my mouth to say anything, Alan gasped sharply. Rapunzel drew back, startled, but then she gasped as well, her green eyes widening in utter shock.

I pressed a hand to my chest, a rush of warmth flooding me. We might be in the real world and not in Enchanted Realm, but Rapunzel's tears still worked. Before our eyes, the scars on Alan's face faded as his flesh knit itself back together.

Within seconds, the prince's clear brown eyes opened and fixed on his wife. He swallowed roughly. "I can see you."

The couple stared at each other, and then Rapunzel abruptly burst into tears and flung herself into his arms again. Alan picked her up and swung her around, narrowly avoiding crashing into my shelving. But I didn't mind. Seeing the pure joy and happiness on both of their faces would have been worth the cleanup.

When Alan finally set Rapunzel back down on the hardwood floor, Maddie stepped forward. She held out her hands to both of them, a teary smile on her face. "Your tears healed him, Rapunzel."

Just like in the story, I thought, but I didn't say anything. I didn't think it was necessary.

"Oh, Maddie!" Rapunzel took both of the fairy godmother's hands and squeezed them tightly before she turned to me and flung her arms around me. "Oh, Celia. Thank you! Thank you so much."

I hugged Rapunzel back, tears leaking down my cheeks again. "You're welcome."

When she pulled back, Alan gave me a deep bow. His newly-healed brown eyes were also filled with tears. "Yes, Lady Celia. Thank you. I don't know how we can ever repay you."

"It's perfectly fine." I waved a hand, wishing I'd had the foresight to a box of tissues behind my front counter. "Please, don't worry about it. I am so happy that Zel has you back. She's missed you, even if she couldn't remember what happened."

Rapunzel and I shared a watery smile, before Rapunzel turned back to her husband and kissed him once more. "Oh, my love. I'm so glad we're back together. I'm so glad our children will grow up with you in their lives."

"Our children," Alan repeated softly, joy filling his face. Returning to the stroller, he knelt down beside the twins and studied them for a long moment. Then he smiled at Zel. "Our son looks just like you."

"And our daughter looks like you." Rapunzel came up beside him and smoothed a hand over his brown hair. "Oh, I missed you." A watery half-sob, half-laugh escaped her. "Even though I didn't remember who you were, I missed you."

Wordlessly, Alan rose and gathered her up in his arms once more. "We'll never be parted again, my love. Not now that we've found each other."

Off to the side, I pressed a hand to my heart. The quiet sincerity in those words sent a rush of warmth flooding through me again. It had taken them a while, but Rapunzel and her prince had finally gotten their happy ending.

A slight movement from Maddie caught my eye. I glanced at the older woman in time to see her give me a twinkling smile, though her green eyes remained solemn.

"Well done, Celia," she said softly. "Well done."

CHAPTER

FIFTY-FIVE

Half an hour later, I let myself into my apartment and leaned up against my front door for a moment, unable to help the wide smile stretching across my face. The memory of Rapunzel and Alan reuniting would be one I treasured for the rest of my life. They were a family again, and somehow I'd been a part of that.

Still smiling, I kicked my shoes and socks off and practically floated through the living room into the kitchen. The linoleum was cool beneath my bare feet, but I didn't notice. This called for popcorn. Celebratory popcorn. And a cold Ale-8. I could almost taste that wonderful citrusy ginger already.

I pressed a hand to my heart, which was so full of joy right now I was half-afraid it would burst right out of my chest. Tonight, Rapunzel, Alan, and their twins would be under the same roof for the first time. And not only did they have their memories back, but Alan had his sight again as well.

Pulling out a bag of microwave popcorn from the pantry, I danced over to the microwave. The whole story was absolutely *amazing* and I couldn't *wait* to share it...

...except that I couldn't share it with anyone.

For the first time, my smile slipped. In all of my joy and excitement, I hadn't realized that part. Of *course* I couldn't share it with anyone. Who would believe me?

I blew out a sigh, resting a hip against the kitchen counter. Bianca was my first choice, but she'd think I was crazy. And, under normal circumstances, rightfully so.

My parents might have texted me a few times since I left Louisville and moved here, but we weren't close enough for a lot of conversations, let alone one like this. Same for most of my friends from Louisville.

It was only then, standing at my kitchen counter with a bag of un-popped popcorn in my hands, that I realized how small my circle of friends had really become. The reality was sobering.

Oh, well, I thought, rallying with a shrug. *At least I can talk to Maddie.* And, once she came back down from cloud nine, I'd be able to talk to Zel too.

Besides, Bianca was my friend, regardless of whether or not I could talk to her about crazy things like amnesiac, cursed fairytale characters.

I put the popcorn into the microwave and retrieved a bottle of Ale-8 from the refrigerator. I don't drink a lot of soft drink, but every once in a while, I enjoy an Ale 8 or a Dr.

Pepper. And even though I'd had a Dr. Pepper earlier with the pizza, I thought the occasion warranted a treat.

I enjoyed those first few gingery sips while I waited for the popcorn to finish popping. When the microwave finally dinged, I set the bottle of Ale-8 down and retrieved the popcorn bag so I could dump it into a large metal bowl.

"So you're a curse breaker now, are you?"

I should probably be used to it at this point, but the sound of Agnes's reedy little voice still startled me. I almost dropped the bag of popcorn. Almost. (She didn't startle me as much as she had a few weeks earlier. We were making progress.)

Turning around, I found the little brownie standing on the counter next to my bottle of Ale-8, hands on her hips, eyeing me as though I had made some sort of strange transformation —and she was not entirely sure she approved of the result.

"Maybe?" I offered her some popcorn. The smell had apparently lured her in again. "Accidentally, I think. I really don't know how I managed it."

Agnes took a piece of popcorn from the bag, but did not eat. She held it in both hands, eying me over the top of it. "You know the story," she said thoughtfully. "*Storykeeper.*"

The title startled a laugh out of me. "Agnes..." I raised a hand to rub the back of my neck. "You make it sound like I'm some sort of—"

"No, no. *You* are the Storykeeper." She nodded to my phone where I'd set it on the counter. "With the help of your magic box."

It was hard to argue with that. I didn't have the mental

energy to attempt to explain the concept of telephones to her again, let alone smartphones and the internet.

Instead, I just shrugged and dumped the popcorn into the bowl on the counter. "Well, their story didn't turn out to be *exactly* like the stories I'd read. But…" I trailed off with a frown, struck by that thought. Actually, now that I had time to think about it, there were a more differences than I'd realized.

Parts of the story Rapunzel had told me matched the Grimm's version of her fairytale, but…my frown deepened. I didn't recall her mentioning anything about the prince bringing her silk strands to weave into a ladder, for one. (Which was *still* ridiculous, because if he was visiting her, why couldn't he just bring her an actual rope ladder?) Nor had Rapunzel given away her secret by commenting on how much faster Alan climbed up the tower than her mother. In fact…

"Celia?"

Dimly, I became aware that Agnes was talking to me again. Blinking, I refocused on the little brownie. "Sorry. I was thinking." I waved a hand, brushing my thoughts aside. I'd have to ponder them later. "I'm very happy for Zel, Alan, and their children."

Maddie had offered to escort them home for tonight, with the promise of sorting out everything else tomorrow. I reached for my Ale-8 and took an absent sip. It was a good thing the newly-recovered fairy godmother worked for the Starhaven Community Foundation—I wasn't sure how else she'd manage to help Alan integrate into Starhaven society properly.

"Hmm." Agnes polished off the last bit of her piece of popcorn and then marched over to the popcorn bowl to select another. "Wasn't sure about you when you got here," she said without looking at me. "But you'll do."

With that prognosis, she turned around, popcorn in hand, and promptly disappeared, leaving me standing in the kitchen, holding a bottle of Ale-8 and shaking my head.

"I really can't believe this is my life," I said into the empty air.

A loud purr greeted this pronouncement. Sassy emerged from beneath my little kitchen table and rubbed against my ankles, clearly angling for some popcorn for herself.

"Here you go." I dropped a few pieces onto the linoleum. "Probably shouldn't eat the whole bag myself anyway."

The cat eagerly snapped them up. I gave her a couple more pieces and then carried my soft drink and the bowl of popcorn into the living room. Sassy followed me and lightly leaped up onto the back of my armchair, where she proceeded to stretch out and go to sleep.

As I curled up in the corner of my couch, Agnes's words floated through my mind again. *Storyteller.*

I pressed my lips into a thin line. Was this really going to be a recurring thing here in Starhaven? Breaking curses?

Celia O'Malley, craft shop owner and fairytale curse breaker. I had to stifle a slightly hysterical giggle at the thought.

That was probably yet another question for Maddie. I added it to the list I had started keeping in my phone, and then resolutely grabbed my laptop from its place on the little end table beside the couch. I really needed to think about something else for a while.

One of the ladies who'd come into the shop in the last few days had asked about patterns for crocheting dolls and other little things like fruit or animals, but I'd been too distracted by the possibility that Zel was actually a cursed Rapunzel to give it much thought. Now, I decided it was a fantastic idea. Crocheting dolls sounded like a lot of fun—I'd definitely have to look into it.

I started googling patterns while I munched popcorn. Within moments, I'd lost myself in a joyful, colorful world of creativity. It was amazing, and I didn't think about anything else.

But when I finally went to bed that night, my dreams were full of little crocheted fairytale princes and princesses wandering around in a dark forest, completely lost. There was, apparently, no escaping the subject.

FIFTY-SIX

The next day found me behind the counter in my shop, sorting through a stack of interesting crochet patterns that I had downloaded and printed the night before. I had actual booklets on order—I figured I would stock a few and see what kind of interest they garnered. But I wanted to test several of the patterns out myself so that when people asked, I would have some idea of what I was talking about.

Every so often, my gaze strayed to the spot near the back where I'd broken Alan's curse and Rapunzel had healed his eyesight. In the cool light of this crisp fall morning, the events of last night took on a slightly surreal cast. I probably could have convinced myself I'd imagined the whole thing...except for the fact that cursed amnesiac fairytale characters appearing in the real world was not something I'd ever imagine.

Nor was a live-in brownie who kept my apartment immaculately clean for me.

No, this was my reality—for better or for worse.

A pattern for a cute little pumpkin caught my eye. Pulling it out of the stack, I set it down on the counter to study it. The pumpkin's design was clever, but not overly complicated. I nodded to myself. This would be fun.

Pattern selected, I headed over to my shelves of yarn to figure out what yarn would work best for these pumpkins. Since I'd opened Celia's Craft Shop, I'd made a pact with myself not to make it a habit to knit or crochet from my inventory unless I paid myself back. But there were times I'd decided I could pull from it.

Today would be one of them. This would go down as an advertising expense. Besides, it was officially fall anyway, so in addition to being advertising, a row of little crocheted pumpkins on my front counter with some autumn leaves would be the perfect decoration.

I was in the middle of trying to decide if I wanted to use a shimmery orange yarn or a regular matte for the pumpkins when the little bell above the front door jingled.

"Hello," I called, leaning around the shelving long enough to pop my head out and greet whoever had just walked into my shop.

To my surprise, it was Maddie. She looked fresh and serene, her gray hair in its usual riot of lovely curls. She'd added a cream cardigan over her pink floral dress to combat the crisp morning air.

"Oh, hi," I said brightly. "Give me just a moment." Quickly, I returned the matte orange yarn to its rack, grabbed another skein of the shimmery orange, and then grabbed a skein of a matching shimmery green yarn.

"What are you doing?" Maddie eyed the collection as I carried it all to the front counter.

"Oh, I'm going to crochet pumpkins," I said cheerfully. Dropping the yarn onto the counter, I tapped the pattern with my index finger. "Trying a new marketing tactic. And I think it would be fun."

Maddie's eyebrows rose and then she smiled. "That sounds exactly like something you should do." There was a fondness to her voice that warmed something in my chest.

"Anyway," I swept the yarn to one side of the counter. "What can I do for you?"

"I wanted to congratulate you again, Celia." Maddie leaned a hip up against the counter, her gaze drifting around my store as though checking for other customers before she turned her bright green eyes back to me. "And I wanted to caution you."

"Well..." Bemused and a little unsettled, I swept a hand through the air. "Congratulate and caution away."

Maddie smiled again, but then her expression grew serious. "Celia, you are exactly what this town needs. You single-handedly changed the trajectory of Rapunzel's and Alan's lives—and their children." She took a deep breath. "And for that reason, I must ask you to be very circumspect about... everything."

Ah. So *that* was what this was about. I offered the fairy godmother a wry smile. "Believe it or not, Maddie, I was going to be discreet anyway. The whole thing sounds rather crazy." My smile widened into an equally wry grin. "Not exactly a story you want to go around telling the whole town."

"True." Maddie inclined her head. "Especially when not everyone in this town is from the Enchanted Realm."

That brought to mind another question I'd been meaning to ask Maddie. I straightened with interest. "Do you know who is?" I turned one hand palm up. "I mean, you work with the Starhaven Community Foundation, and the Foundation helps people like Rapunzel and Alan after they come through the portal. So you must have a list of those people."

The look on Maddie's face told me that the Foundation did indeed have such a list—and I had the distinct impression that she had no intention of sharing it with me. I kept that thought to myself, however, as Maddie offered me a grandmotherly smile.

"You, Celia O'Malley, are a very sharp young lady. The Foundation does indeed have a list of some...new arrivals... but not everyone." Her gaze drifted off into the distance as though seeing something beyond mortal understanding. "We don't find everyone. Or every *thing*," she added, a little darkly.

That sent a faint shiver of alarm down my spine, but before I could question her about it, Maddie sailed on.

"Unfortunately, it is against Foundation policy to hand out personal information." She sighed. "As much as I would love to have you set to work attempting to identify some of them. Besides..." her forehead scrunched in a frown. "I am not entirely sure the curse and the magic behind it will allow that."

Of course they didn't. Otherwise, it would be too easy for somebody like me to break said curse. I nodded in understanding. "Right. So I can't just randomly walk up to people and tell them which character from a fairytale I think they are."

I expected Maddie to laugh, but she did not. "No," she said thoughtfully. "I don't think you can."

"Okay, good to know." I offered her a reassuring smile. "So does that mean what I did for Zel and Alan was more of a one-off?"

Again, Maddie surprised me. "No," she said slowly. "Not necessarily. But I don't think we'll know for certain just yet."

I nodded again, and then my eyes lit with a sudden idea. "Maddie." I leaned toward the fairy godmother. "What if I volunteer for the Foundation? Would *that* let me help people?"

I saw the moment that idea sank in—Maddie's green eyes began twinkling. A mischievous smile wrinkled her face. "You know, Celia, that just might work. I shall have to make inquires."

She looked like she was about to add something else, but at that moment, the bell above the door jingled. Mrs. Yates, an older lady who lived three blocks away, walked in and greeted me with a smile and a wave.

I waved back and watched as she made her way to the fabric aisle. Mrs. Yates, I had discovered, was a quilter. One who pieced by machine, but quilted by hand.

"Business has picked up lately, I see," Maddie observed.

"Yes. I'm very grateful for that. I'm starting to feel like I might actually make it here in Starhaven." I turned back to Maddie, a rueful smile twisting my lips. "I've been wondering if maybe Dave's gotten over his little tizzy about newcomers."

"Oh, no, I'm afraid he has not," Maddie said matter-of-factly. "But he *has* been warned that it's in poor taste to run off fellow businesspeople. And that certain steps might be taken if he continues to cause issues."

I lifted my eyebrows in surprise. "That's good to know. Thank you, Maddie."

Maddie waved my thanks aside with a flick of her fingers. "Merely common courtesy. The decent thing to do. The Council would have seen to that even if..." she trailed off, giving me a suggestive look.

I nodded. "Also good to know."

The two of us stood in silence for a moment, listening to the upbeat music playing over my Bluetooth speaker.

Maddie's gaze had gone thoughtful again, but then she turned a mysterious smile on me. "I'm glad you moved to Starhaven. Celia O'Malley. Life will certainly be more interesting with you around." And with that, she nodded briskly and walked out the door, which jingled behind her.

I was glad Maddie thought so, but as I looked around at all the colorful fabrics and yarns and wonderful craft notions filling my shop and then glanced out the large plate glass window at Main Street beyond, I realized that it didn't matter. Regardless of what anybody in this town thought, I was glad to be here.

I had a lot to learn about Starhaven, and I'm sure it would take time to build my business to the point where I felt comfortable that I wasn't going to collapse and have to return to Louisville, but I thought I'd made a good start. I had friends. I had a taciturn brownie willing to clean my apartment for me. (That was a huge win in and of itself—I really don't love cleaning.)

I also had repeat customers, and I'd even broken a curse on a couple of fairytale characters. (Again, not something I could share with my mom if she ever called but...)

A slow smile curved my lips as I nodded to myself, propping my hands on my hips. Not a bad start for my first two months in this town. Eventually, I planned on even winning people like Dave over.

But even if I didn't, I was going to love living life here in Starhaven. I just knew it.

AFTERWORD

I hope you enjoyed reading this book as much as I enjoyed writing it!

I grew up reading—and loving—cozy mysteries and fairytales. I am also an unabashed crafter. Knitting, crocheting, and quilting are three of my favorite crafts, along with counted cross-stitching and a little beading. (If only there was more time in the day for everything I want to do!)

Last year the idea of a cozy mystery series set in a small-town craft shop and featuring fairytale characters walloped me over the head. After I dusted myself off, I realized it was the perfect project for me to write next.

Once Upon a Craft Shop is the first installment in a brand-new cozy fantasy mystery series.

There will be more... *The Glass Slipper Heist* is up next!

Until next time!

~ E. R. Paskey

September 2025

~ E. R. Paskey

ACKNOWLEDGMENTS

Writing may be a solitary endeavor, but it doesn't happen in a vacuum. I am so blessed to have family and friends to cheer me on.

For my husband, Tim. Thanks so much for always encouraging me to keep pursuing the dreams and talents the Lord has given me. Thanks for putting up with a wife who regularly writes down what the voices in her head say. ::grin::

For my children—thanks for keeping things to a (mostly) dull roar while I'm working.

For my mom and siblings—thanks for your encouragement and support.

For Lori Christie and the many, many hours spent knitting or crocheting while geeking out.

Thank you also to Kim Burns and Heather Stearns for being excited readers, great friends, and great listening ears.

Kickstarter Acknowledgments

A very special thanks to everyone who backed my 2025 Kickstarter campaign for *Once Upon a Craft Shop*. In particular, I would like to thank the following people:

R Sarty, Amanda Thompson, Beth Barany, Michelle L,

Kai'lee, Madelyn S., MichelleG, Cortney Babcock, Amanda Eschmeyer, Kat Fey Diehl, Scarlett Luna Strange, Amanda Balter, Talitha Italiano, polinchka, Laura Eaton, suettle, R.S. Kellogg, Simon Mark de Wolfe, Andrew Kaplan, Jasmine C, Alexis W, Rachael Barcellano, Susan K., ValerieAnne, Emerald Bruce, Catherine Holmes, Kat Tipton, Florentina, Charlotte P., Kristen Schleif, Elleemmenno, Zilla, Dwayne Plain, Nalamba, Nivita Starling, John Idlor, Nikkii Thompson, Chumyshka, EL, Michelle Brenner, Amber Willoe, Meow, Karen MacIntosh, Ellie, Julie Seas All, Kira Bolding, Allegra, Melisa V, Jeffrey Tristan Thyme, Sarah Faith, Axel KNG, Liana, Anon <3, Zephyr Mini, Gabrielle Landi, Julia A Paskey, Mary Caite, Nancy Y., Terry Steinke, Molly Fessel, Nichole Heydenburg, Corrie Pelc, Antoinetta Aquila, Christy S, Kimberly Burns, Carol MacLennan-Gonzales, Nicole Folsom, Samantha Newberry, Lauren Govert, Louise Bergin, Robert Miller, Lisa Grant, Dragonologest, Carla Bermudez, Katie Killam, Alexandra Corrsin, Brytney Hobson, Erin Davis, J.S. Baehr, Nicole, Gail Cu, Caty Garcia, Isabel Bauer, Elisabeth Aimee Brown, Kasey Cooksey, Claire Smith-Simmons, The Lovely Miss Oye, Galasso, K. "Cyanide" Stauffer, Kaarin Borel, Winnie, Maggie Rusch, Angela P, Jennifer Corry, Kendra, Douglas Bargfield, Alycia Baker, Cristine Patrick, Melissa Graham, Ashley, Becky Carr, J.L. Hendricks, Ana Lewis, Ashley Hill, Amanda Tallon, Liz Donnell, Stacy Ward, Nic Haratyk, Katherine Malloy, Rebecca P, Samantha, Mirage, L. B. Mickson, Natalie Manahan, Rebecca O'Neill, Annarose Willhite, Sarah Gaertner, Crystal Oldham, Sandra Peyton, Suzanne Zoumbaris, Dominic Hilsbos, McKenzie Paulsen, Richard Libera, Liz Semkiu, Heather S, Danielle K Bird, Brian Daniels,

Shelli, Victoria Wash, Stacey Andrews, Katelyn Hester, Amy Trent, Sax is my Axe, Ivy Ru, Natalie Munford, Johanna Miller, Karina Krogh, Christine Schulz, Allee Snyder, Alexandrina Cambria, Rachel Simpson, Midnightmare, Lee Knickle, Dawn Blair, Anna Marie Stern, Linda van der Wolf, Jackie Lopez, Sara Liming, Erin Ratelle, Rebecca M. Senese, Meyari McFarland, Preslee Marshall, Sergey Kochergan, Anonymous Reader, Yesi, Carissa Boehmer, J Dunaway, Stevie Hosler, and Kathryn Kirmess.

In addition, an extra special thanks to Danielle Bird, who named Rafe Levan, the owner of Starhaven Grill, and Brian Daniels, who named Marie Claire, the owner of Vine Life.

Y'all are amazing, and I am so grateful for each and every one of you! Thank you again for your enthusiastic support!

COMING SPRING 2026!

NEWSLETTER SIGN-UP

I value honest feedback and would love to hear your opinion in a review, if you're so inclined, on your favorite retailer's site. Thank you!

Be the first to know!

Just sign up for the E.R. Paskey newsletter and keep up with the latest news, releases, and so much more, including the occasional giveaway.

Go to Erpaskey.com/newsletter-signup/ or scan this QR code:

About the Author

E. R. Paskey is the author of seventeen novels, including the *Finder* series and a Christian science fiction series, *The Guardians*. She writes across multiple genres, from science fiction and mystery to romance.

Writing/storytelling has been her passion most of her life. Being able to share her books with the world is a dream come true. She currently lives in Southern Indiana with her husband, six children, four cats, and a dog.

You can find her website at: ERPaskey.com or scan this QR code:

facebook.com/erpaskey

ALSO BY E. R. PASKEY

The Guardians

Bad Faith

Portal Woes

Treason's Edge

Freedom's Children

Ink Realm Duology

Lady Ink

Finder Series

Head Case

Magna

Old Wounds

Overload

Blowback

Wild Sea Novels

The Other Side of the Horizon

A Tale of Star-Crossed Hearts

Standalone Novels

Galaxy's Way

In Plain Sight

The Spy at the Embassy

The Spy at the Embassy Special Edition